CARTOON NETWORK

STEVEN UNIVERSE

TO BE HAPPY

kaboom!

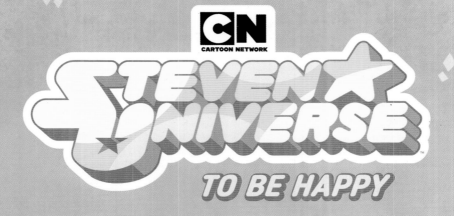

Ross Richie CEO & Founder
Joy Huffman CFO
Matt Gagnon Editor-in-Chief
Filip Sablik President, Publishing & Marketing
Stephen Christy President, Development
Lance Kreiter Vice President, Licensing & Merchandising
Arune Singh Vice President, Marketing
Bryce Carlson Vice President, Editorial & Creative Strategy
Kate Henning Director, Operations
Spencer Simpson Director, Sales
Scott Newman Manager, Production Design
Elyse Strandberg Manager, Finance
Sierra Hahn Executive Editor
Jeanine Schaefer Executive Editor
Dafna Pleban Senior Editor
Shannon Watters Senior Editor
Eric Harburn Senior Editor
Matthew Levine Editor
Sophie Philips-Roberts Associate Editor
Amanda LaFranco Associate Editor
Jonathan Manning Associate Editor
Gavin Gronenthal Assistant Editor
Gwen Waller Assistant Editor
Allyson Gronowitz Assistant Editor
Ramiro Portnoy Assistant Editor
Shelby Netschke Editorial Assistant
Michelle Ankley Design Coordinator
Marie Krupina Production Designer
Grace Park Production Designer
Chelsea Roberts Production Designer
Samantha Knapp Production Design Assistant
José Meza Live Events Lead
Stephanie Hocutt Digital Marketing Lead
Esther Kim Marketing Coordinator
Cat O'Grady Digital Marketing Coordinator
Breanna Sarpy Live Events Coordinator
Amanda Lawson Marketing Assistant
Holly Aitchison Digital Sales Coordinator
Morgan Perry Retail Sales Coordinator
Megan Christopher Operations Coordinator
Rodrigo Hernandez Mailroom Assistant
Zipporah Smith Operations Assistant
Jason Lee Senior Accountant
Sabrina Lesin Accounting Assistant

WWW.BOOM-STUDIOS.COM

STEVEN UNIVERSE ONGOING Volume Eight, September 2020.
Published by KaBOOM!, a division of Boom Entertainment, Inc.
STEVEN UNIVERSE, CARTOON NETWORK, the logos, and all related
characters and elements are trademarks of and © Cartoon Network.
A WarnerMedia Company. All rights reserved. (S20) Originally
published in single magazine form as STEVEN UNIVERSE ONGOING
No. 29-32 © Cartoon Network. A WarnerMedia Company. All rights
reserved. (S19) KaBOOM! and the KaBOOM! logo are trademarks
of Boom Entertainment, Inc., registered in various countries
and categories. All characters, events, and institutions depicted
herein are fictional. Any similarity between any of the names,
characters, persons, events, and/or institutions in this publication
to actual names, characters, and persons, whether living or dead,
events, and/or institutions is unintended and purely coincidental.
KaBOOM! does not read or accept unsolicited submissions of ideas,
stories, or artwork.

BOOM! Studios, 5670 Wilshire Boulevard, Suite 400, Los Angeles,
CA 90036-5679. Printed in China. First Printing.

ISBN: 978-1-68415-626-9, eISBN: 978-1-64668-038-2

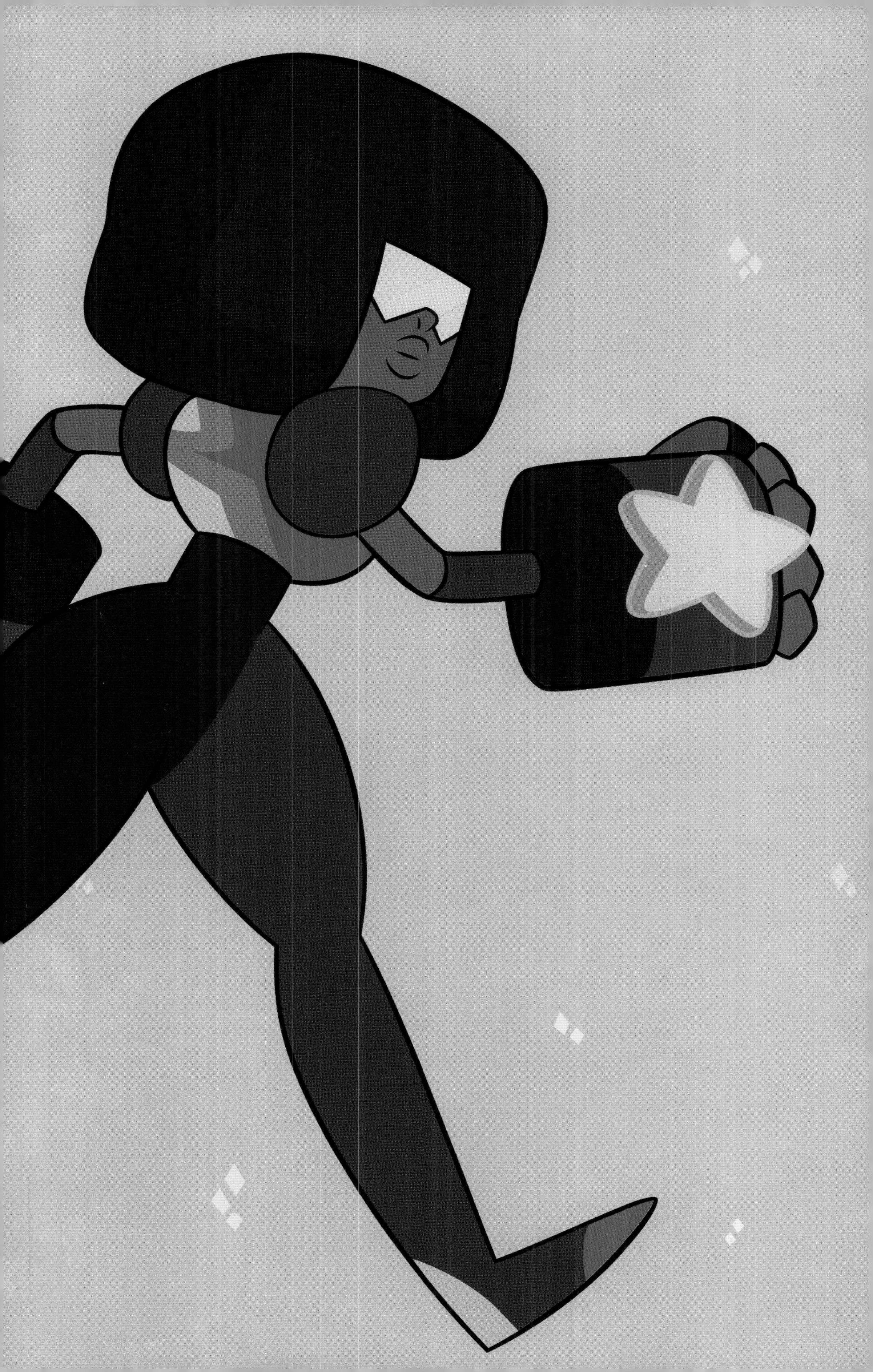

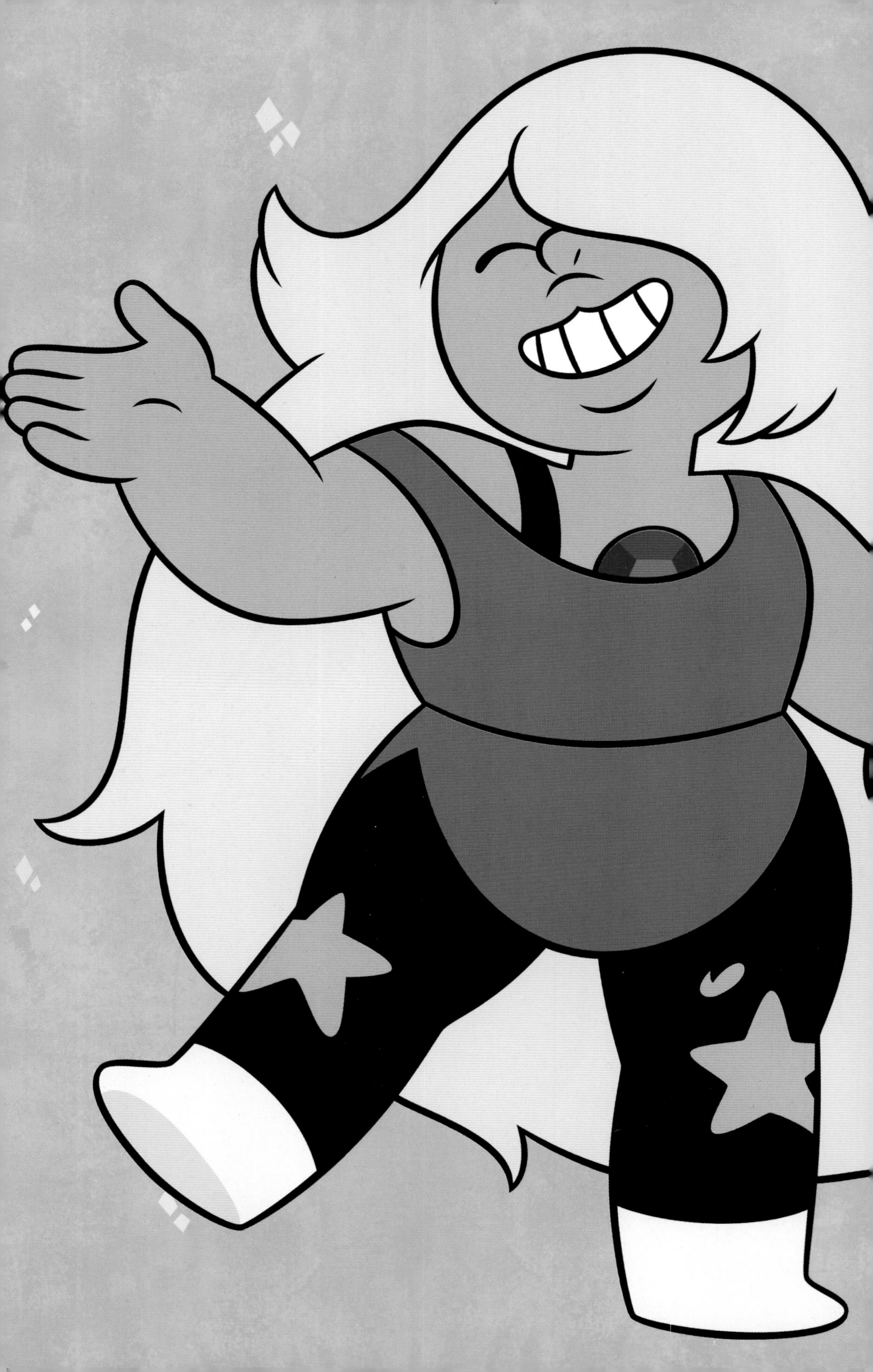

STEVEN ★ UNIVERSE

TO BE HAPPY

created by
REBECCA SUGAR

written by
SARAH GAILEY

illustrated by
RII ABREGO

colors by
WHITNEY COGAR

letters by
MIKE FIORENTINO

cover by
MISSY PEÑA

series designer
GRACE PARK

collection designer
MARIE KRUPINA

editor
MATTHEW LEVINE

Special thanks to
Marisa Marionakis, Janet No, Austin Page,
Conrad Montgomery, Jackie Buscarino and the
wonderful folks at Cartoon Network.

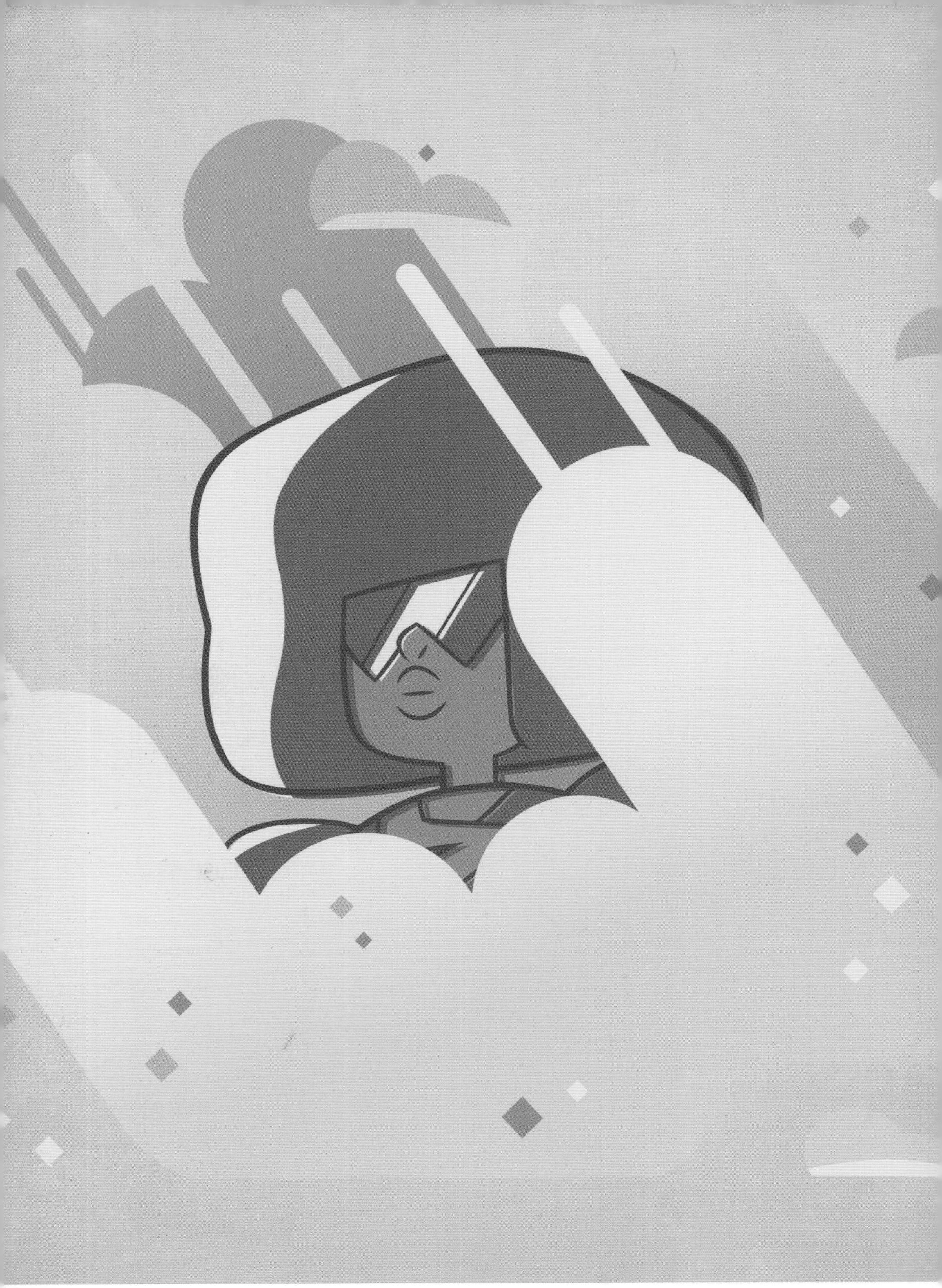

CHAPTER TWENTY-NINE

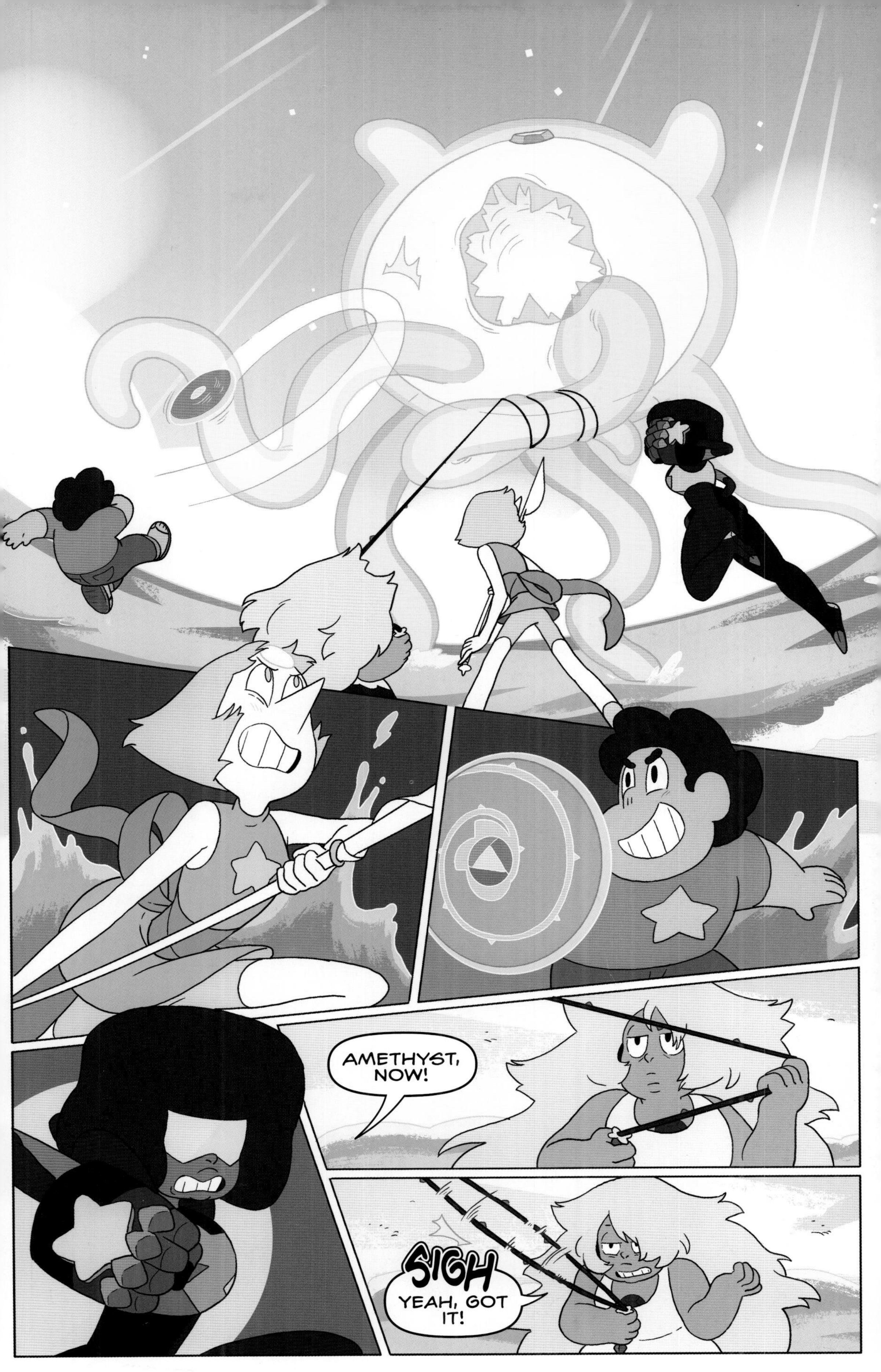
AMETHYST, NOW!
SIGH
YEAH, GOT IT!

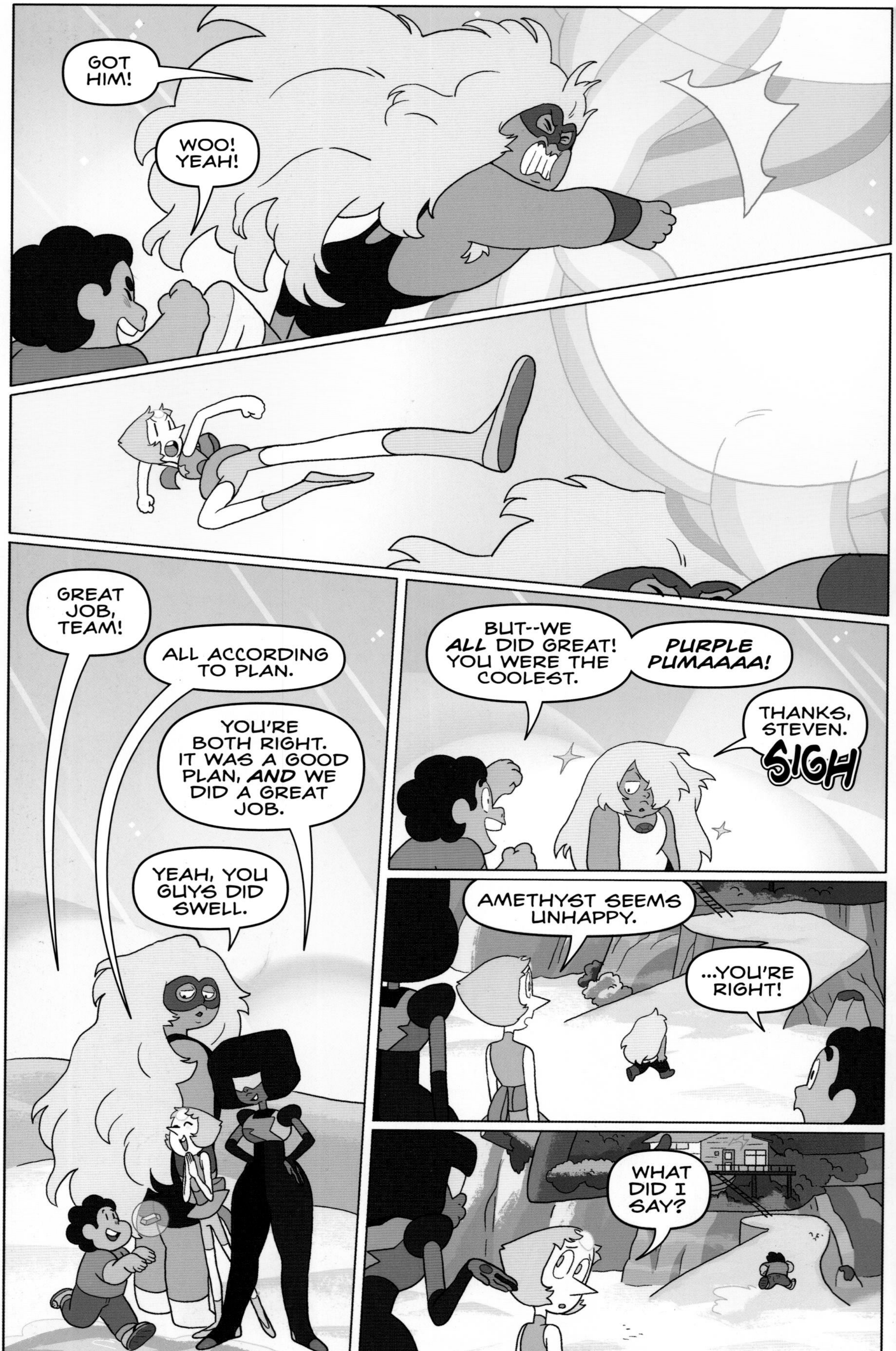
GOT HIM!
WOO! YEAH!
GREAT JOB, TEAM!
ALL ACCORDING TO PLAN.
YOU'RE BOTH RIGHT. IT WAS A GOOD PLAN, *AND* WE DID A GREAT JOB.
YEAH, YOU GUYS DID SWELL.
BUT--WE *ALL* DID GREAT! YOU WERE THE COOLEST.
PURPLE PUMAAAA!
THANKS, STEVEN.
SIGH
AMETHYST SEEMS UNHAPPY.
...YOU'RE RIGHT!
WHAT DID I SAY?

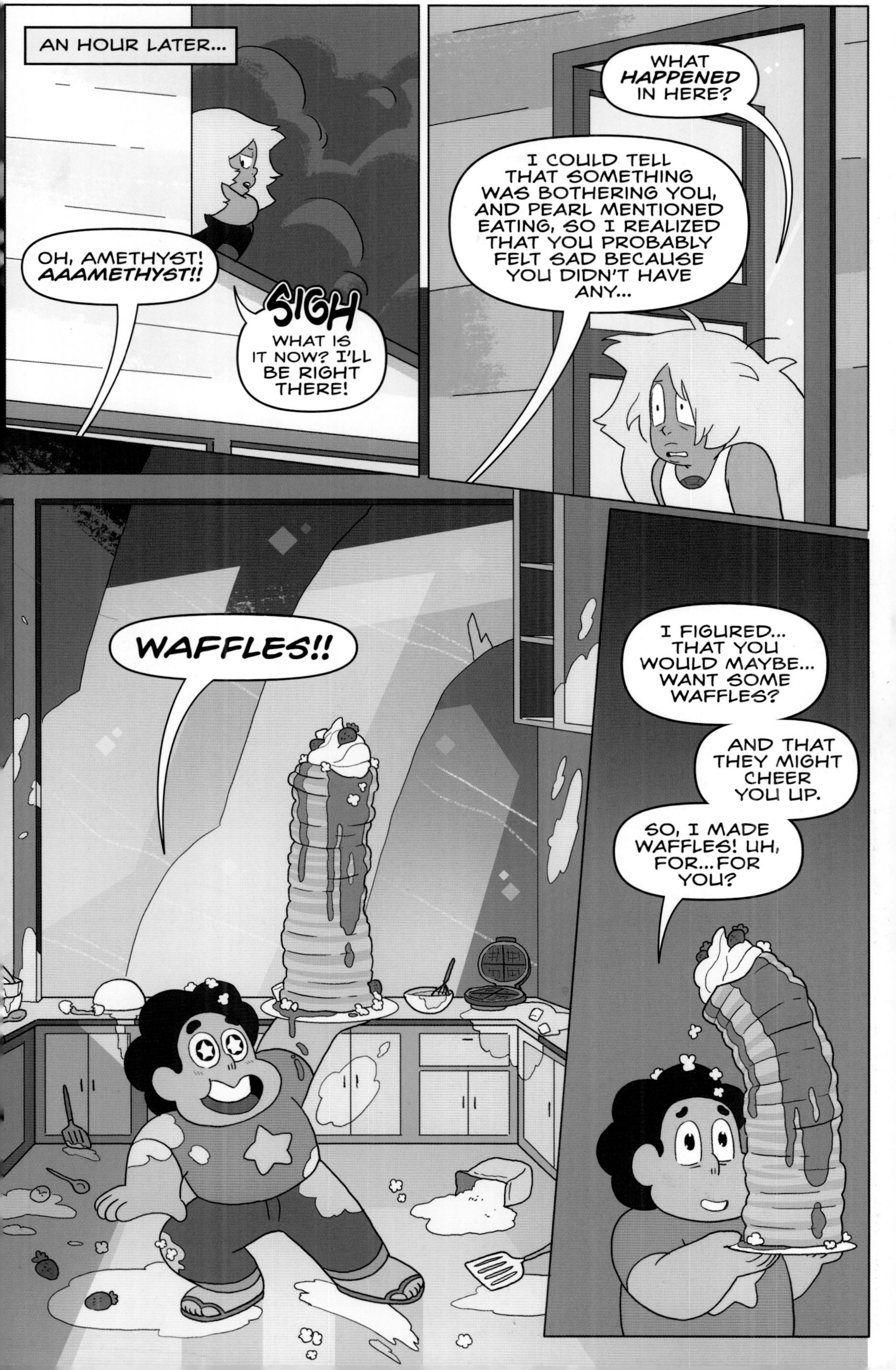
AN HOUR LATER...
OH, AMETHYST! AAAMETHYST!!
SIGH
WHAT IS IT NOW? I'LL BE RIGHT THERE!
WHAT HAPPENED IN HERE?
I COULD TELL THAT SOMETHING WAS BOTHERING YOU, AND PEARL MENTIONED EATING, SO I REALIZED THAT YOU PROBABLY FELT SAD BECAUSE YOU DIDN'T HAVE ANY...
WAFFLES!!
I FIGURED... THAT YOU WOULD MAYBE... WANT SOME WAFFLES?
AND THAT THEY MIGHT CHEER YOU UP.
SO, I MADE WAFFLES! UH, FOR...FOR YOU?

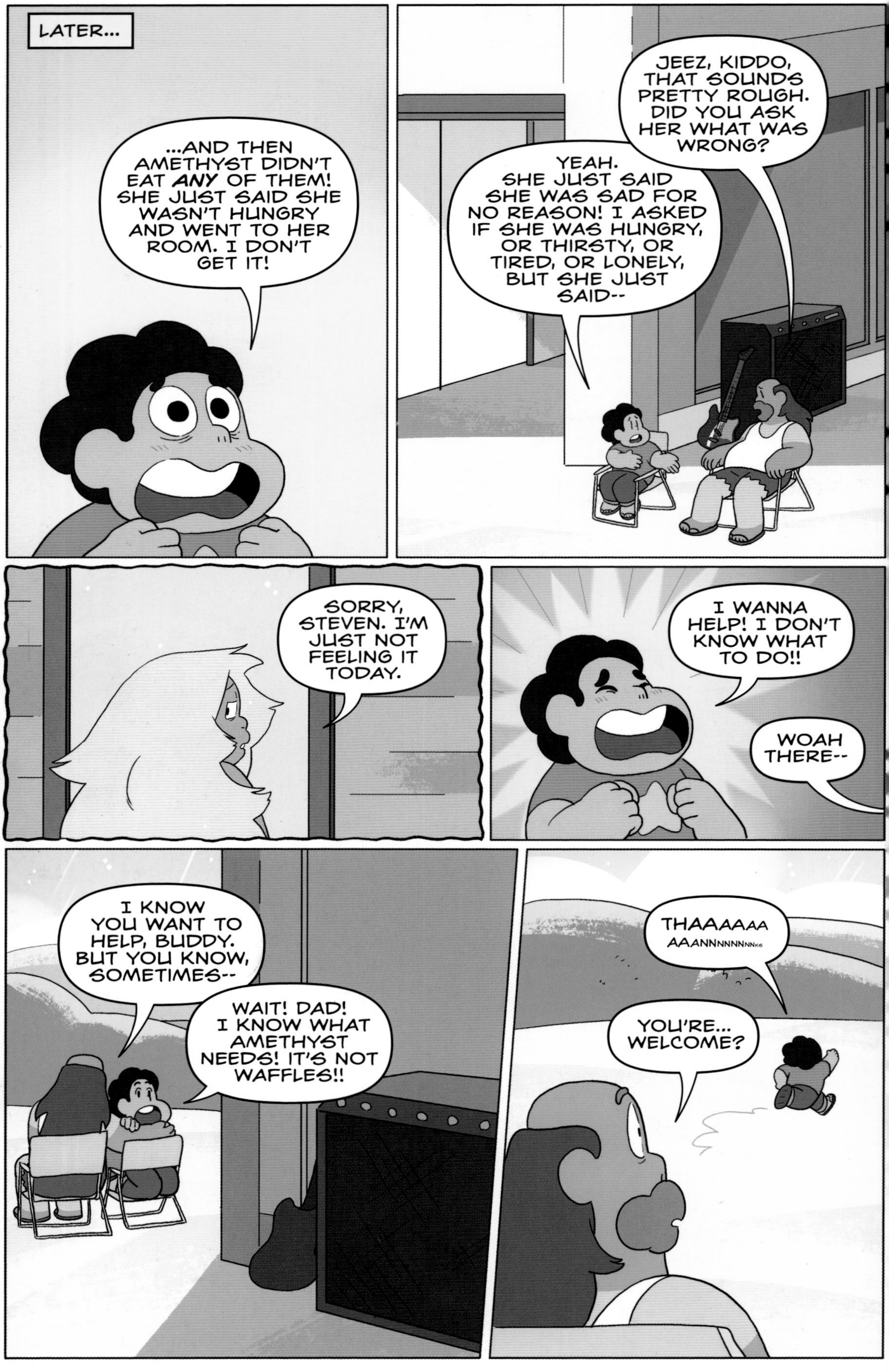

LATER...
...AND THEN AMETHYST DIDN'T EAT ANY OF THEM! SHE JUST SAID SHE WASN'T HUNGRY AND WENT TO HER ROOM. I DON'T GET IT!
JEEZ, KIDDO, THAT SOUNDS PRETTY ROUGH. DID YOU ASK HER WHAT WAS WRONG?
YEAH. SHE JUST SAID SHE WAS SAD FOR NO REASON! I ASKED IF SHE WAS HUNGRY, OR THIRSTY, OR TIRED, OR LONELY, BUT SHE JUST SAID--
SORRY, STEVEN. I'M JUST NOT FEELING IT TODAY.
I WANNA HELP! I DON'T KNOW WHAT TO DO!!
WOAH THERE--
I KNOW YOU WANT TO HELP, BUDDY. BUT YOU KNOW, SOMETIMES--
WAIT! DAD! I KNOW WHAT AMETHYST NEEDS! IT'S NOT WAFFLES!!
THAAAAAA AAANNNNNNNKS
YOU'RE... WELCOME?

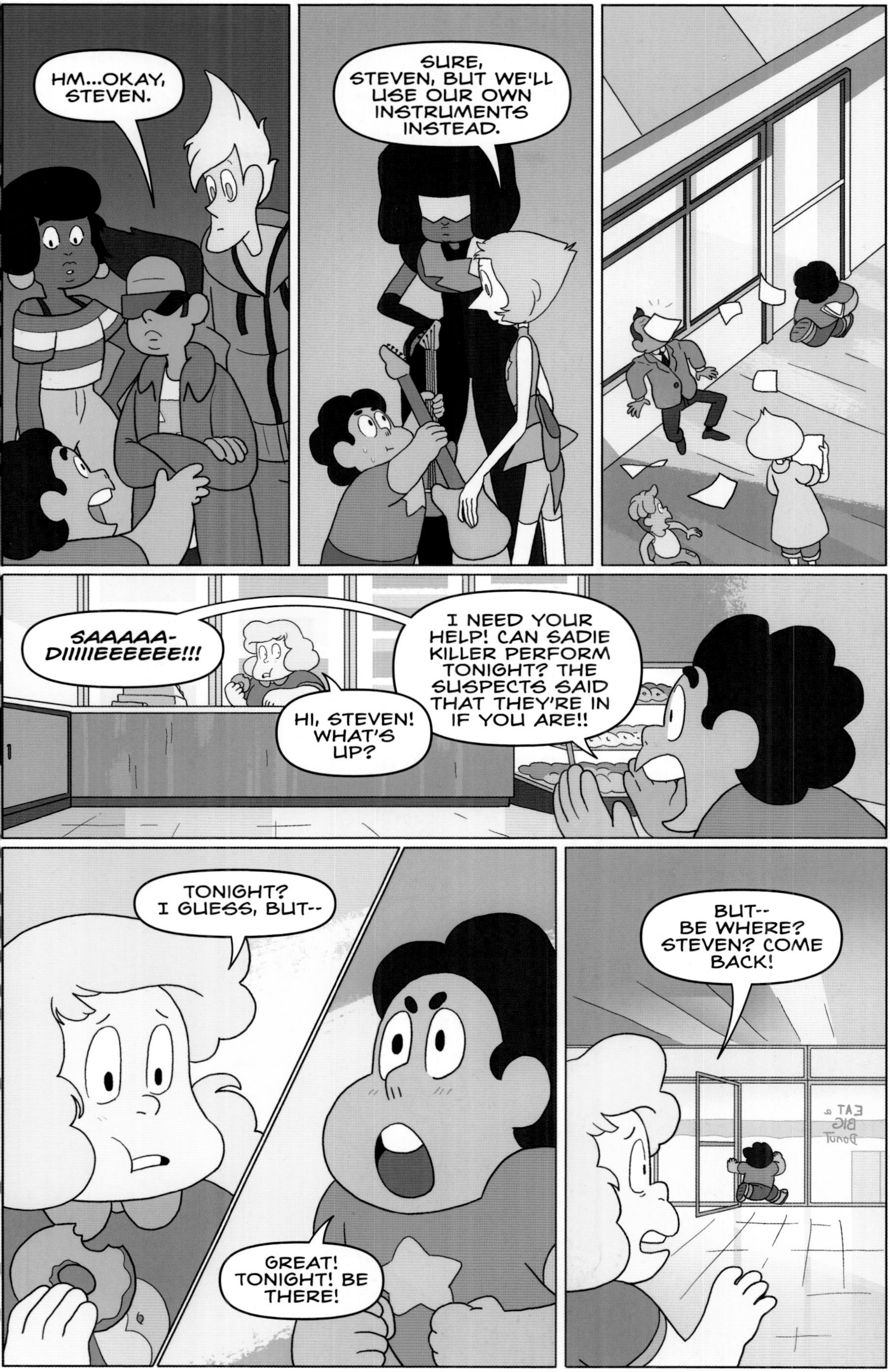
HM...OKAY, STEVEN.
SURE, STEVEN, BUT WE'LL USE OUR OWN INSTRUMENTS INSTEAD.
SAAAAAA-DIIIIIEEEEEE!!!
I NEED YOUR HELP! CAN SADIE KILLER PERFORM TONIGHT? THE SUSPECTS SAID THAT THEY'RE IN IF YOU ARE!!
HI, STEVEN! WHAT'S UP?
TONIGHT? I GUESS, BUT--
GREAT! TONIGHT! BE THERE!
BUT-- BE WHERE? STEVEN? COME BACK!

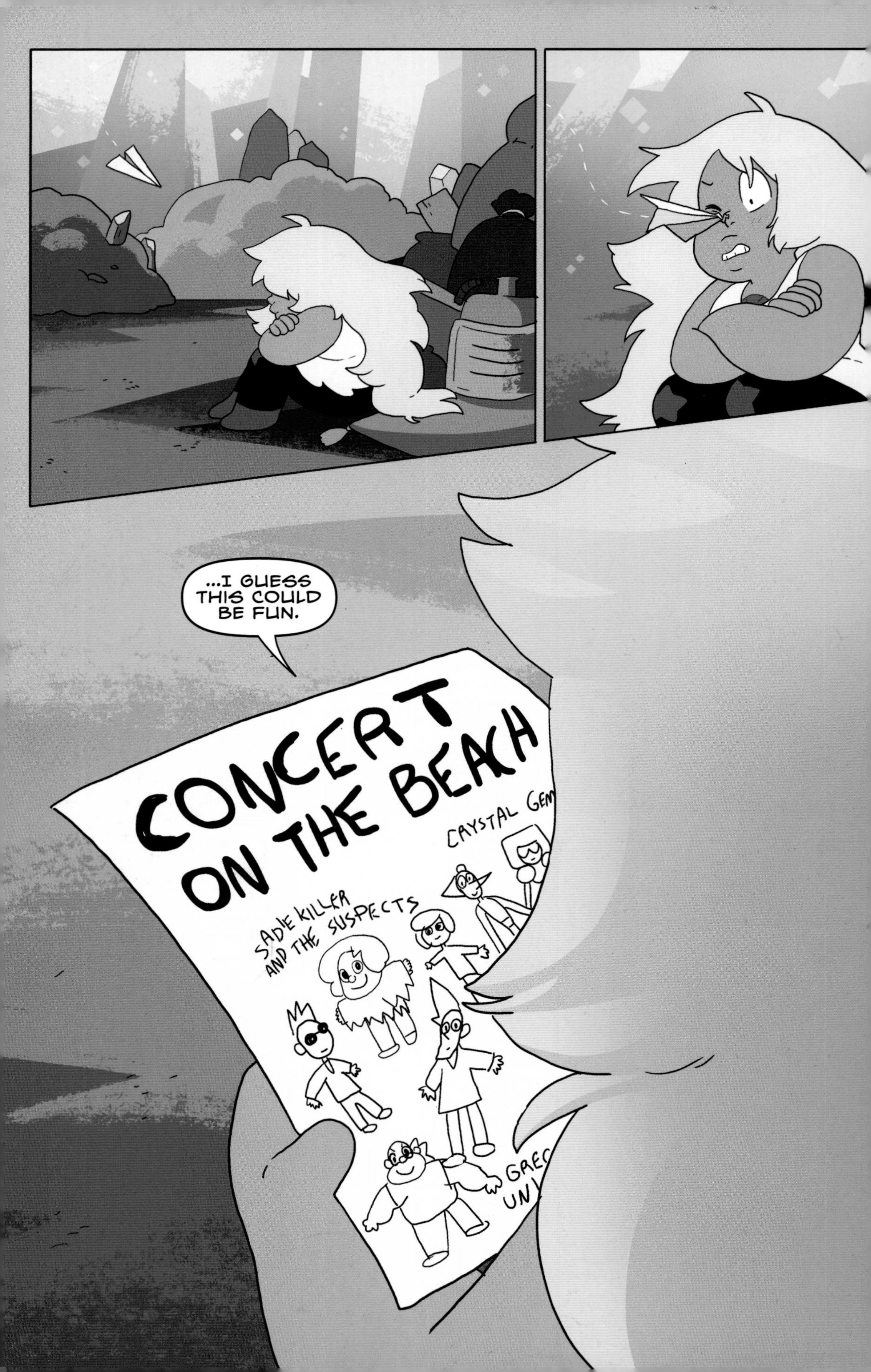
...I GUESS THIS COULD BE FUN.
CONCERT ON THE BEACH
CRYSTAL GEM
SADIE KILLER AND THE SUSPECTS

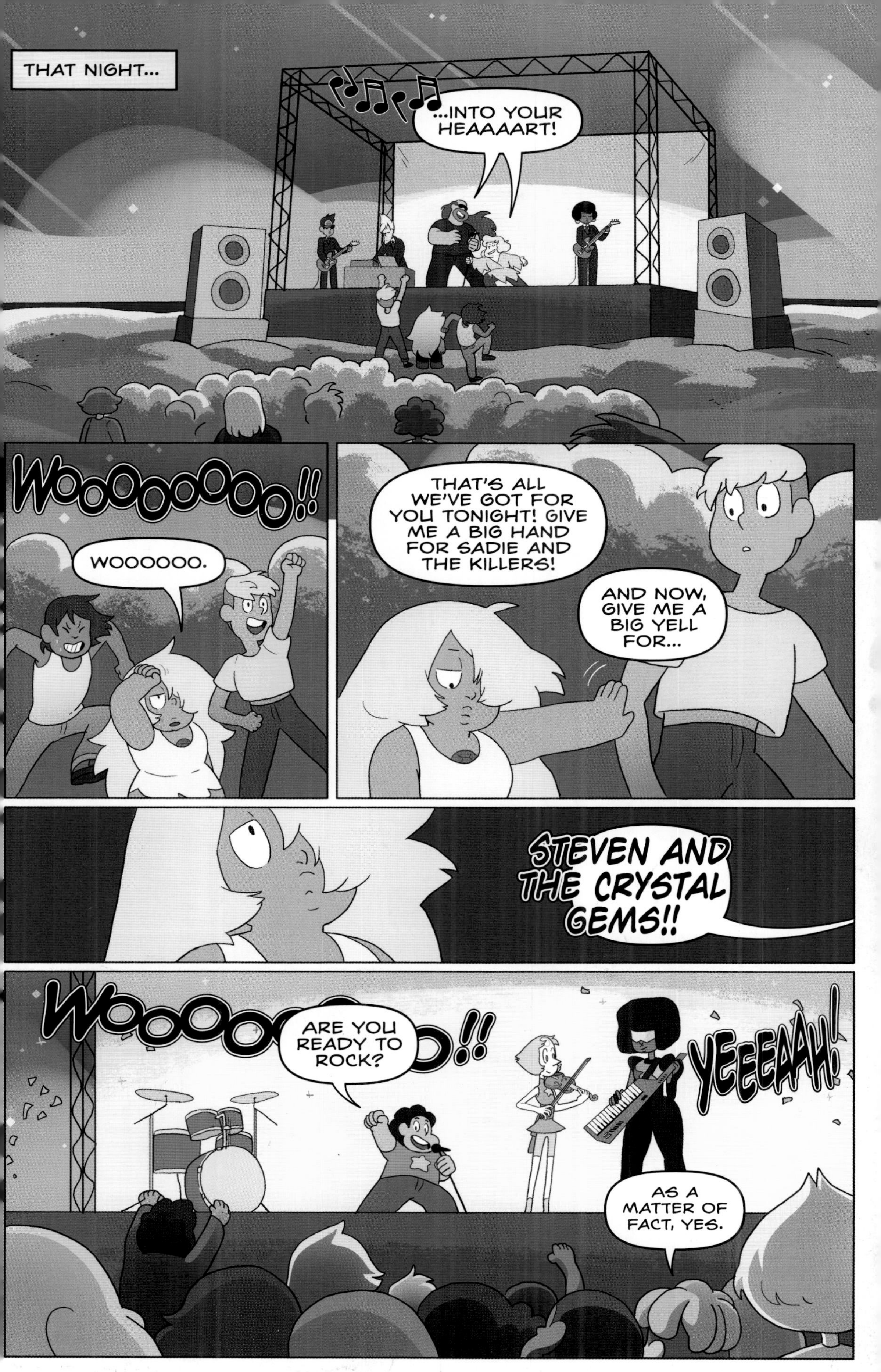
THAT NIGHT...
...INTO YOUR HEAAAART!
WOOOOOOOOO!!
WOOOOOO.
THAT'S ALL WE'VE GOT FOR YOU TONIGHT! GIVE ME A BIG HAND FOR SADIE AND THE KILLERS!
AND NOW, GIVE ME A BIG YELL FOR...
STEVEN AND THE CRYSTAL GEMS!!
ARE YOU READY TO ROCK?
YEEEAAH!
AS A MATTER OF FACT, YES.

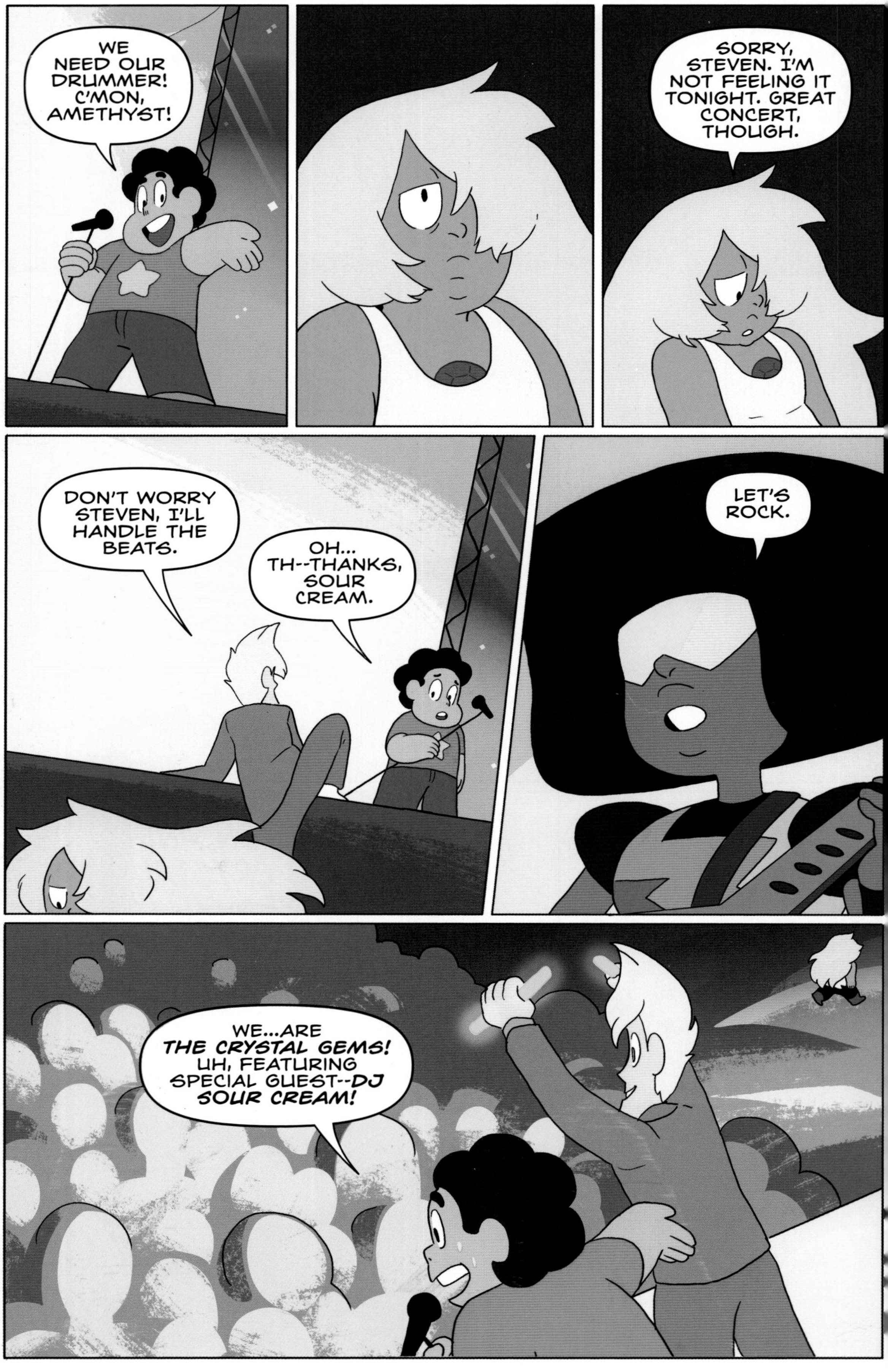
WE NEED OUR DRUMMER! C'MON, AMETHYST!
SORRY, STEVEN. I'M NOT FEELING IT TONIGHT. GREAT CONCERT, THOUGH.
DON'T WORRY STEVEN, I'LL HANDLE THE BEATS.
OH... TH--THANKS, SOUR CREAM.
LET'S ROCK.
WE...ARE *THE CRYSTAL GEMS!* UH, FEATURING SPECIAL GUEST--*DJ SOUR CREAM!*

LATER...

GREAT CONCERT, BUDDY. I THINK I HAVE GLITTER IN MY NOSE. AND MY EARS. AND...

...WELL, EVERYWHERE!

IT DIDN'T WORK THOUGH!

WHAT DO YOU MEAN?

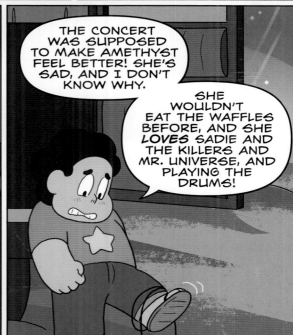

THE CONCERT WAS SUPPOSED TO MAKE AMETHYST FEEL BETTER! SHE'S SAD, AND I DON'T KNOW WHY.

SHE WOULDN'T EAT THE WAFFLES BEFORE, AND SHE *LOVES* SADIE AND THE KILLERS AND MR. UNIVERSE, AND PLAYING THE DRUMS!

I DON'T KNOW WHAT TO *DO*.

OH, STEVEN...

SOMETIMES, THERE'S NOTHING *TO* DO. SOMETIMES PEOPLE ARE JUST SAD.

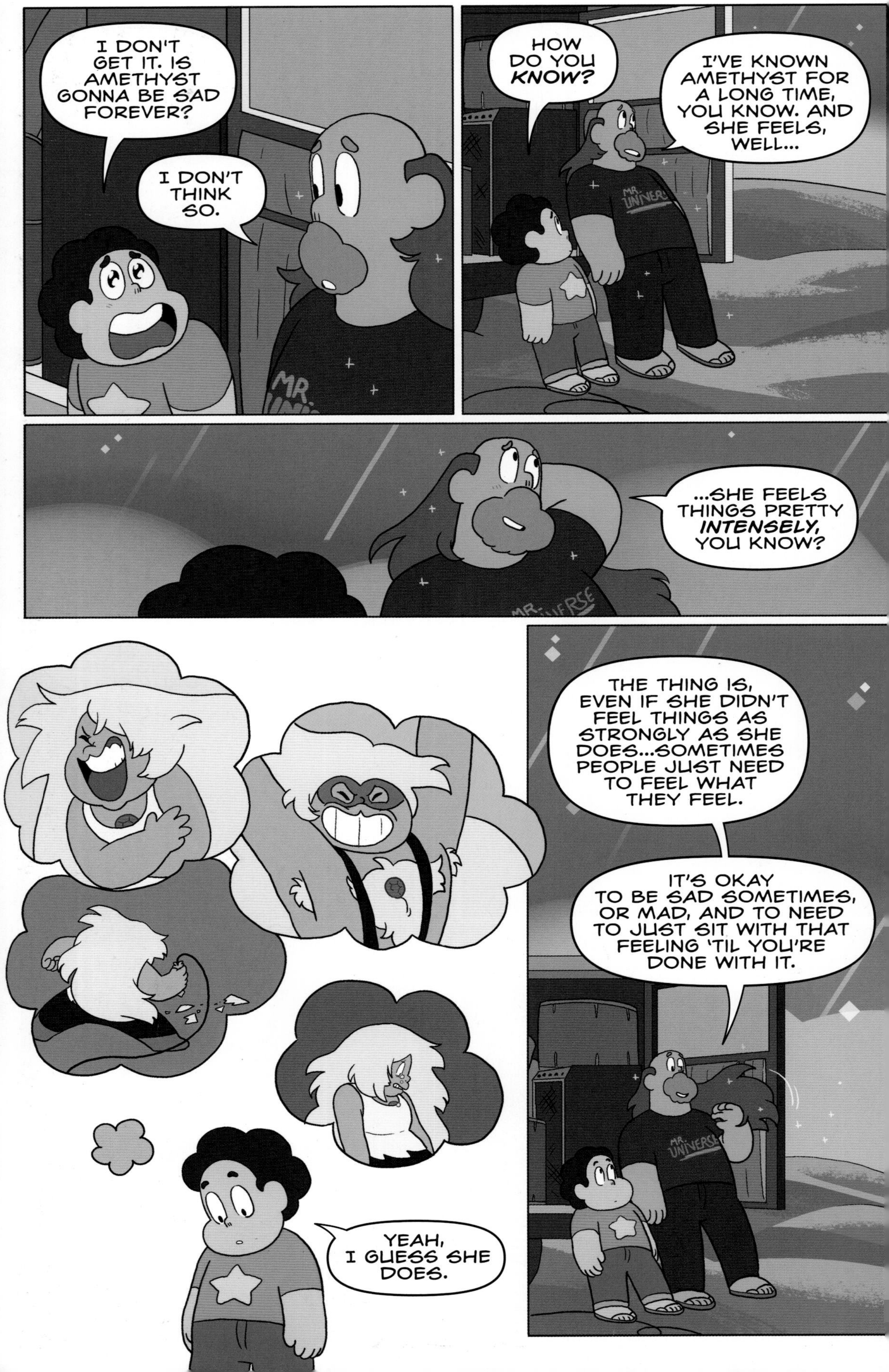
I DON'T GET IT. IS AMETHYST GONNA BE SAD FOREVER?
I DON'T THINK SO.
HOW DO YOU KNOW?
I'VE KNOWN AMETHYST FOR A LONG TIME, YOU KNOW. AND SHE FEELS, WELL...
MR. UNIVERSE
...SHE FEELS THINGS PRETTY INTENSELY, YOU KNOW?
MR. UNIVERSE
THE THING IS, EVEN IF SHE DIDN'T FEEL THINGS AS STRONGLY AS SHE DOES...SOMETIMES PEOPLE JUST NEED TO FEEL WHAT THEY FEEL.
IT'S OKAY TO BE SAD SOMETIMES, OR MAD, AND TO NEED TO JUST SIT WITH THAT FEELING 'TIL YOU'RE DONE WITH IT.
MR. UNIVERSE
YEAH, I GUESS SHE DOES.

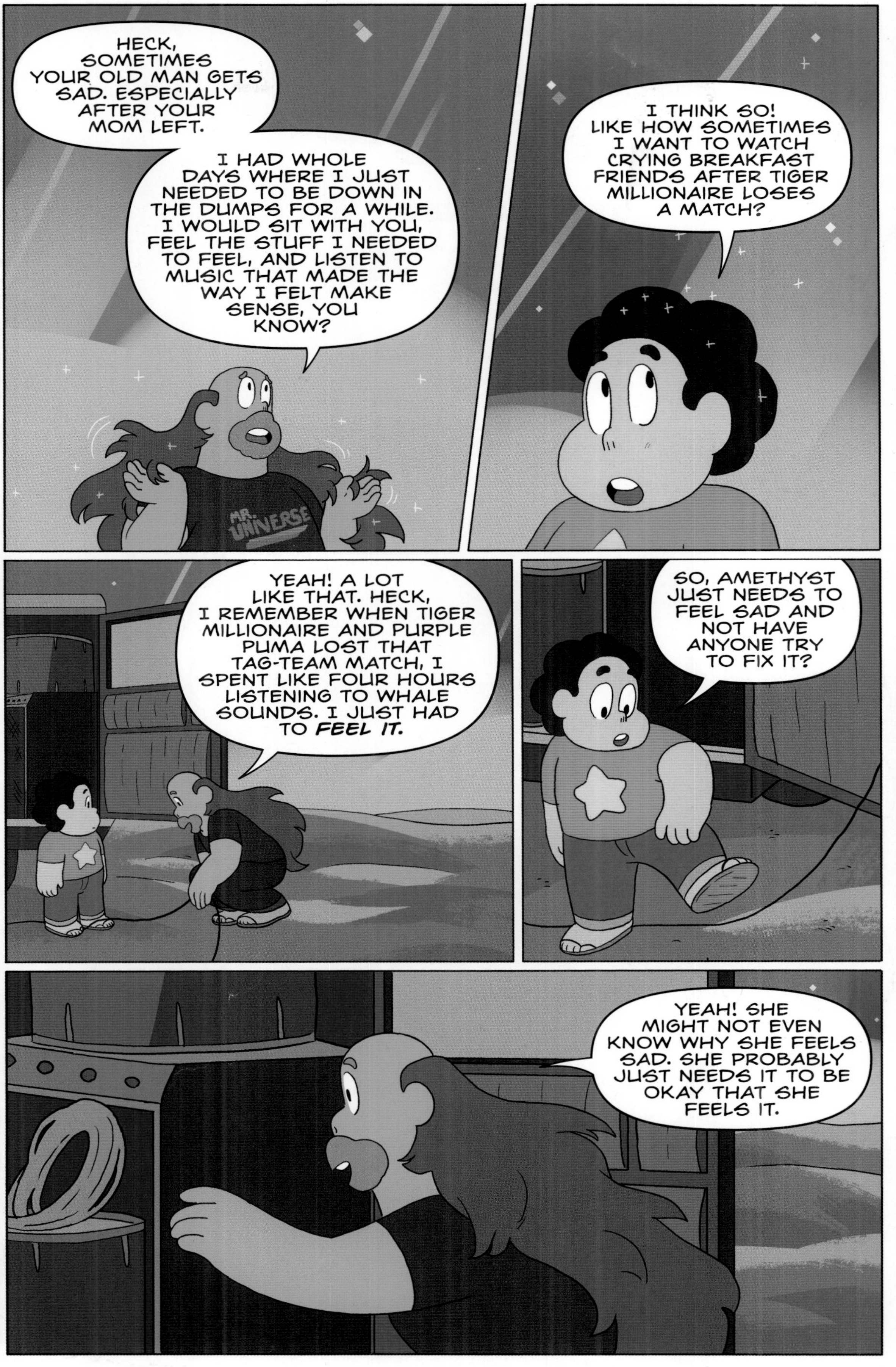
HECK, SOMETIMES YOUR OLD MAN GETS SAD. ESPECIALLY AFTER YOUR MOM LEFT.
I HAD WHOLE DAYS WHERE I JUST NEEDED TO BE DOWN IN THE DUMPS FOR A WHILE. I WOULD SIT WITH YOU, FEEL THE STUFF I NEEDED TO FEEL, AND LISTEN TO MUSIC THAT MADE THE WAY I FELT MAKE SENSE, YOU KNOW?
MR. UNIVERSE
I THINK SO! LIKE HOW SOMETIMES I WANT TO WATCH CRYING BREAKFAST FRIENDS AFTER TIGER MILLIONAIRE LOSES A MATCH?
YEAH! A LOT LIKE THAT. HECK, I REMEMBER WHEN TIGER MILLIONAIRE AND PURPLE PUMA LOST THAT TAG-TEAM MATCH, I SPENT LIKE FOUR HOURS LISTENING TO WHALE SOUNDS. I JUST HAD TO *FEEL IT.*
SO, AMETHYST JUST NEEDS TO FEEL SAD AND NOT HAVE ANYONE TRY TO FIX IT?
YEAH! SHE MIGHT NOT EVEN KNOW WHY SHE FEELS SAD. SHE PROBABLY JUST NEEDS IT TO BE OKAY THAT SHE FEELS IT.

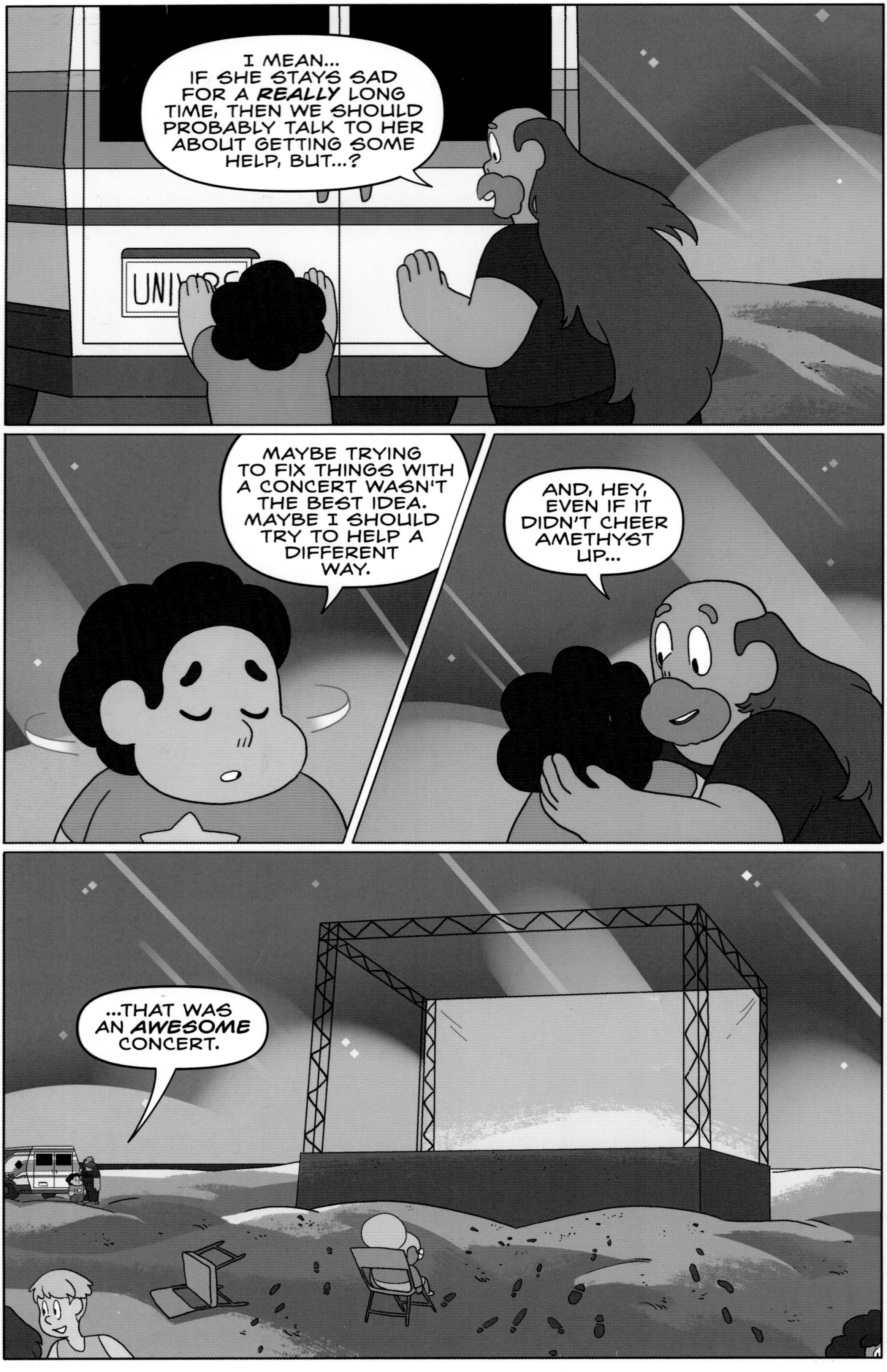
I MEAN... IF SHE STAYS SAD FOR A *REALLY* LONG TIME, THEN WE SHOULD PROBABLY TALK TO HER ABOUT GETTING SOME HELP, BUT...?
UNIV
MAYBE TRYING TO FIX THINGS WITH A CONCERT WASN'T THE BEST IDEA. MAYBE I SHOULD TRY TO HELP A DIFFERENT WAY.
AND, HEY, EVEN IF IT DIDN'T CHEER AMETHYST UP...
...THAT WAS AN *AWESOME* CONCERT.

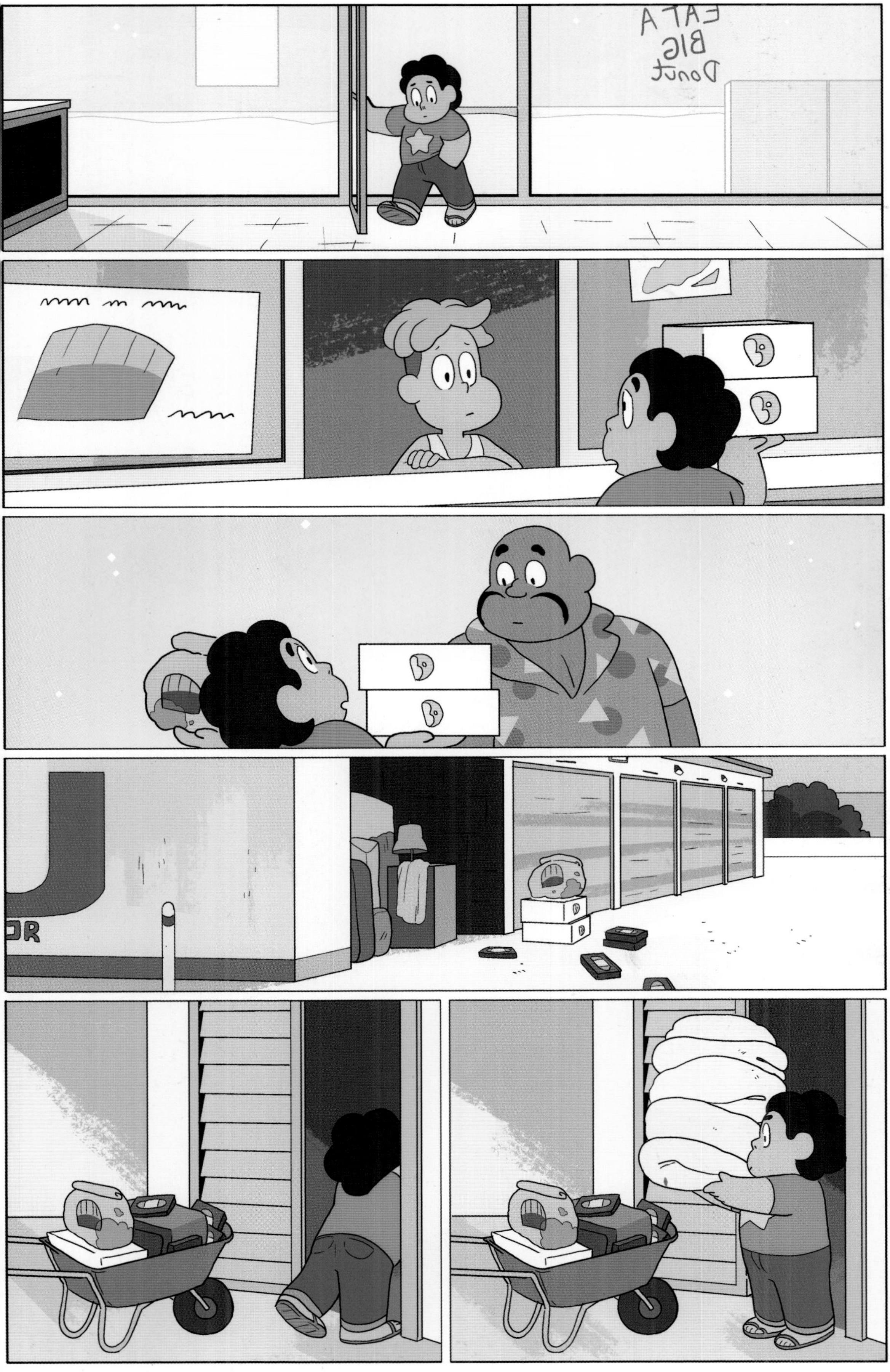
EAT A BIG Donut

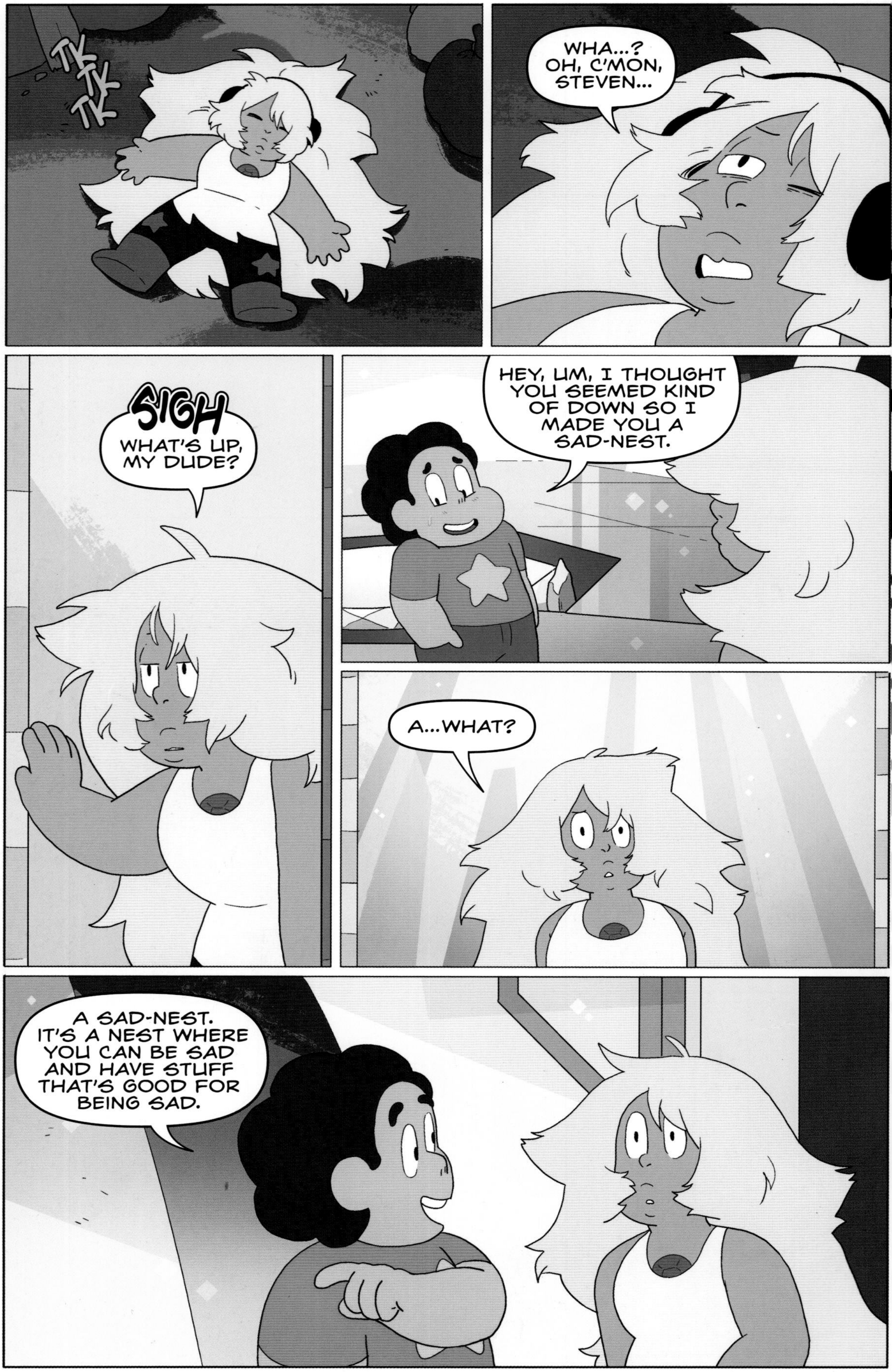
TK TK TK
WHA...? OH, C'MON, STEVEN...
SIGH
WHAT'S UP, MY DUDE?
HEY, UM, I THOUGHT YOU SEEMED KIND OF DOWN SO I MADE YOU A SAD-NEST.
A...WHAT?
A SAD-NEST. IT'S A NEST WHERE YOU CAN BE SAD AND HAVE STUFF THAT'S GOOD FOR BEING SAD.

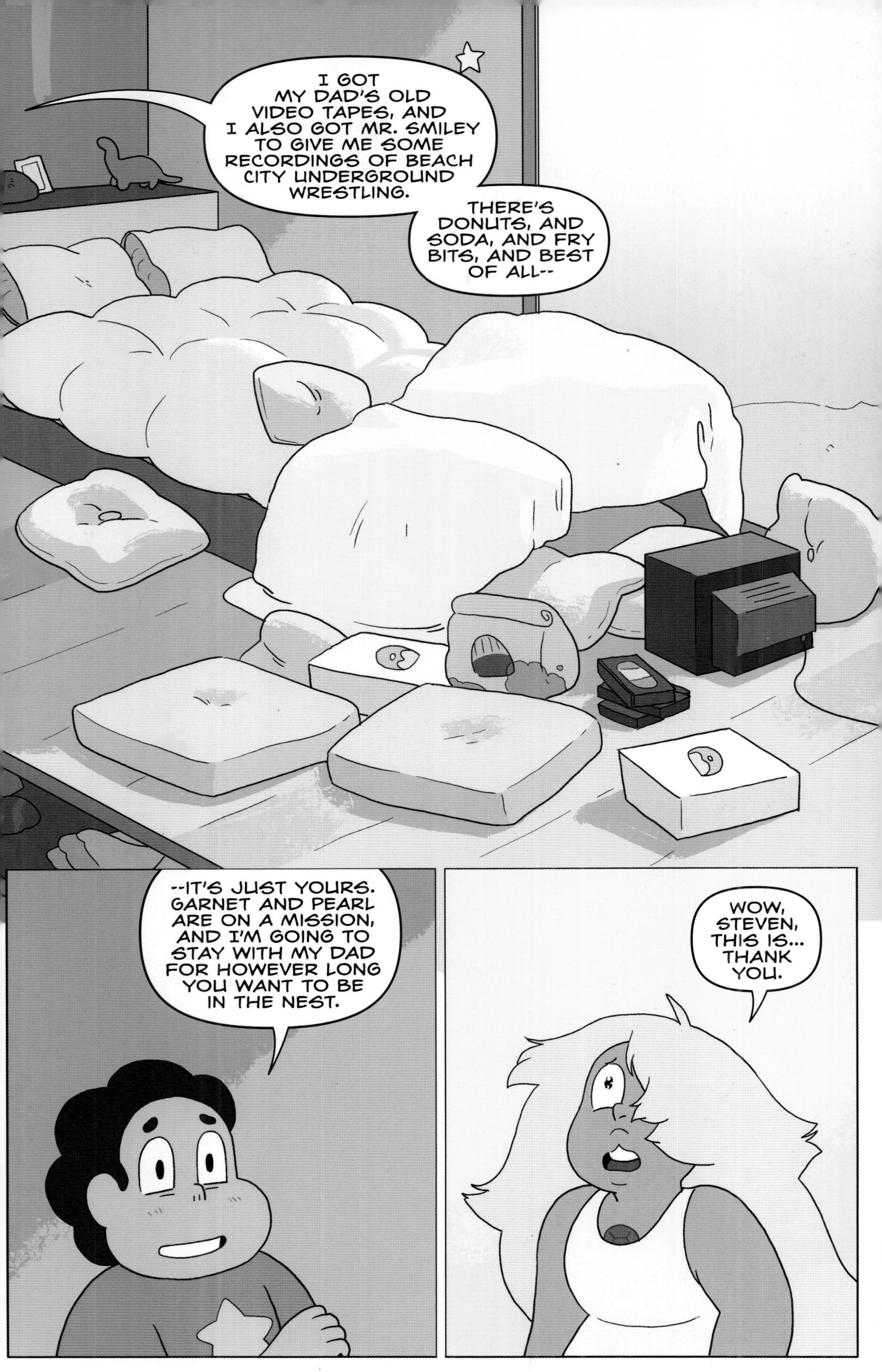
I GOT MY DAD'S OLD VIDEO TAPES, AND I ALSO GOT MR. SMILEY TO GIVE ME SOME RECORDINGS OF BEACH CITY UNDERGROUND WRESTLING.
THERE'S DONUTS, AND SODA, AND FRY BITS, AND BEST OF ALL--
--IT'S JUST YOURS. GARNET AND PEARL ARE ON A MISSION, AND I'M GOING TO STAY WITH MY DAD FOR HOWEVER LONG YOU WANT TO BE IN THE NEST.
WOW, STEVEN, THIS IS... THANK YOU.

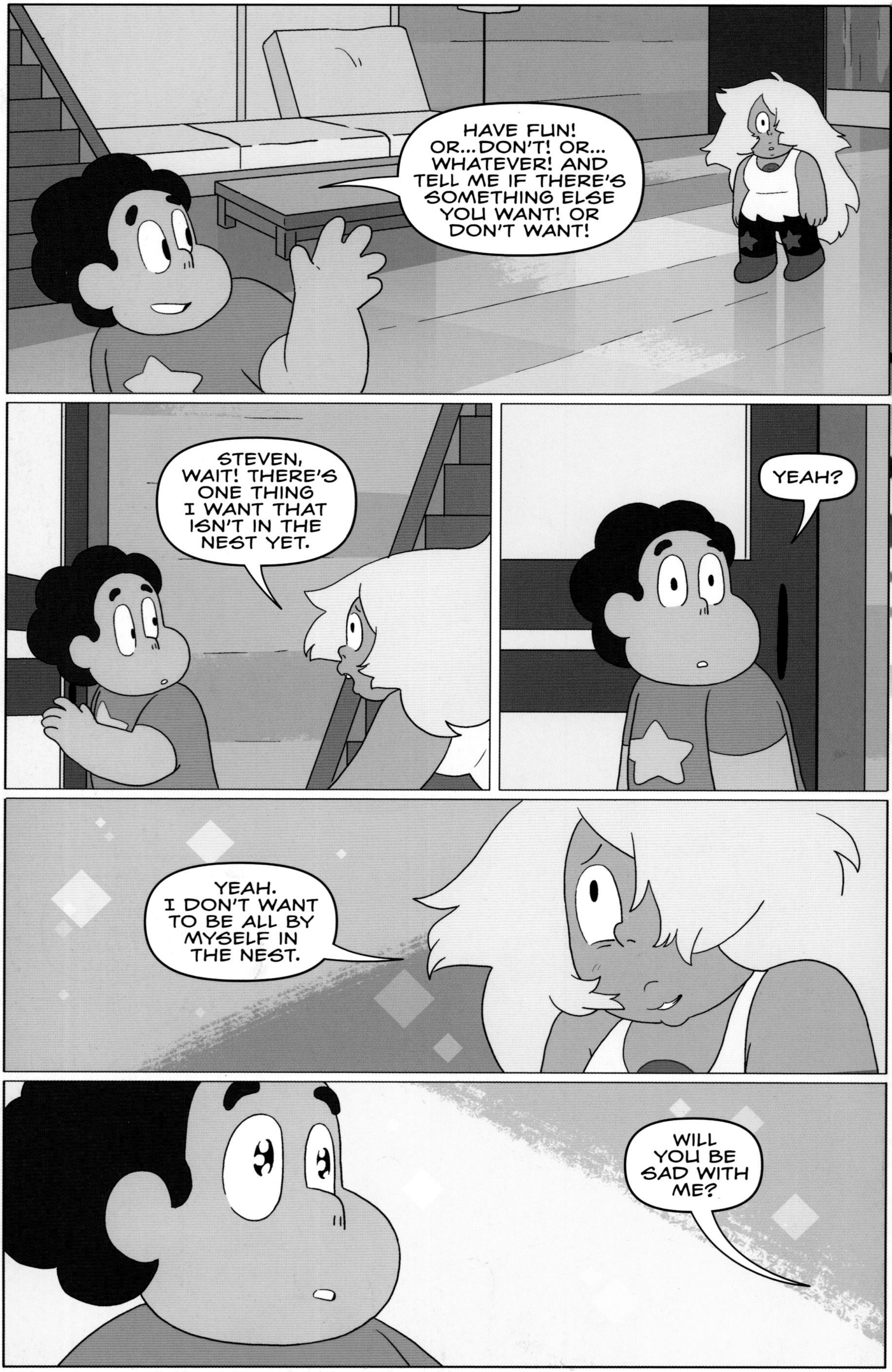
HAVE FUN! OR...DON'T! OR... WHATEVER! AND TELL ME IF THERE'S SOMETHING ELSE YOU WANT! OR DON'T WANT!
STEVEN, WAIT! THERE'S ONE THING I WANT THAT ISN'T IN THE NEST YET.
YEAH?
YEAH. I DON'T WANT TO BE ALL BY MYSELF IN THE NEST.
WILL YOU BE SAD WITH ME?

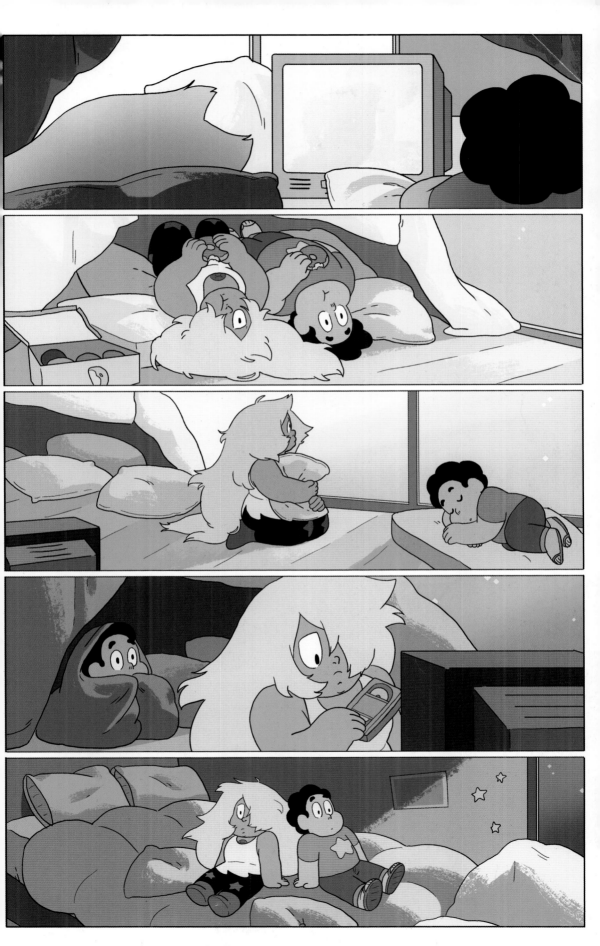

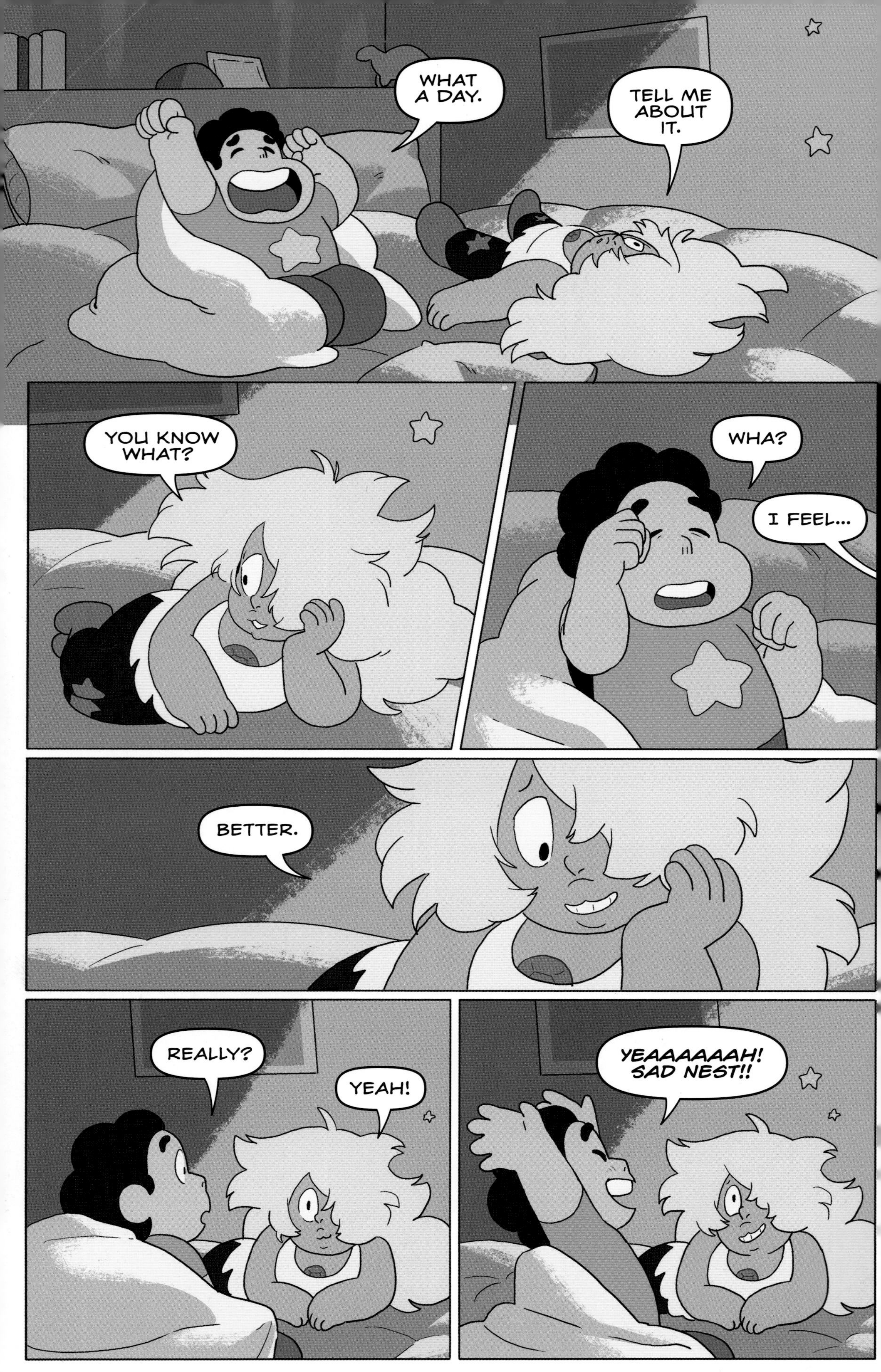
WHAT A DAY.
TELL ME ABOUT IT.
YOU KNOW WHAT?
WHA?
I FEEL...
BETTER.
REALLY?
YEAH!
YEAAAAAAH! SAD NEST!!

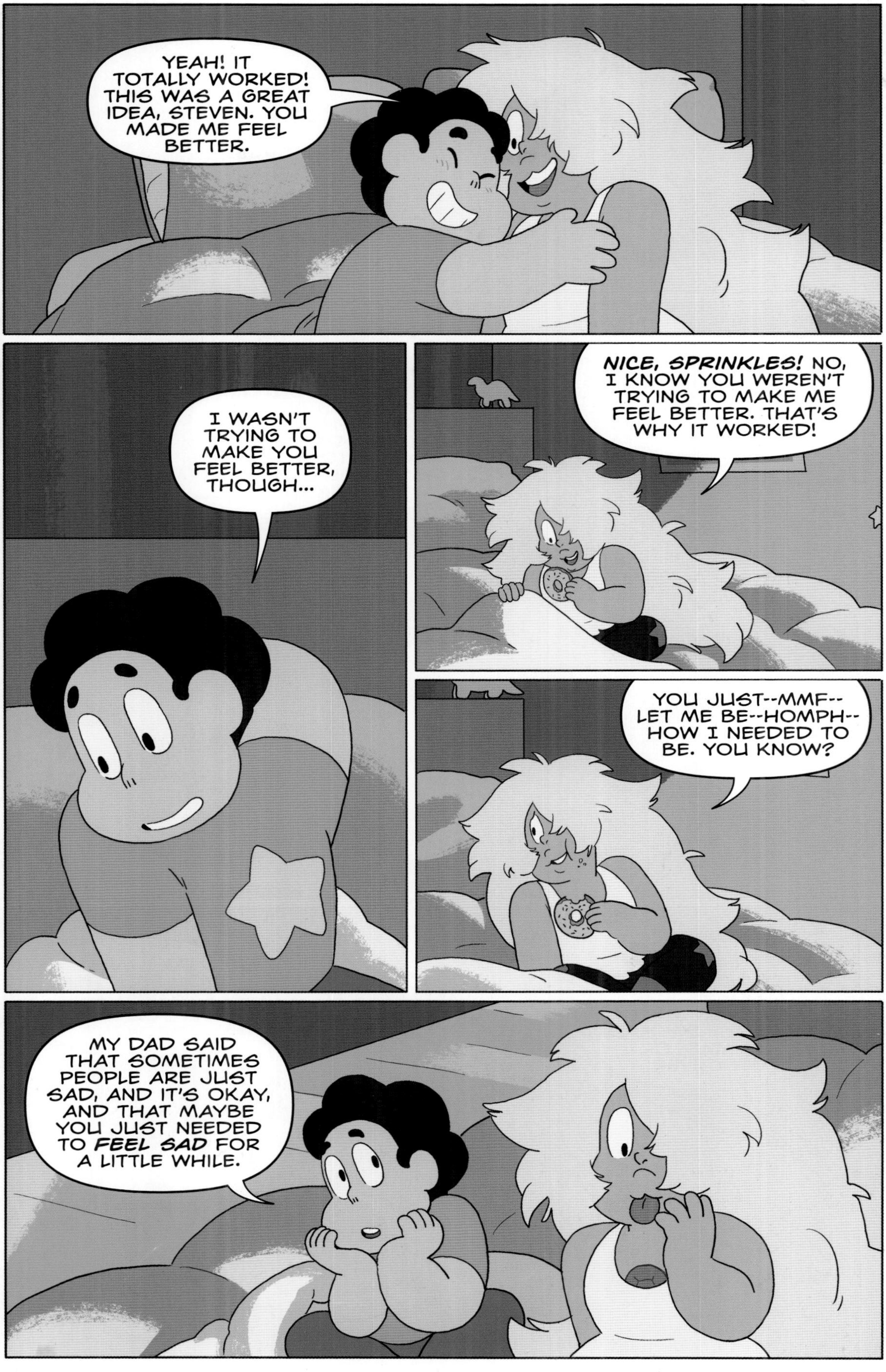
YEAH! IT TOTALLY WORKED! THIS WAS A GREAT IDEA, STEVEN. YOU MADE ME FEEL BETTER.
I WASN'T TRYING TO MAKE YOU FEEL BETTER, THOUGH...
NICE, SPRINKLES! NO, I KNOW YOU WEREN'T TRYING TO MAKE ME FEEL BETTER. THAT'S WHY IT WORKED!
YOU JUST--MMF-- LET ME BE--HOMPH-- HOW I NEEDED TO BE. YOU KNOW?
MY DAD SAID THAT SOMETIMES PEOPLE ARE JUST SAD, AND IT'S OKAY, AND THAT MAYBE YOU JUST NEEDED TO FEEL SAD FOR A LITTLE WHILE.

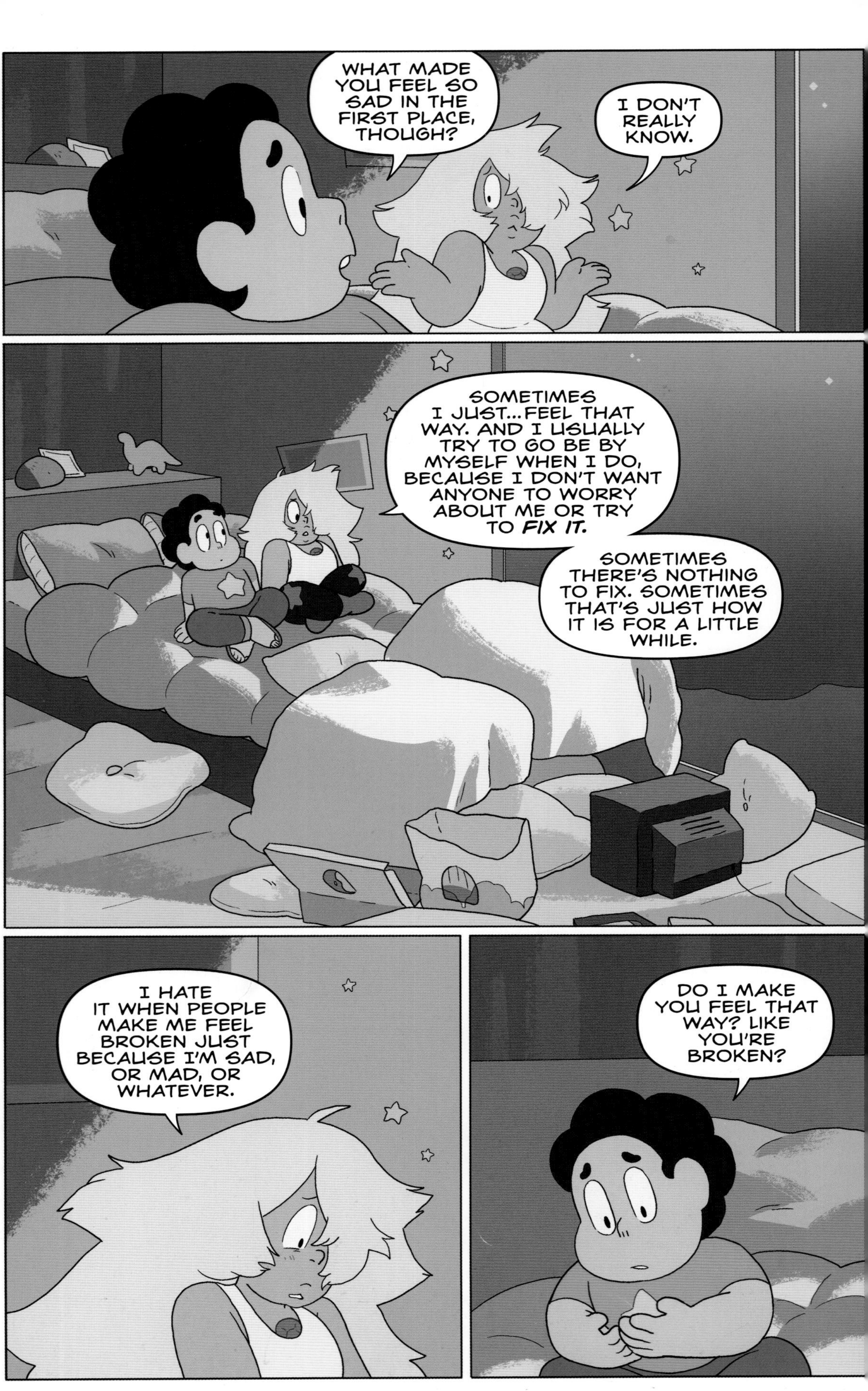
WHAT MADE YOU FEEL SO SAD IN THE FIRST PLACE, THOUGH?
I DON'T REALLY KNOW.
SOMETIMES I JUST...FEEL THAT WAY. AND I USUALLY TRY TO GO BE BY MYSELF WHEN I DO, BECAUSE I DON'T WANT ANYONE TO WORRY ABOUT ME OR TRY TO FIX IT.
SOMETIMES THERE'S NOTHING TO FIX. SOMETIMES THAT'S JUST HOW IT IS FOR A LITTLE WHILE.
I HATE IT WHEN PEOPLE MAKE ME FEEL BROKEN JUST BECAUSE I'M SAD, OR MAD, OR WHATEVER.
DO I MAKE YOU FEEL THAT WAY? LIKE YOU'RE BROKEN?

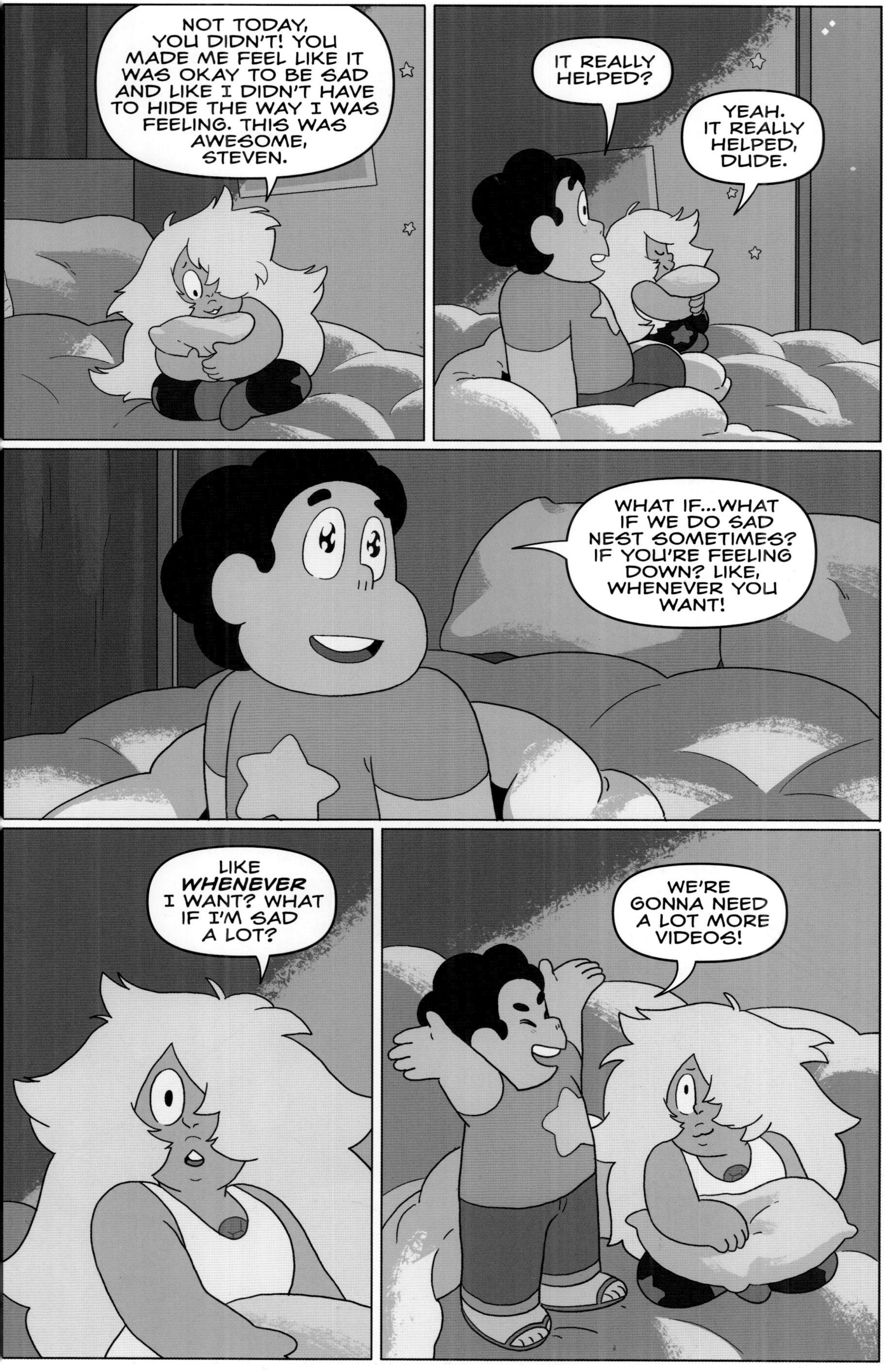
NOT TODAY, YOU DIDN'T! YOU MADE ME FEEL LIKE IT WAS OKAY TO BE SAD AND LIKE I DIDN'T HAVE TO HIDE THE WAY I WAS FEELING. THIS WAS AWESOME, STEVEN.
IT REALLY HELPED?
YEAH. IT REALLY HELPED, DUDE.
WHAT IF...WHAT IF WE DO SAD NEST SOMETIMES? IF YOU'RE FEELING DOWN? LIKE, WHENEVER YOU WANT!
LIKE *WHENEVER* I WANT? WHAT IF I'M SAD A LOT?
WE'RE GONNA NEED A LOT MORE VIDEOS!

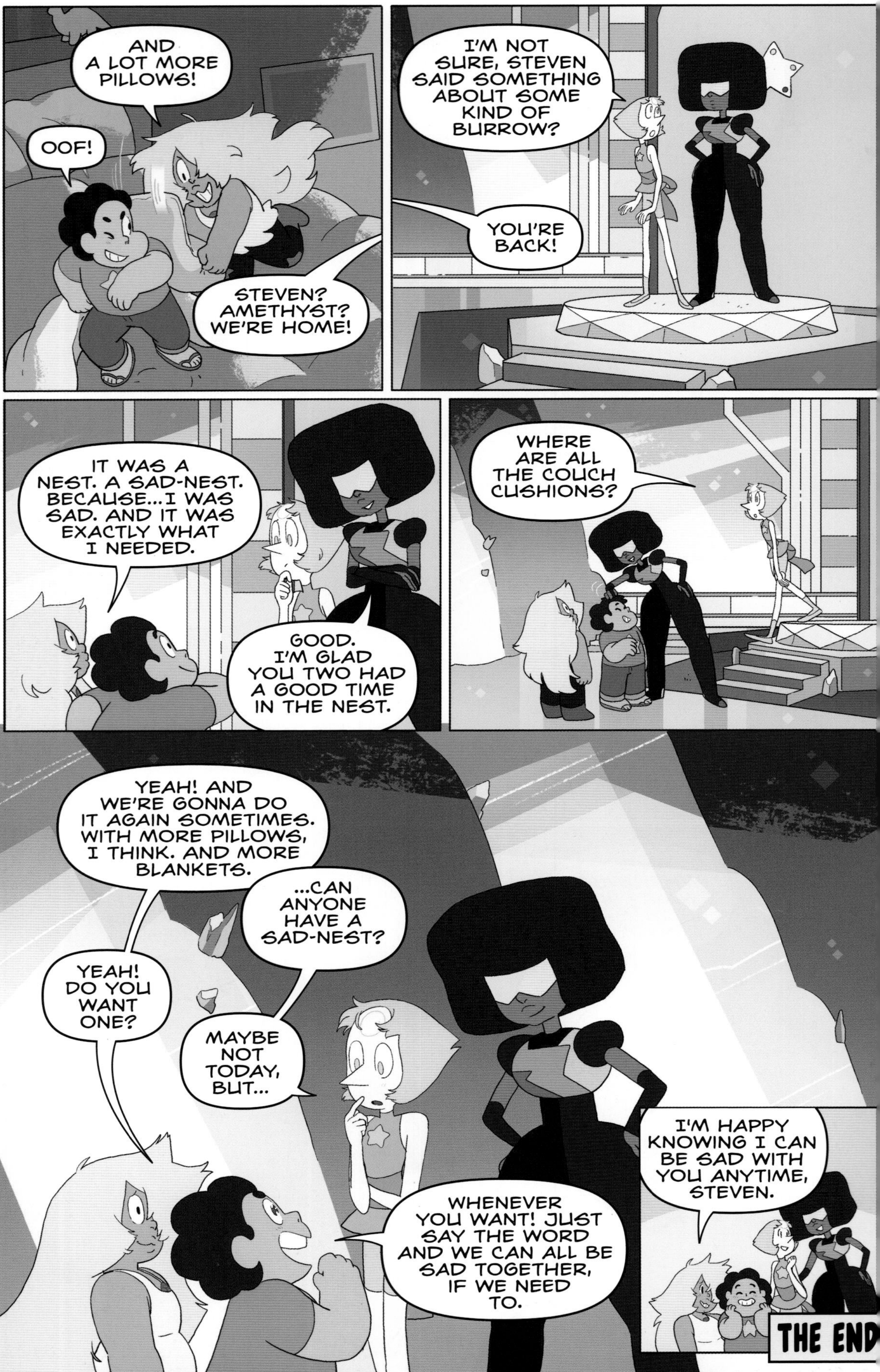
AND A LOT MORE PILLOWS!
OOF!
STEVEN? AMETHYST? WE'RE HOME!
I'M NOT SURE, STEVEN SAID SOMETHING ABOUT SOME KIND OF BURROW?
YOU'RE BACK!
IT WAS A NEST. A SAD-NEST. BECAUSE...I WAS SAD. AND IT WAS EXACTLY WHAT I NEEDED.
GOOD. I'M GLAD YOU TWO HAD A GOOD TIME IN THE NEST.
WHERE ARE ALL THE COUCH CUSHIONS?
YEAH! AND WE'RE GONNA DO IT AGAIN SOMETIMES. WITH MORE PILLOWS, I THINK. AND MORE BLANKETS.
...CAN ANYONE HAVE A SAD-NEST?
YEAH! DO YOU WANT ONE?
MAYBE NOT TODAY, BUT...
WHENEVER YOU WANT! JUST SAY THE WORD AND WE CAN ALL BE SAD TOGETHER, IF WE NEED TO.
I'M HAPPY KNOWING I CAN BE SAD WITH YOU ANYTIME, STEVEN.
THE END

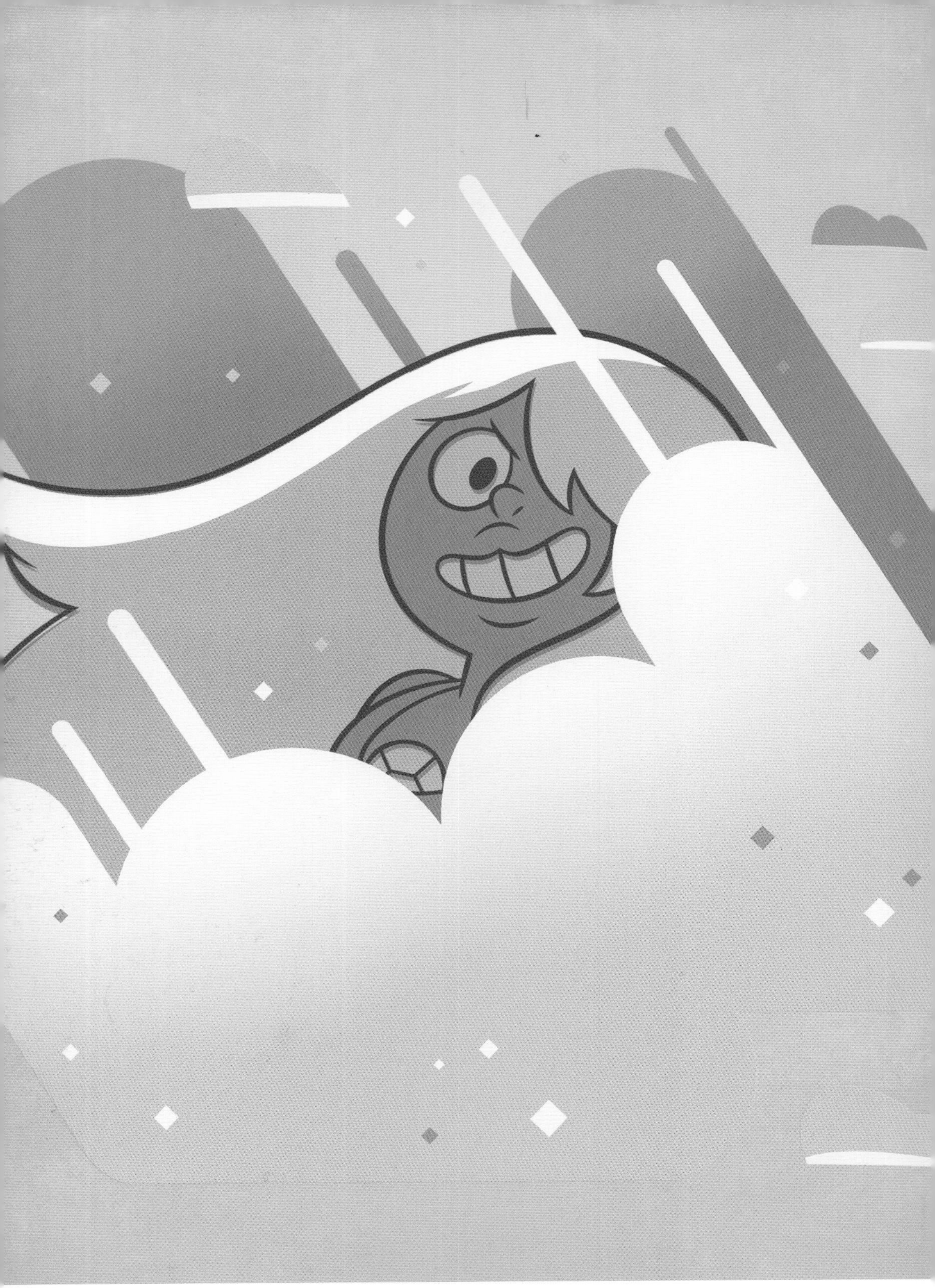

CHAPTER THIRTY

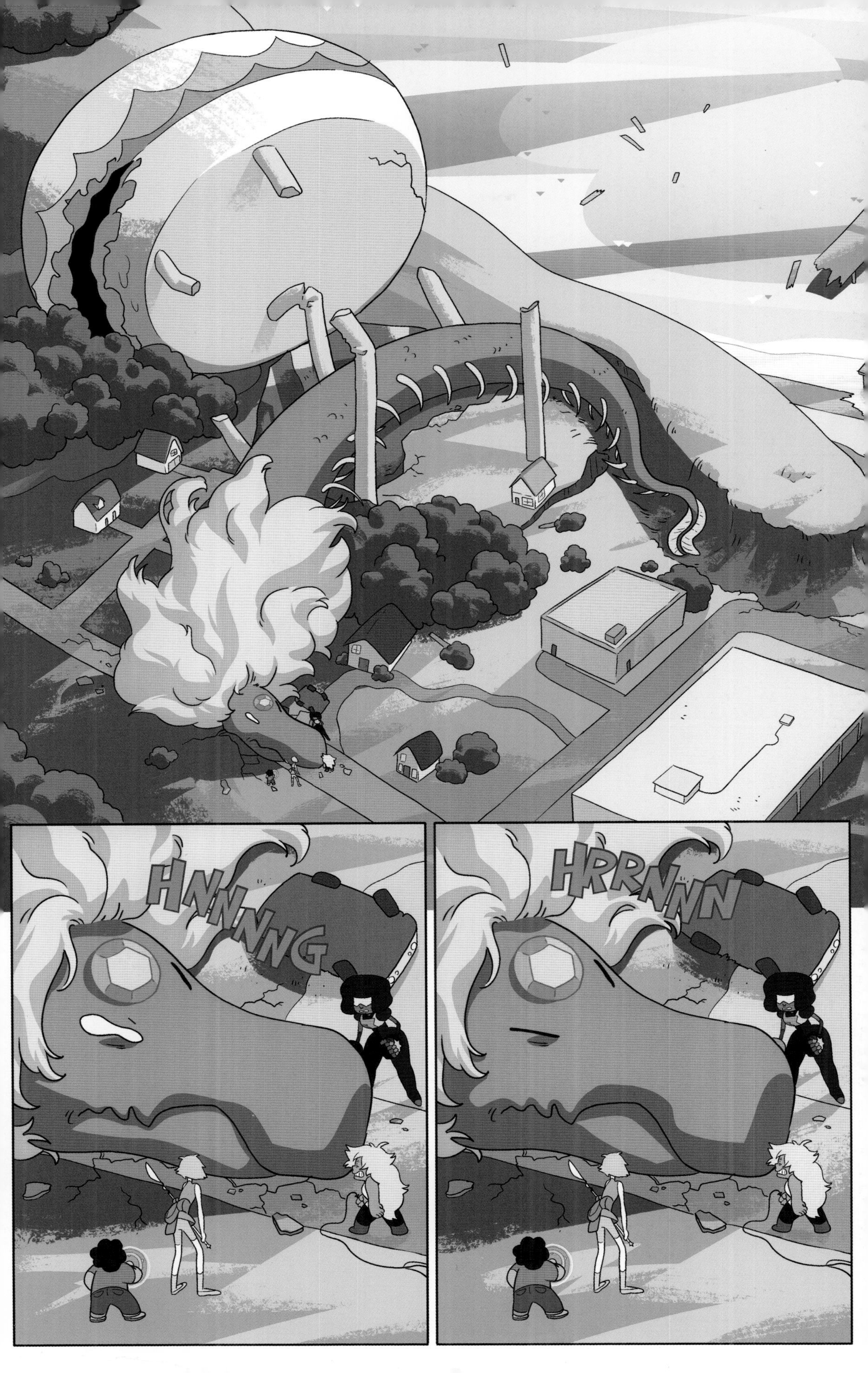
HNNNNG
HRRNNN

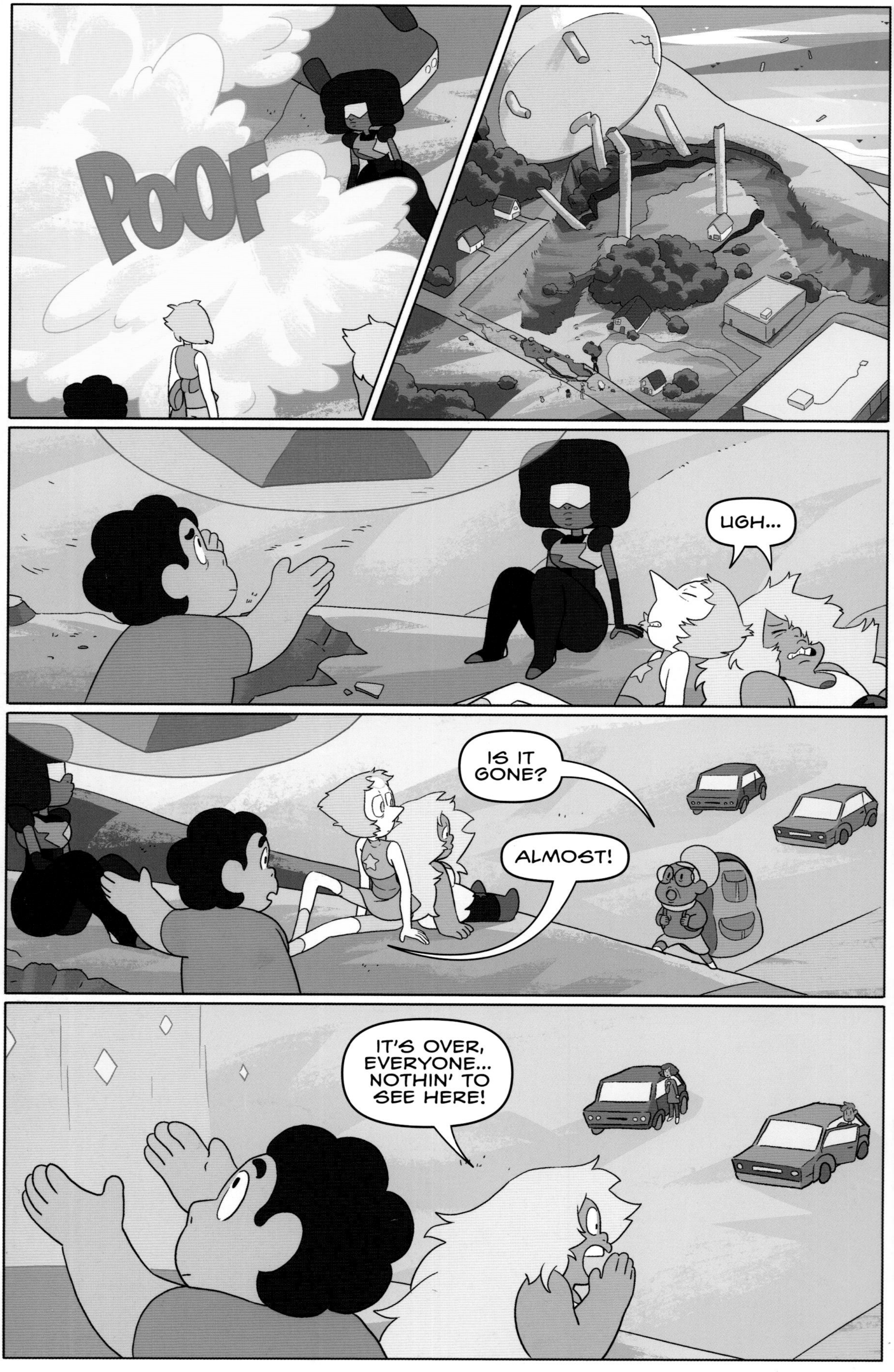
POOF
UGH...
IS IT GONE?
ALMOST!
IT'S OVER, EVERYONE... NOTHIN' TO SEE HERE!

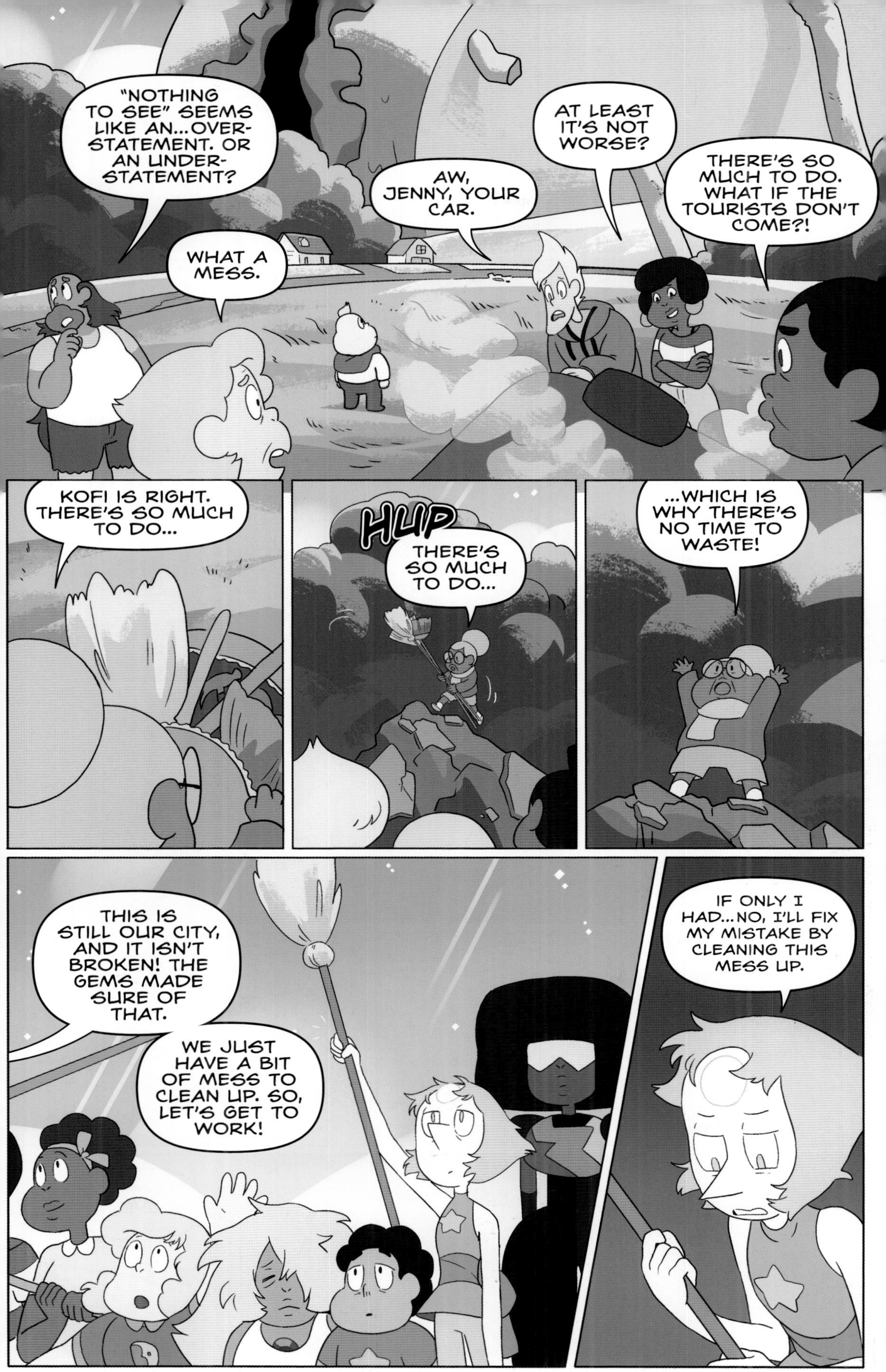
"NOTHING TO SEE" SEEMS LIKE AN...OVER-STATEMENT. OR AN UNDER-STATEMENT?
WHAT A MESS.
AW, JENNY, YOUR CAR.
AT LEAST IT'S NOT WORSE?
THERE'S SO MUCH TO DO. WHAT IF THE TOURISTS DON'T COME?!
KOFI IS RIGHT. THERE'S SO MUCH TO DO...
HUP
THERE'S SO MUCH TO DO...
...WHICH IS WHY THERE'S NO TIME TO WASTE!
THIS IS STILL OUR CITY, AND IT ISN'T BROKEN! THE GEMS MADE SURE OF THAT.
WE JUST HAVE A BIT OF MESS TO CLEAN UP. SO, LET'S GET TO WORK!
IF ONLY I HAD...NO, I'LL FIX MY MISTAKE BY CLEANING THIS MESS UP.

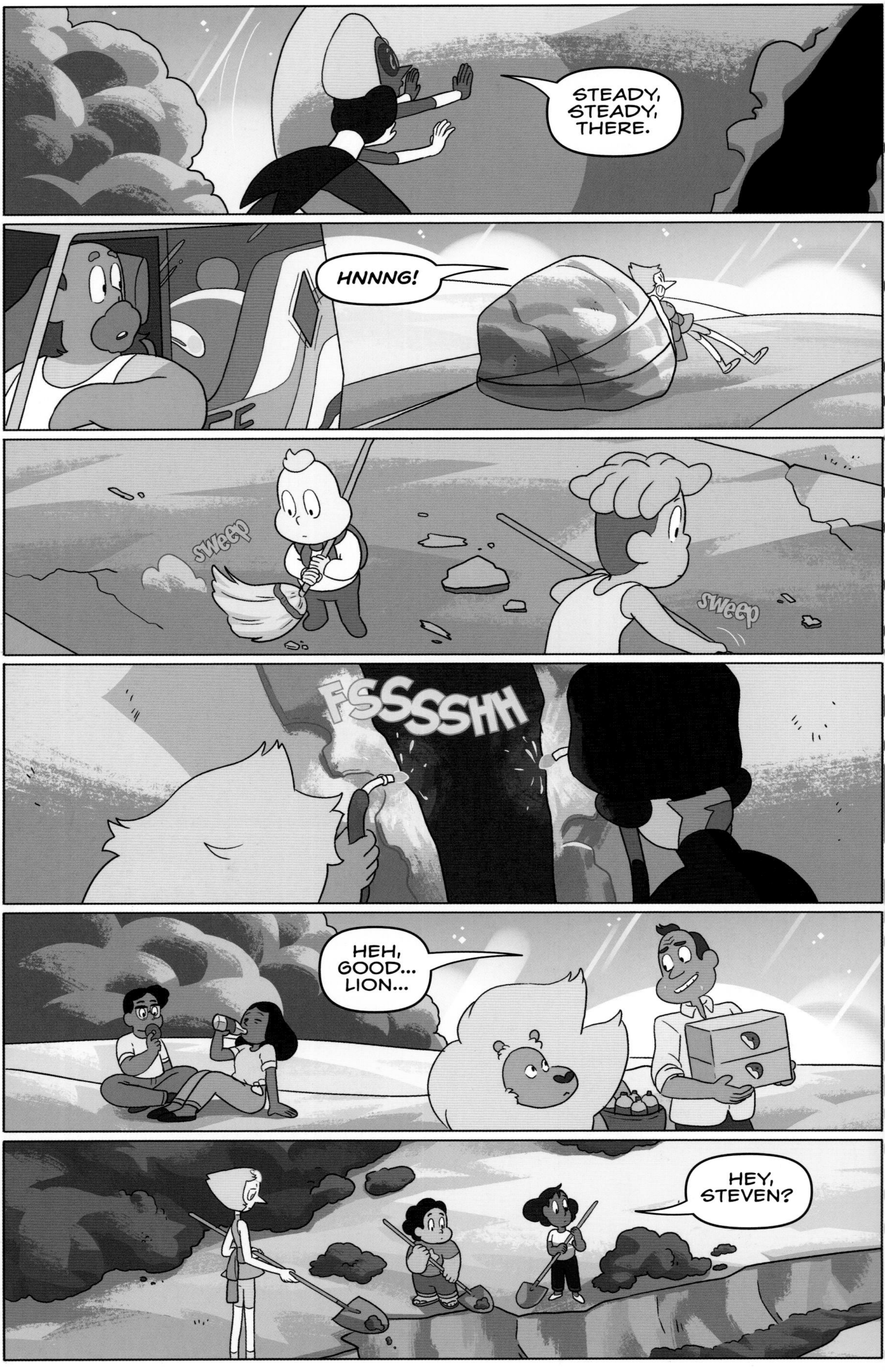
STEADY, STEADY, THERE.
HNNNG!
SWEEP
SWEEP
FSSSSHH
HEH, GOOD... LION...
HEY, STEVEN?

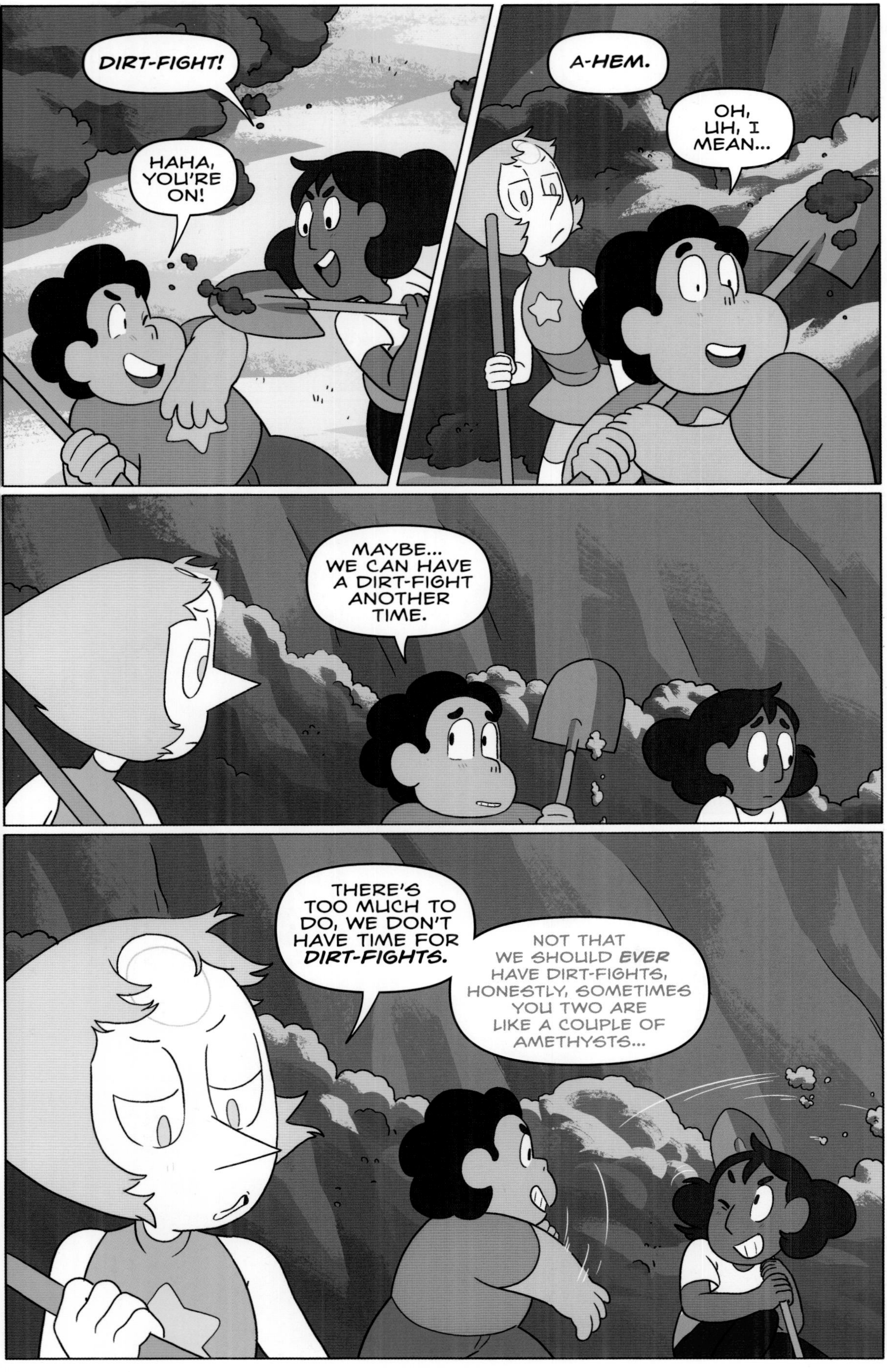
DIRT-FIGHT!
HAHA, YOU'RE ON!
A-HEM.
OH, UH, I MEAN...
MAYBE... WE CAN HAVE A DIRT-FIGHT ANOTHER TIME.
THERE'S TOO MUCH TO DO, WE DON'T HAVE TIME FOR DIRT-FIGHTS.
NOT THAT WE SHOULD EVER HAVE DIRT-FIGHTS, HONESTLY, SOMETIMES YOU TWO ARE LIKE A COUPLE OF AMETHYSTS...

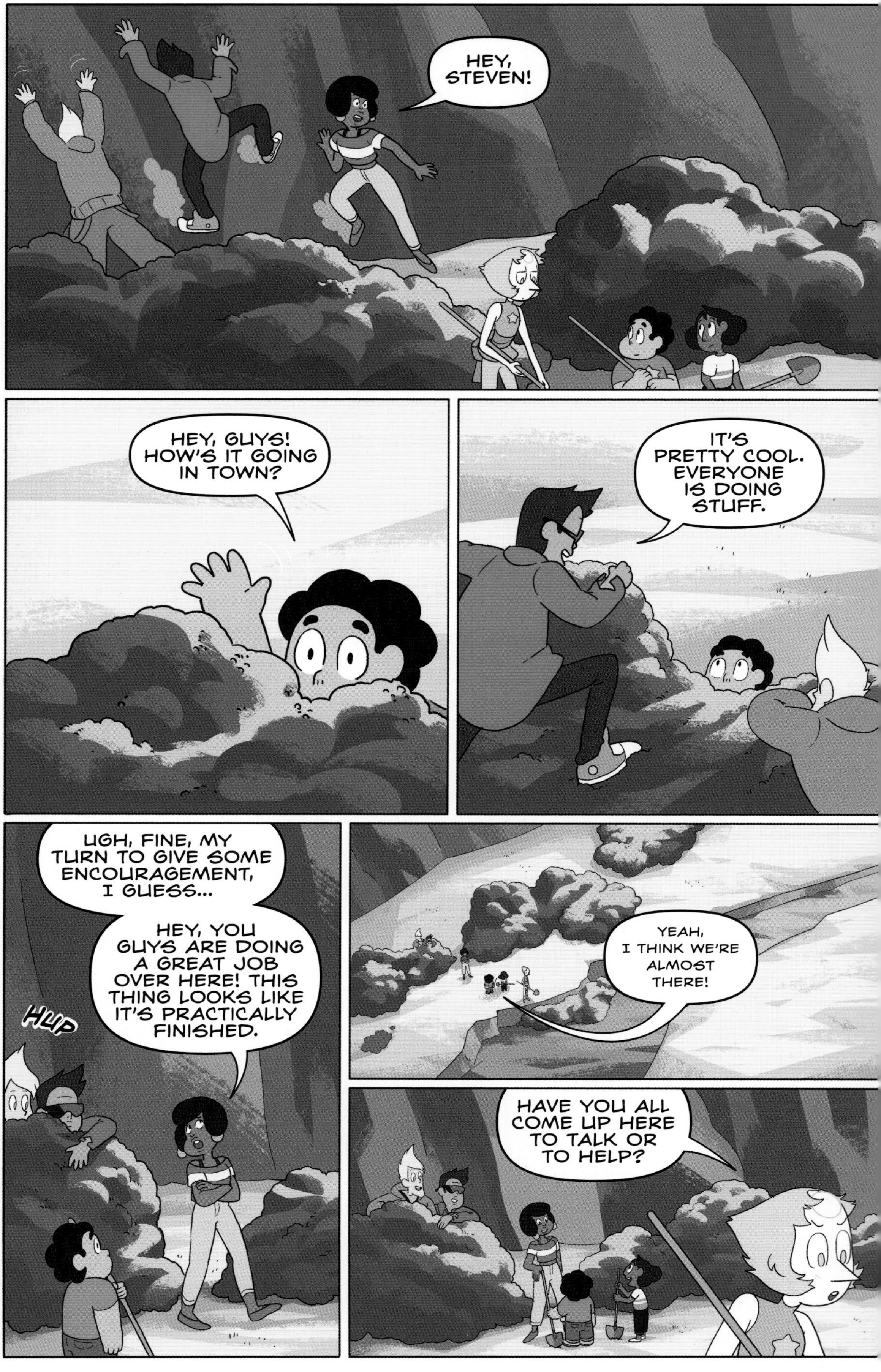
HEY, STEVEN!
HEY, GUYS! HOW'S IT GOING IN TOWN?
IT'S PRETTY COOL. EVERYONE IS DOING STUFF.
UGH, FINE, MY TURN TO GIVE SOME ENCOURAGEMENT, I GUESS...
HEY, YOU GUYS ARE DOING A GREAT JOB OVER HERE! THIS THING LOOKS LIKE IT'S PRACTICALLY FINISHED.
HUP
YEAH, I THINK WE'RE ALMOST THERE!
HAVE YOU ALL COME UP HERE TO TALK OR TO HELP?

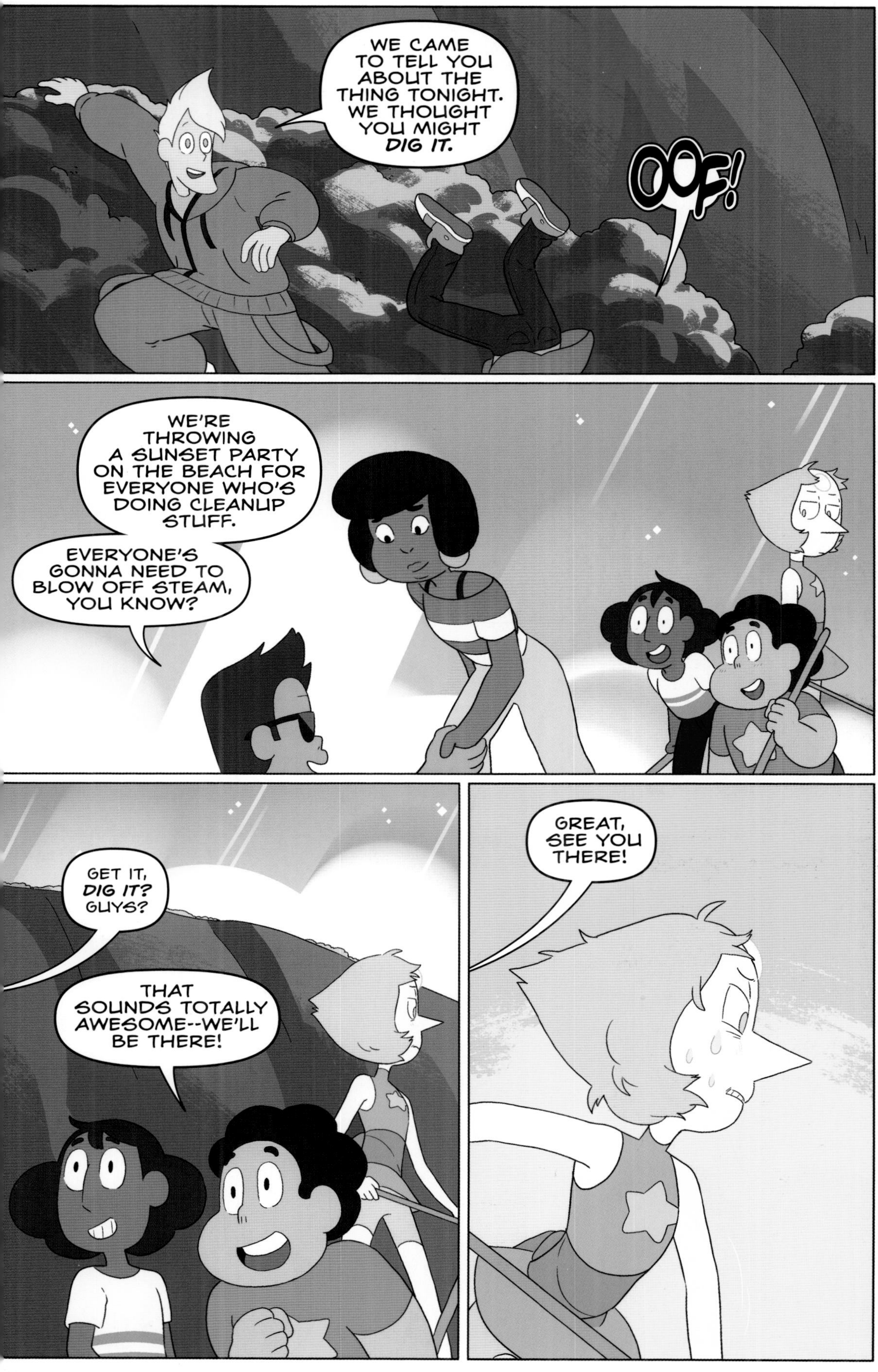
WE CAME TO TELL YOU ABOUT THE THING TONIGHT. WE THOUGHT YOU MIGHT *DIG IT.*
OOF!
WE'RE THROWING A SUNSET PARTY ON THE BEACH FOR EVERYONE WHO'S DOING CLEANUP STUFF.
EVERYONE'S GONNA NEED TO BLOW OFF STEAM, YOU KNOW?
GET IT, *DIG IT?* GUYS?
THAT SOUNDS TOTALLY AWESOME--WE'LL BE THERE!
GREAT, SEE YOU THERE!

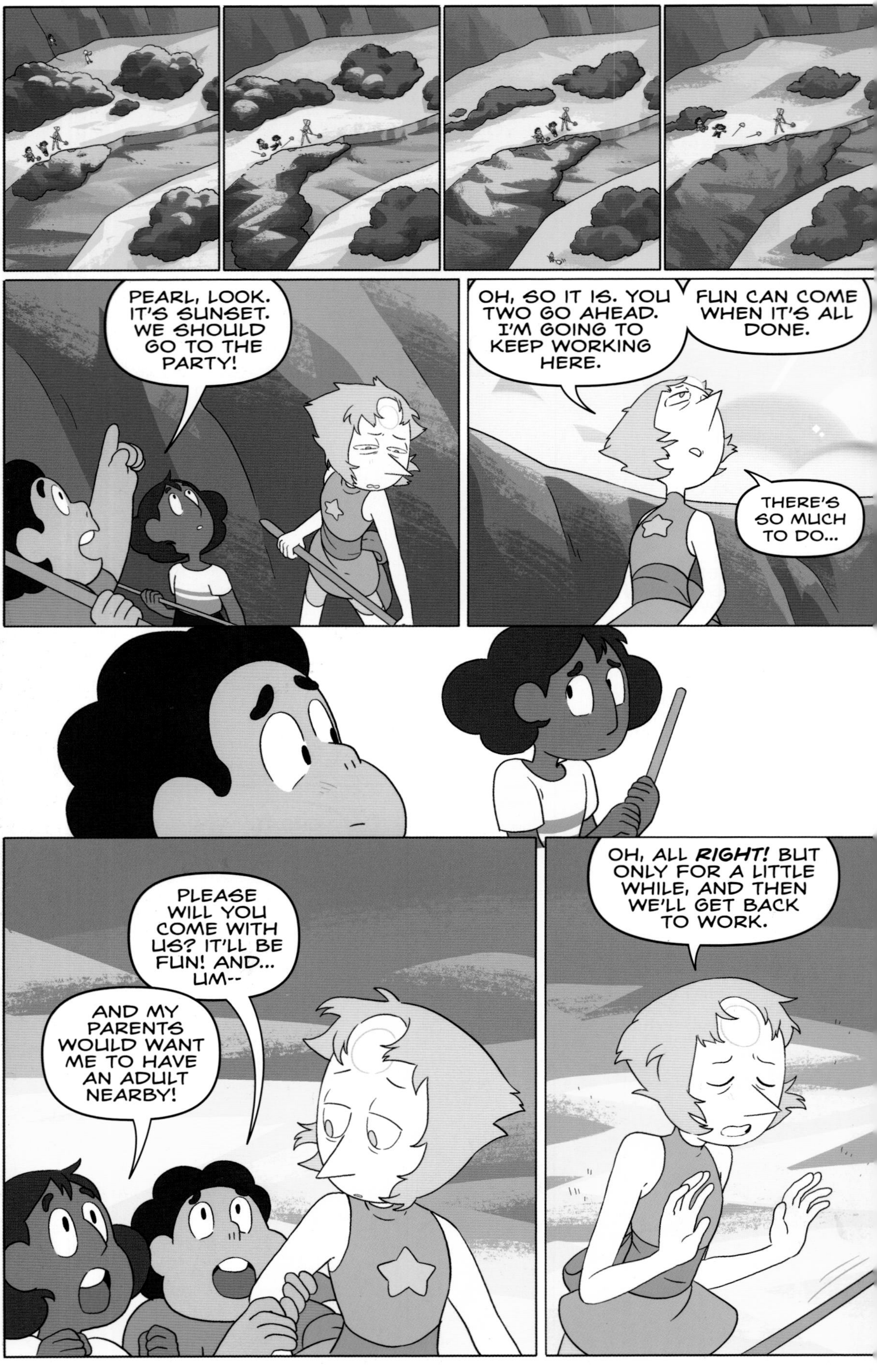
PEARL, LOOK. IT'S SUNSET. WE SHOULD GO TO THE PARTY!
OH, SO IT IS. YOU TWO GO AHEAD. I'M GOING TO KEEP WORKING HERE.
FUN CAN COME WHEN IT'S ALL DONE.
THERE'S SO MUCH TO DO...
PLEASE WILL YOU COME WITH US? IT'LL BE FUN! AND... UM--
AND MY PARENTS WOULD WANT ME TO HAVE AN ADULT NEARBY!
OH, ALL RIGHT! BUT ONLY FOR A LITTLE WHILE, AND THEN WE'LL GET BACK TO WORK.

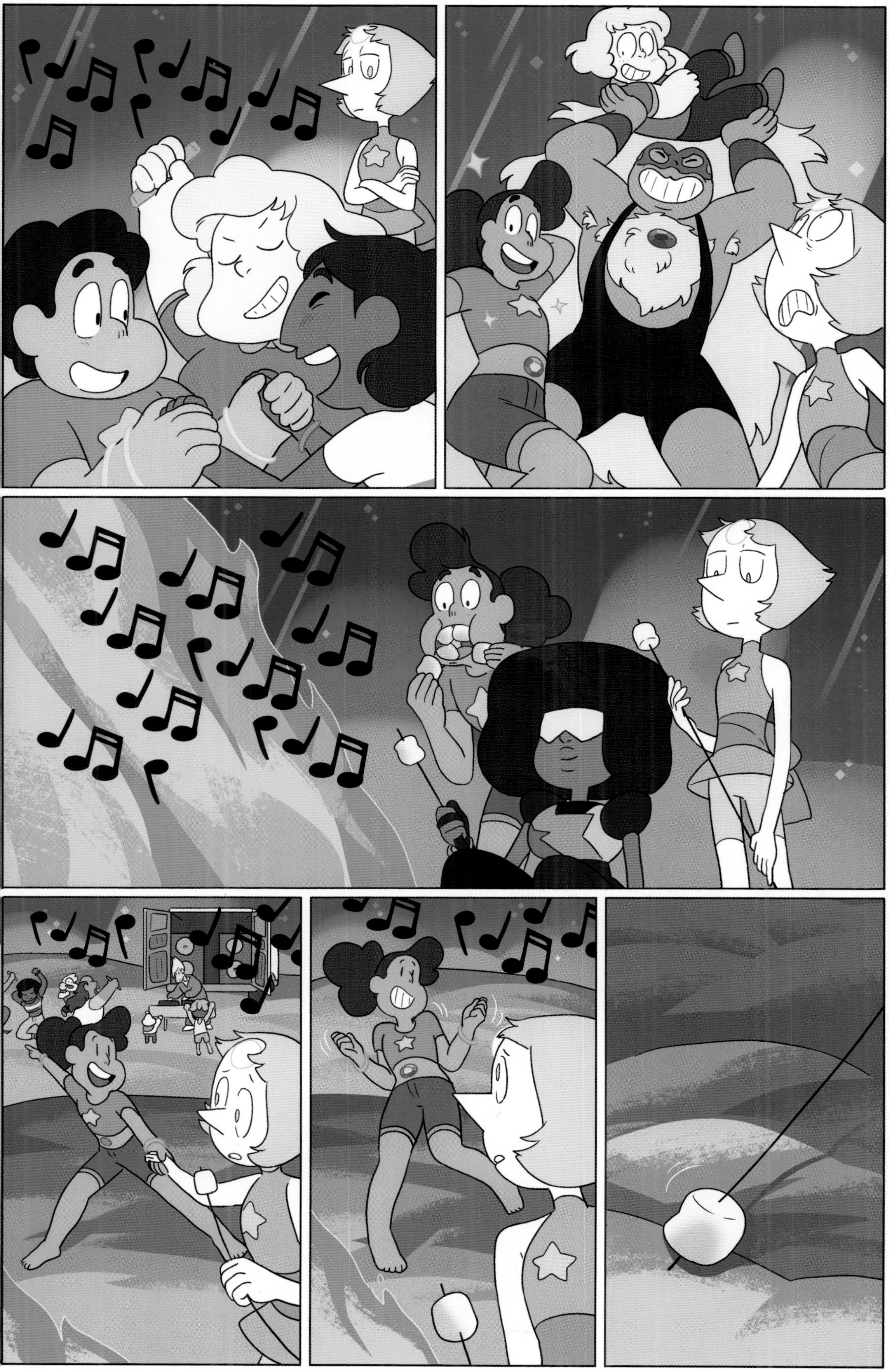

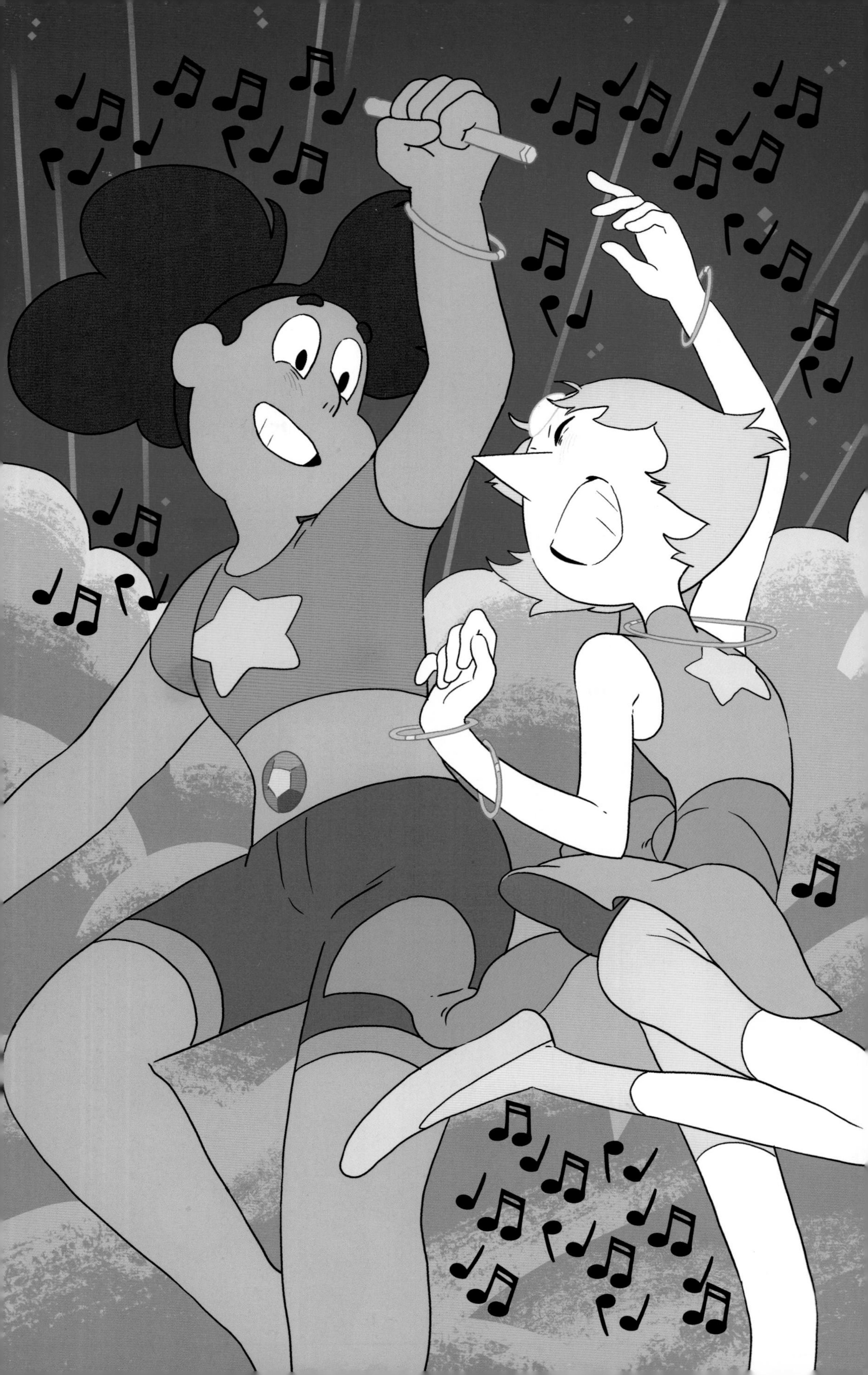

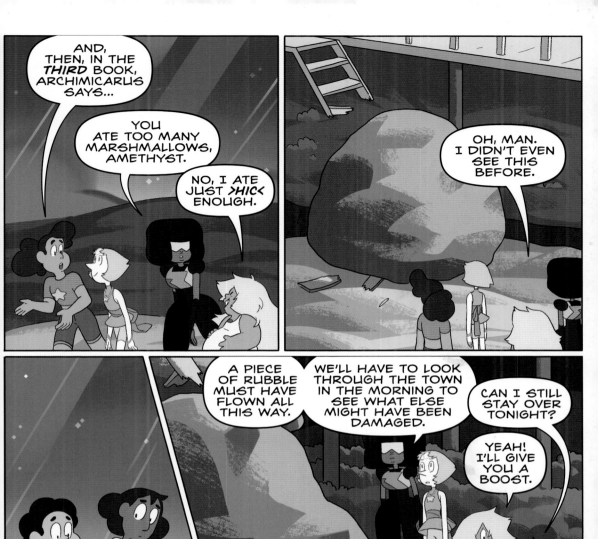

AND, THEN, IN THE *THIRD* BOOK, ARCHIMICARUS SAYS...

YOU ATE TOO MANY MARSHMALLOWS, AMETHYST.

NO, I ATE JUST >HIC< ENOUGH.

OH, MAN. I DIDN'T EVEN SEE THIS BEFORE.

A PIECE OF RUBBLE MUST HAVE FLOWN ALL THIS WAY.

WE'LL HAVE TO LOOK THROUGH THE TOWN IN THE MORNING TO SEE WHAT ELSE MIGHT HAVE BEEN DAMAGED.

CAN I STILL STAY OVER TONIGHT?

YEAH! I'LL GIVE YOU A BOOST.

I KNEW IT.

HUH?

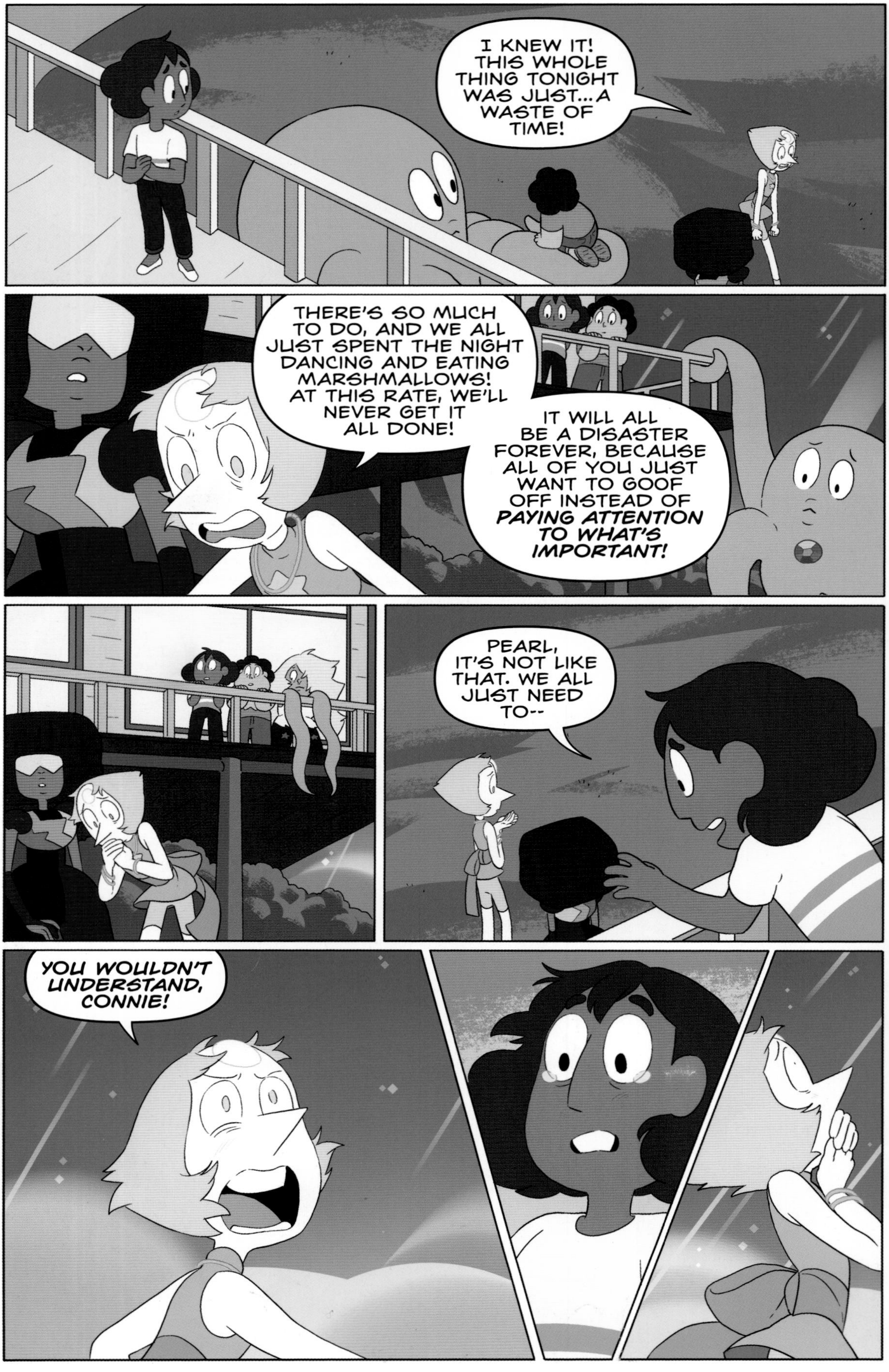
I KNEW IT! THIS WHOLE THING TONIGHT WAS JUST... A WASTE OF TIME!
THERE'S SO MUCH TO DO, AND WE ALL JUST SPENT THE NIGHT DANCING AND EATING MARSHMALLOWS! AT THIS RATE, WE'LL NEVER GET IT ALL DONE!
IT WILL ALL BE A DISASTER FOREVER, BECAUSE ALL OF YOU JUST WANT TO GOOF OFF INSTEAD OF *PAYING ATTENTION TO WHAT'S IMPORTANT!*
PEARL, IT'S NOT LIKE THAT. WE ALL JUST NEED TO--
YOU WOULDN'T UNDERSTAND, CONNIE!

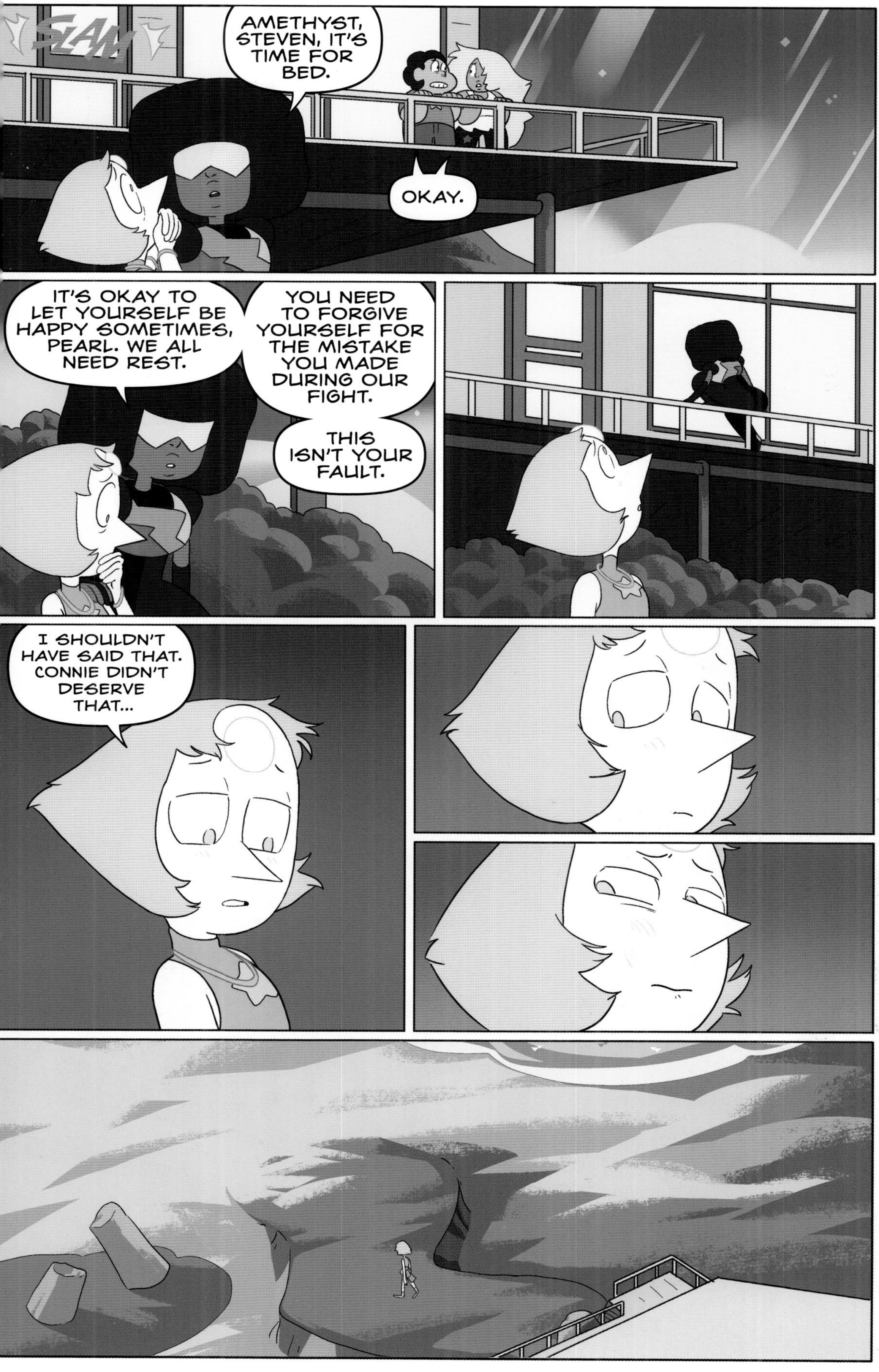
SLAM
AMETHYST, STEVEN, IT'S TIME FOR BED.
OKAY.
IT'S OKAY TO LET YOURSELF BE HAPPY SOMETIMES, PEARL. WE ALL NEED REST.
YOU NEED TO FORGIVE YOURSELF FOR THE MISTAKE YOU MADE DURING OUR FIGHT.
THIS ISN'T YOUR FAULT.
I SHOULDN'T HAVE SAID THAT. CONNIE DIDN'T DESERVE THAT...

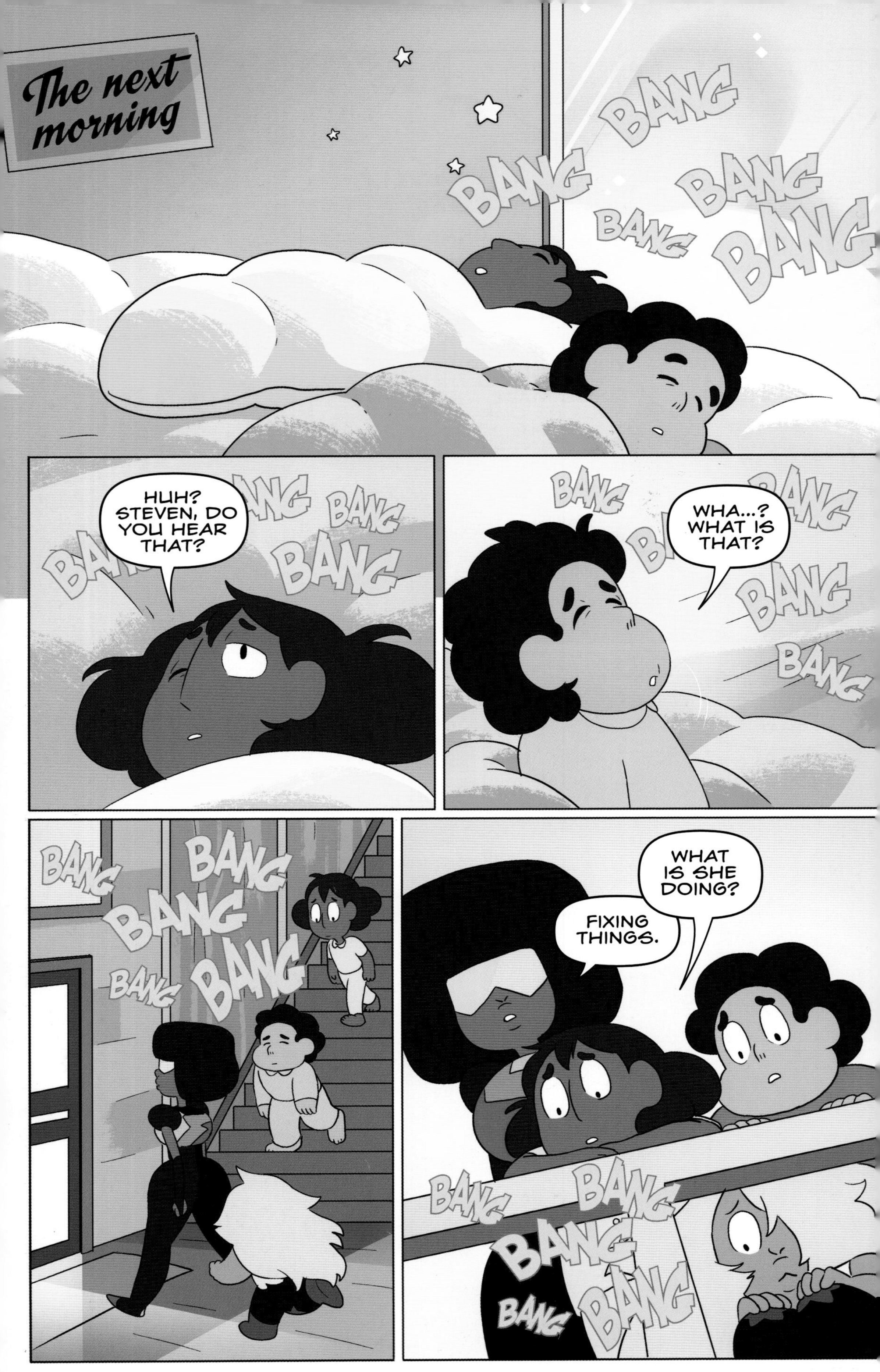
The next morning
BANG
BANG
BANG
BANG
BANG
BANG
HUH? STEVEN, DO YOU HEAR THAT?
BANG
BANG
BANG
BANG
WHA...? WHAT IS THAT?
BANG
BANG
BANG
BANG
BANG
BANG
BANG
BANG
WHAT IS SHE DOING?
FIXING THINGS.
BANG
BANG
BANG
BANG
BANG!

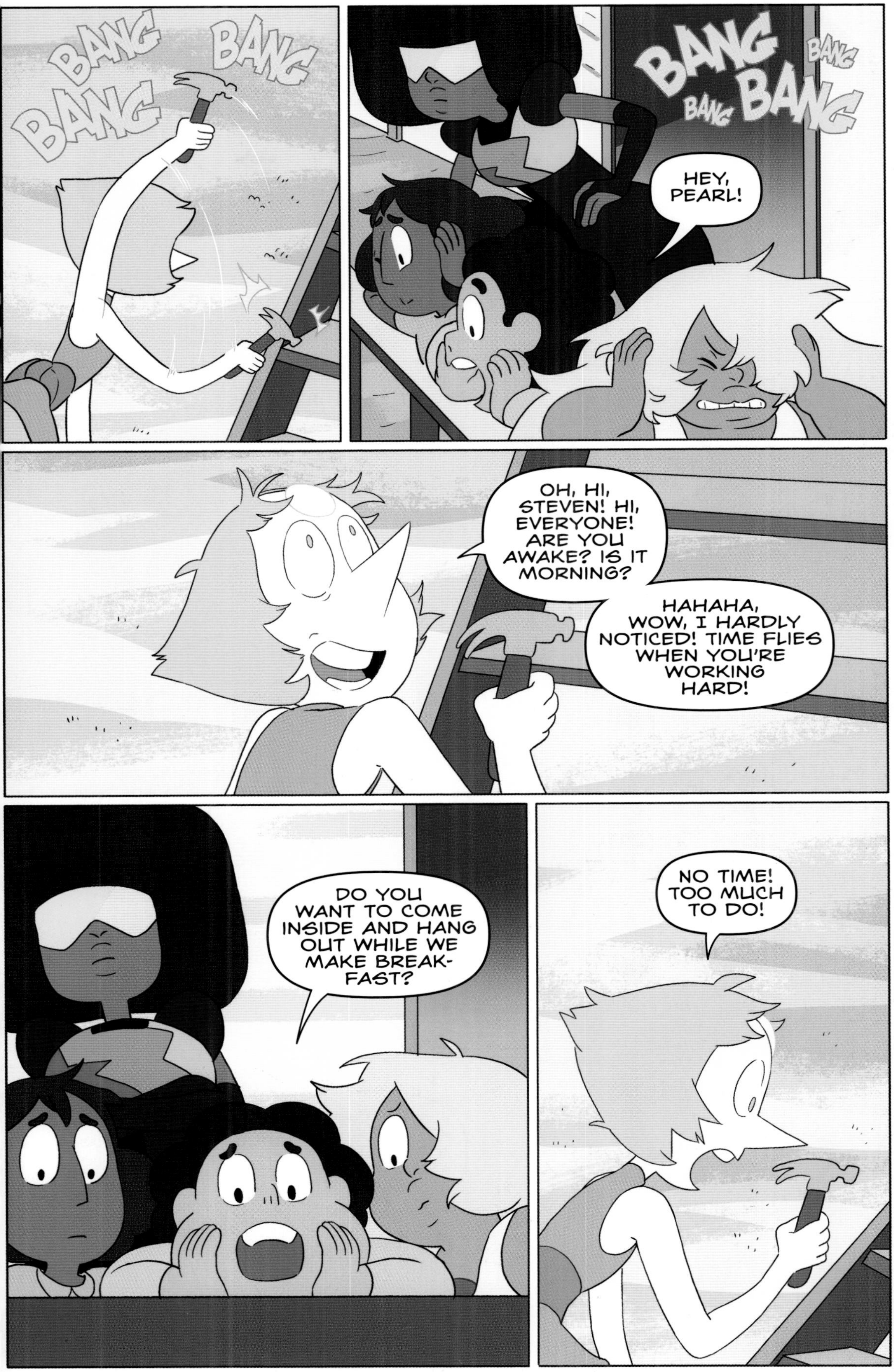
BANG
BANG
BANG
BANG
BANG
BANG
BANG
HEY, PEARL!
OH, HI, STEVEN! HI, EVERYONE! ARE YOU AWAKE? IS IT MORNING?
HAHAHA, WOW, I HARDLY NOTICED! TIME FLIES WHEN YOU'RE WORKING HARD!
DO YOU WANT TO COME INSIDE AND HANG OUT WHILE WE MAKE BREAK-FAST?
NO TIME! TOO MUCH TO DO!

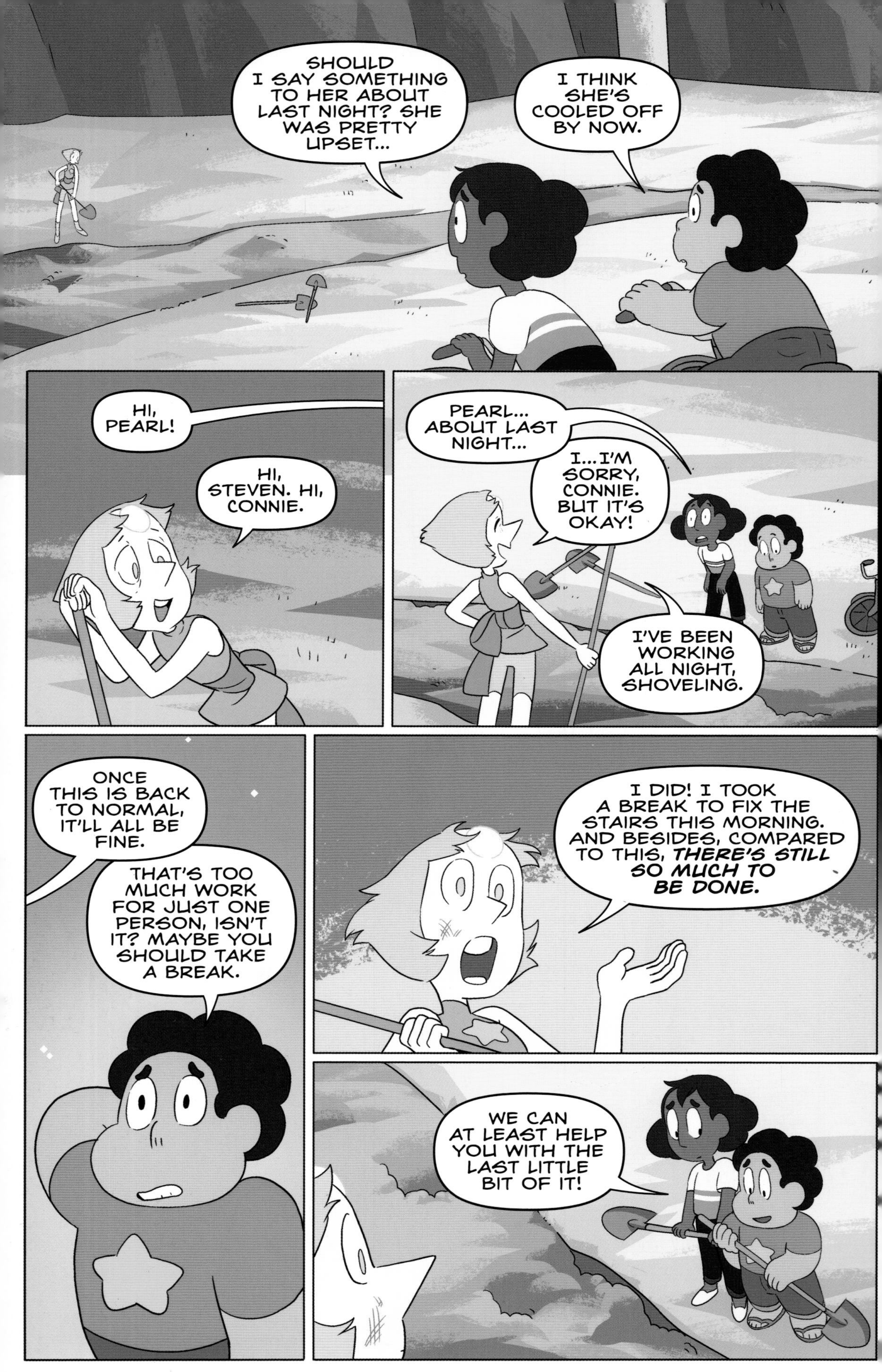

SHOULD I SAY SOMETHING TO HER ABOUT LAST NIGHT? SHE WAS PRETTY UPSET...
I THINK SHE'S COOLED OFF BY NOW.
HI, PEARL!
HI, STEVEN. HI, CONNIE.
PEARL... ABOUT LAST NIGHT...
I...I'M SORRY, CONNIE. BUT IT'S OKAY!
I'VE BEEN WORKING ALL NIGHT, SHOVELING.
ONCE THIS IS BACK TO NORMAL, IT'LL ALL BE FINE.
THAT'S TOO MUCH WORK FOR JUST ONE PERSON, ISN'T IT? MAYBE YOU SHOULD TAKE A BREAK.
I DID! I TOOK A BREAK TO FIX THE STAIRS THIS MORNING. AND BESIDES, COMPARED TO THIS, *THERE'S STILL SO MUCH TO BE DONE.*
WE CAN AT LEAST HELP YOU WITH THE LAST LITTLE BIT OF IT!

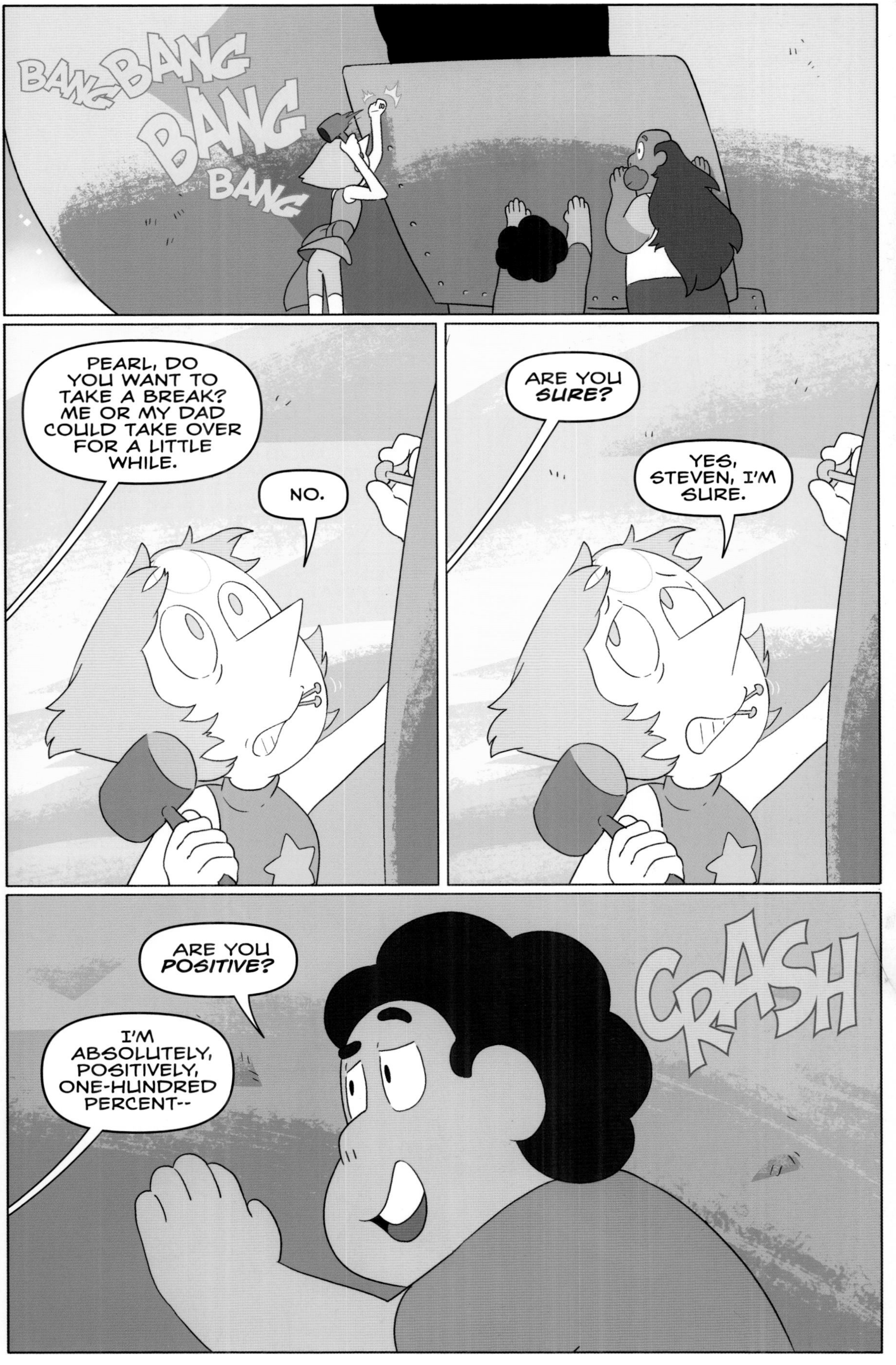
BANG BANG
BANG
BANG
PEARL, DO YOU WANT TO TAKE A BREAK? ME OR MY DAD COULD TAKE OVER FOR A LITTLE WHILE.
NO.
ARE YOU *SURE?*
YES, STEVEN, I'M SURE.
ARE YOU *POSITIVE?*
I'M ABSOLUTELY, POSITIVELY, ONE-HUNDRED PERCENT--
CRASH

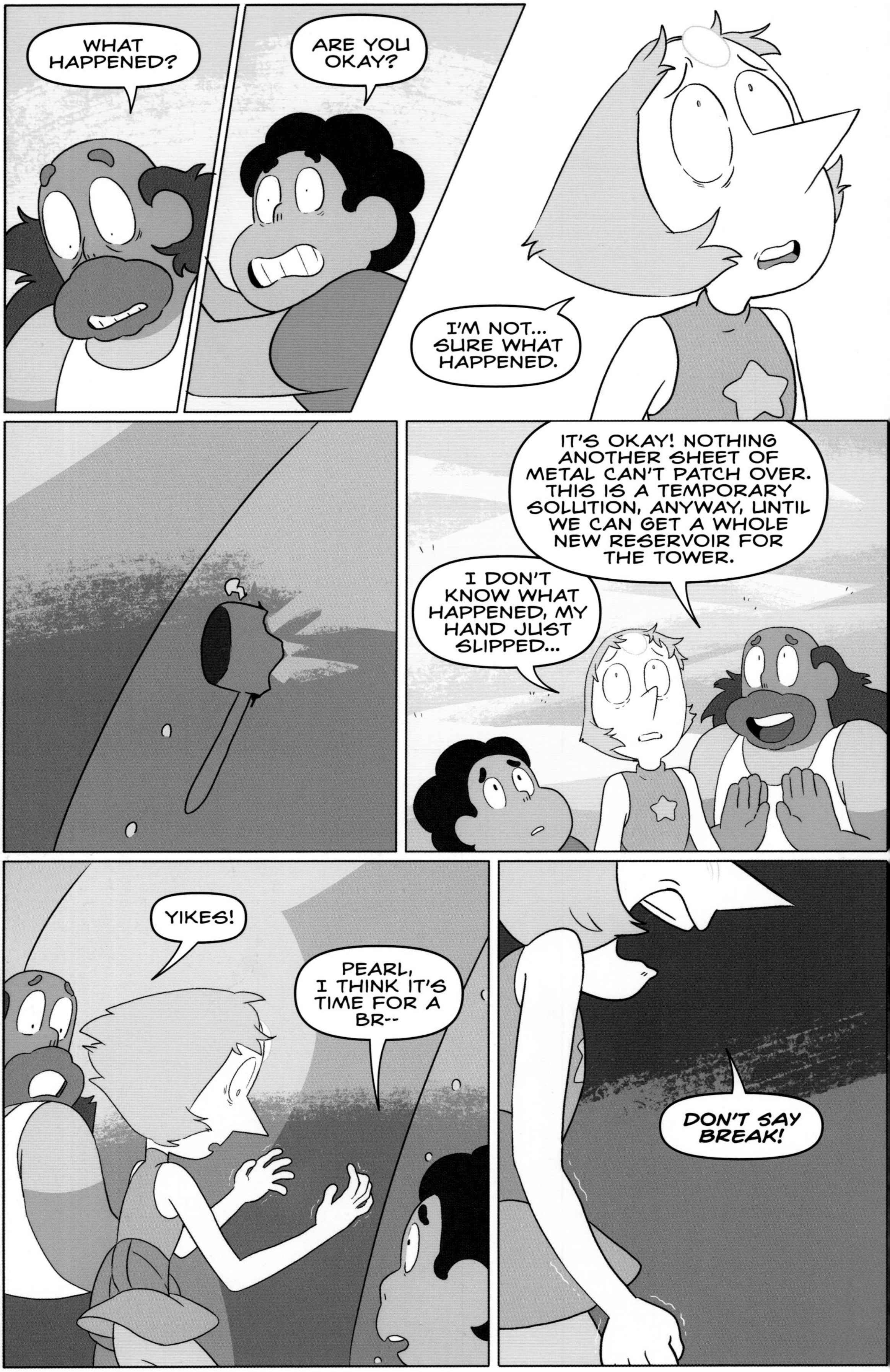
WHAT HAPPENED?
ARE YOU OKAY?
I'M NOT... SURE WHAT HAPPENED.
IT'S OKAY! NOTHING ANOTHER SHEET OF METAL CAN'T PATCH OVER. THIS IS A TEMPORARY SOLUTION, ANYWAY, UNTIL WE CAN GET A WHOLE NEW RESERVOIR FOR THE TOWER.
I DON'T KNOW WHAT HAPPENED, MY HAND JUST SLIPPED...
YIKES!
PEARL, I THINK IT'S TIME FOR A BR--
DON'T SAY BREAK!

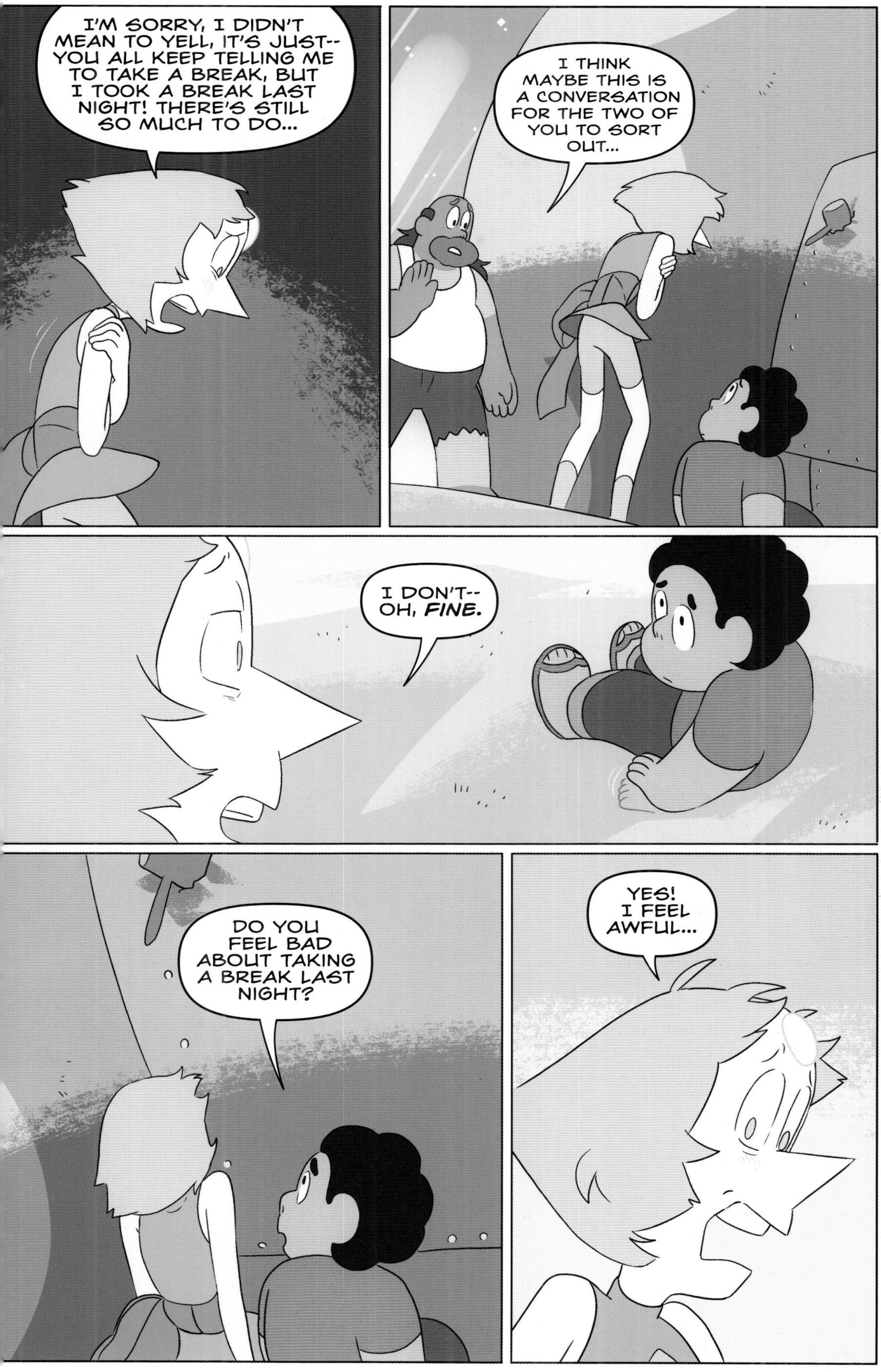
I'M SORRY, I DIDN'T MEAN TO YELL, IT'S JUST-- YOU ALL KEEP TELLING ME TO TAKE A BREAK, BUT I TOOK A BREAK LAST NIGHT! THERE'S STILL SO MUCH TO DO...
I THINK MAYBE THIS IS A CONVERSATION FOR THE TWO OF YOU TO SORT OUT...
I DON'T-- OH, FINE.
DO YOU FEEL BAD ABOUT TAKING A BREAK LAST NIGHT?
YES! I FEEL AWFUL...

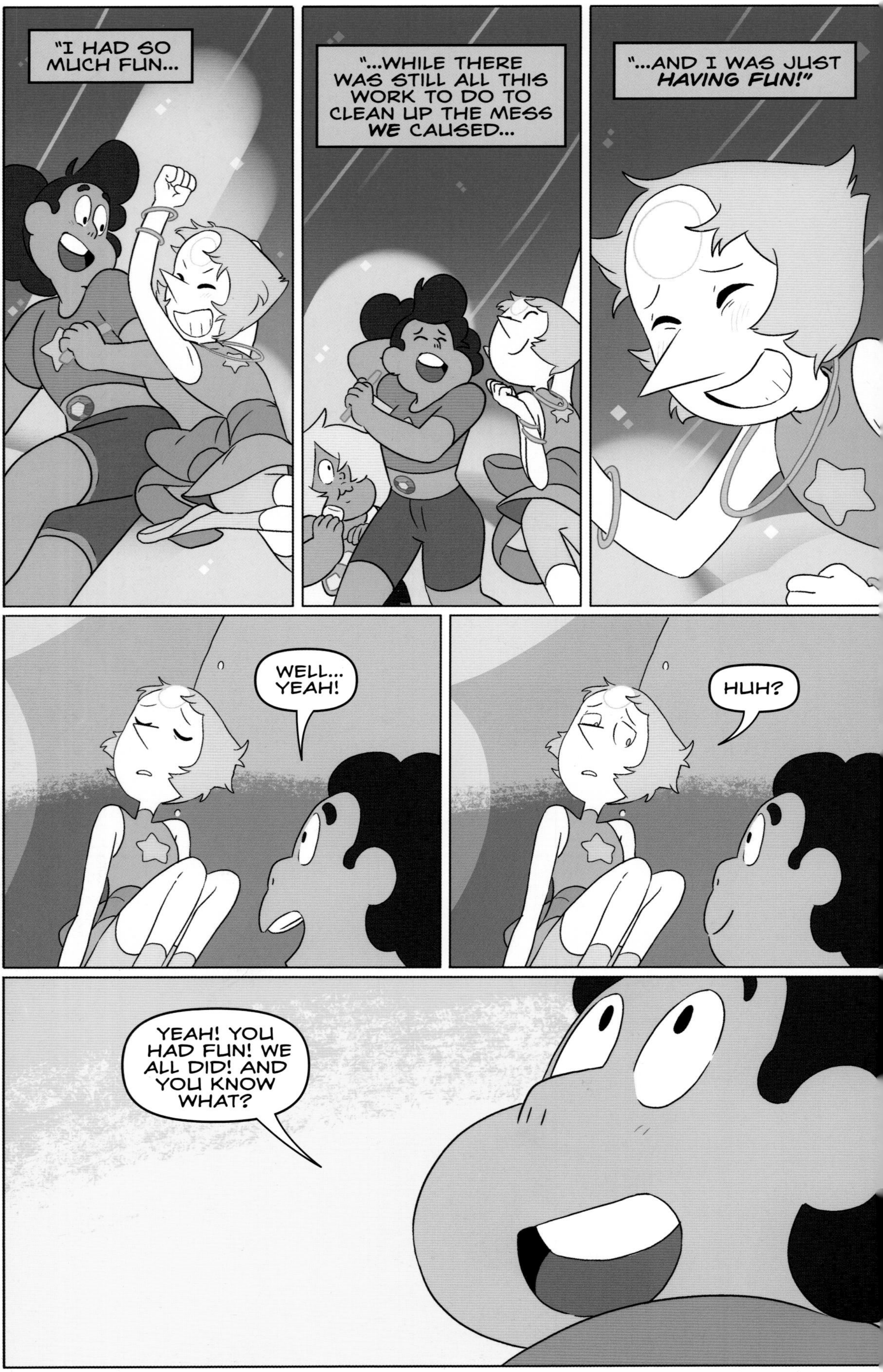
"I HAD SO MUCH FUN...
"...WHILE THERE WAS STILL ALL THIS WORK TO DO TO CLEAN UP THE MESS WE CAUSED...
"...AND I WAS JUST HAVING FUN!"
WELL... YEAH!
HUH?
YEAH! YOU HAD FUN! WE ALL DID! AND YOU KNOW WHAT?

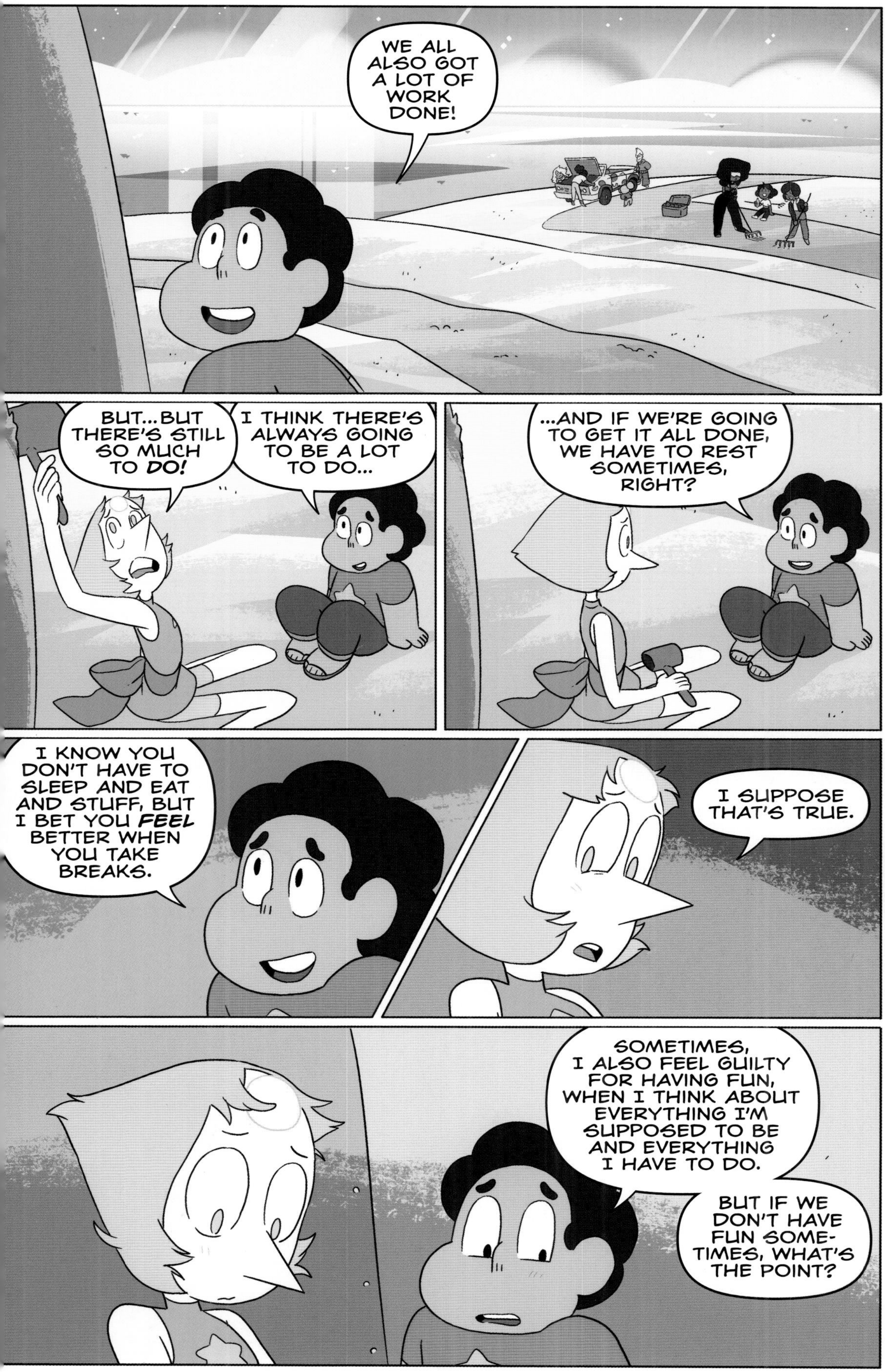
WE ALL ALSO GOT A LOT OF WORK DONE!
BUT...BUT THERE'S STILL SO MUCH TO *DO!*
I THINK THERE'S ALWAYS GOING TO BE A LOT TO DO...
...AND IF WE'RE GOING TO GET IT ALL DONE, WE HAVE TO REST SOMETIMES, RIGHT?
I KNOW YOU DON'T HAVE TO SLEEP AND EAT AND STUFF, BUT I BET YOU *FEEL* BETTER WHEN YOU TAKE BREAKS.
I SUPPOSE THAT'S TRUE.
SOMETIMES, I ALSO FEEL GUILTY FOR HAVING FUN, WHEN I THINK ABOUT EVERYTHING I'M SUPPOSED TO BE AND EVERYTHING I HAVE TO DO.
BUT IF WE DON'T HAVE FUN SOME-TIMES, WHAT'S THE POINT?

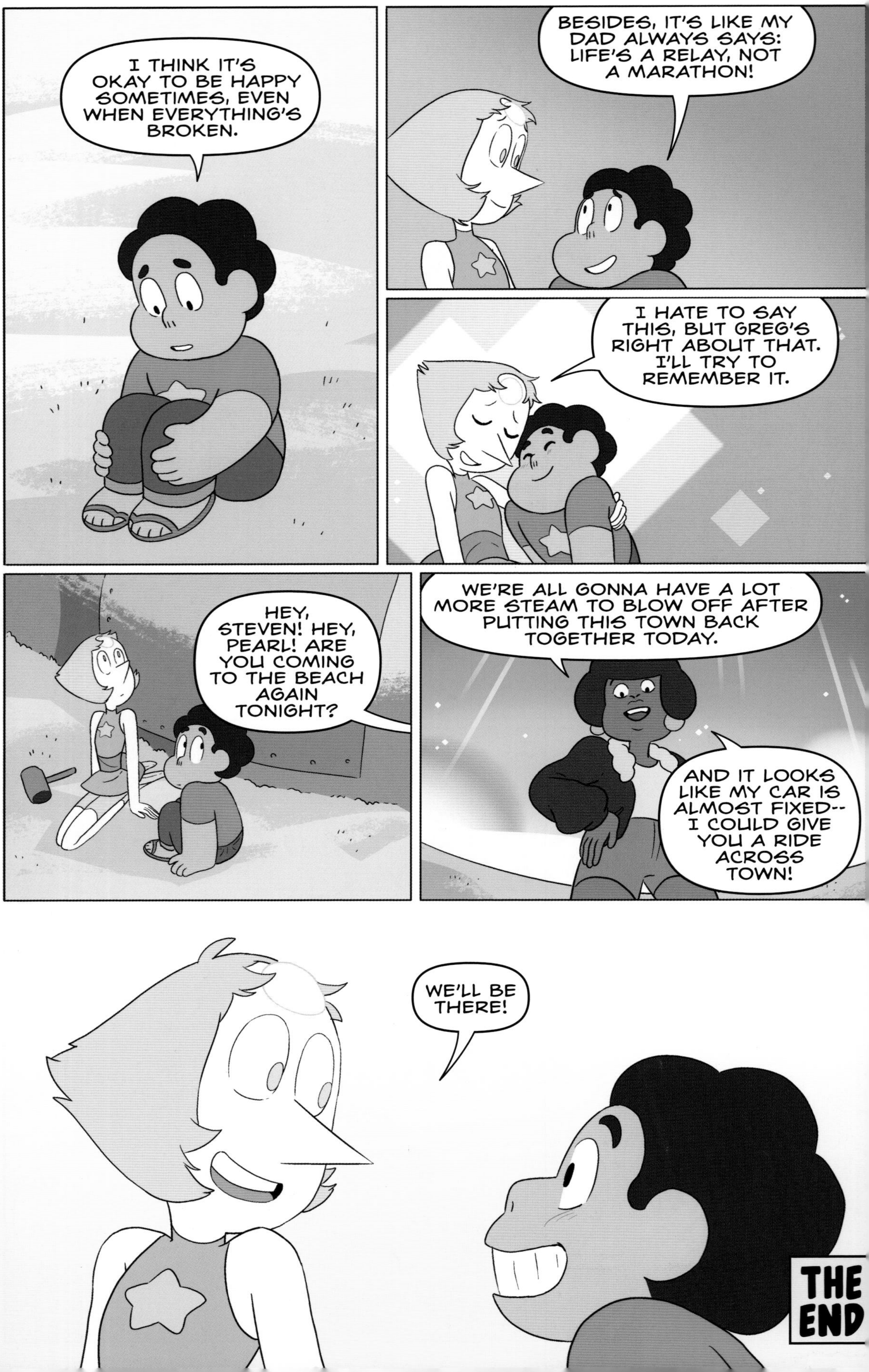
I THINK IT'S OKAY TO BE HAPPY SOMETIMES, EVEN WHEN EVERYTHING'S BROKEN.
BESIDES, IT'S LIKE MY DAD ALWAYS SAYS: LIFE'S A RELAY, NOT A MARATHON!
I HATE TO SAY THIS, BUT GREG'S RIGHT ABOUT THAT. I'LL TRY TO REMEMBER IT.
HEY, STEVEN! HEY, PEARL! ARE YOU COMING TO THE BEACH AGAIN TONIGHT?
WE'RE ALL GONNA HAVE A LOT MORE STEAM TO BLOW OFF AFTER PUTTING THIS TOWN BACK TOGETHER TODAY.
AND IT LOOKS LIKE MY CAR IS ALMOST FIXED-- I COULD GIVE YOU A RIDE ACROSS TOWN!
WE'LL BE THERE!
THE END

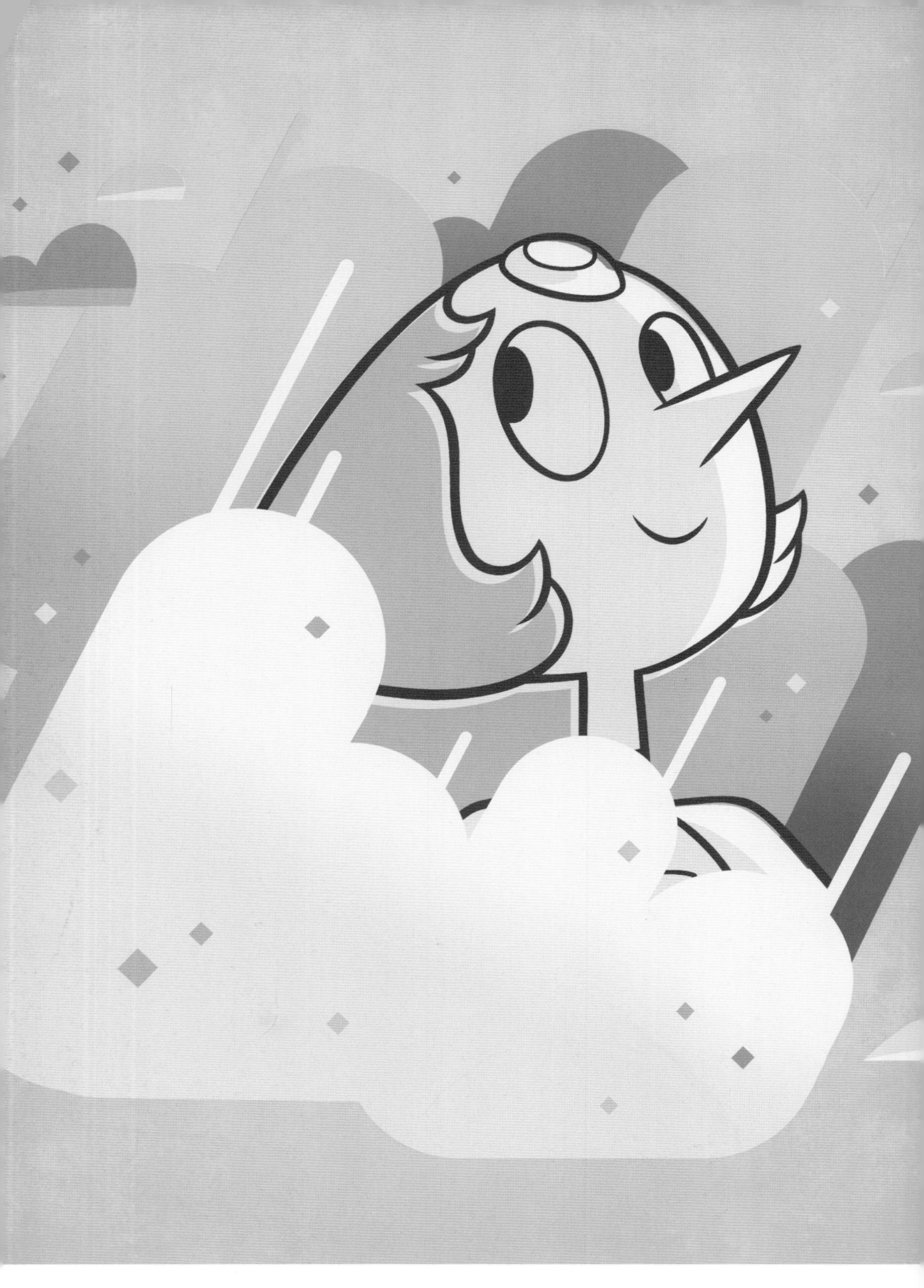

CHAPTER THIRTY-ONE

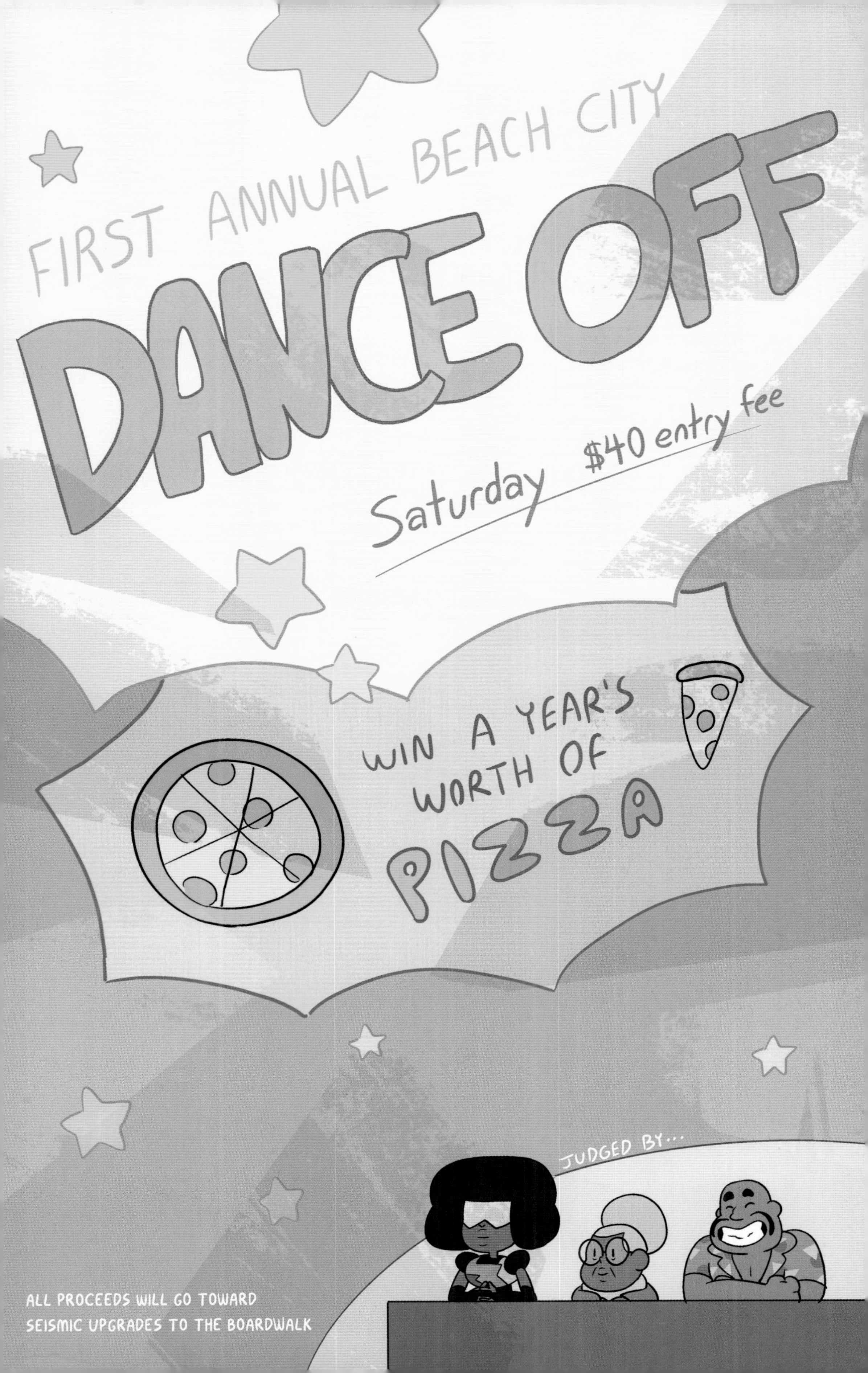
FIRST ANNUAL BEACH CITY
DANCE OFF
Saturday $40 entry fee
WIN A YEAR'S WORTH OF PIZZA
JUDGED BY...
ALL PROCEEDS WILL GO TOWARD SEISMIC UPGRADES TO THE BOARDWALK

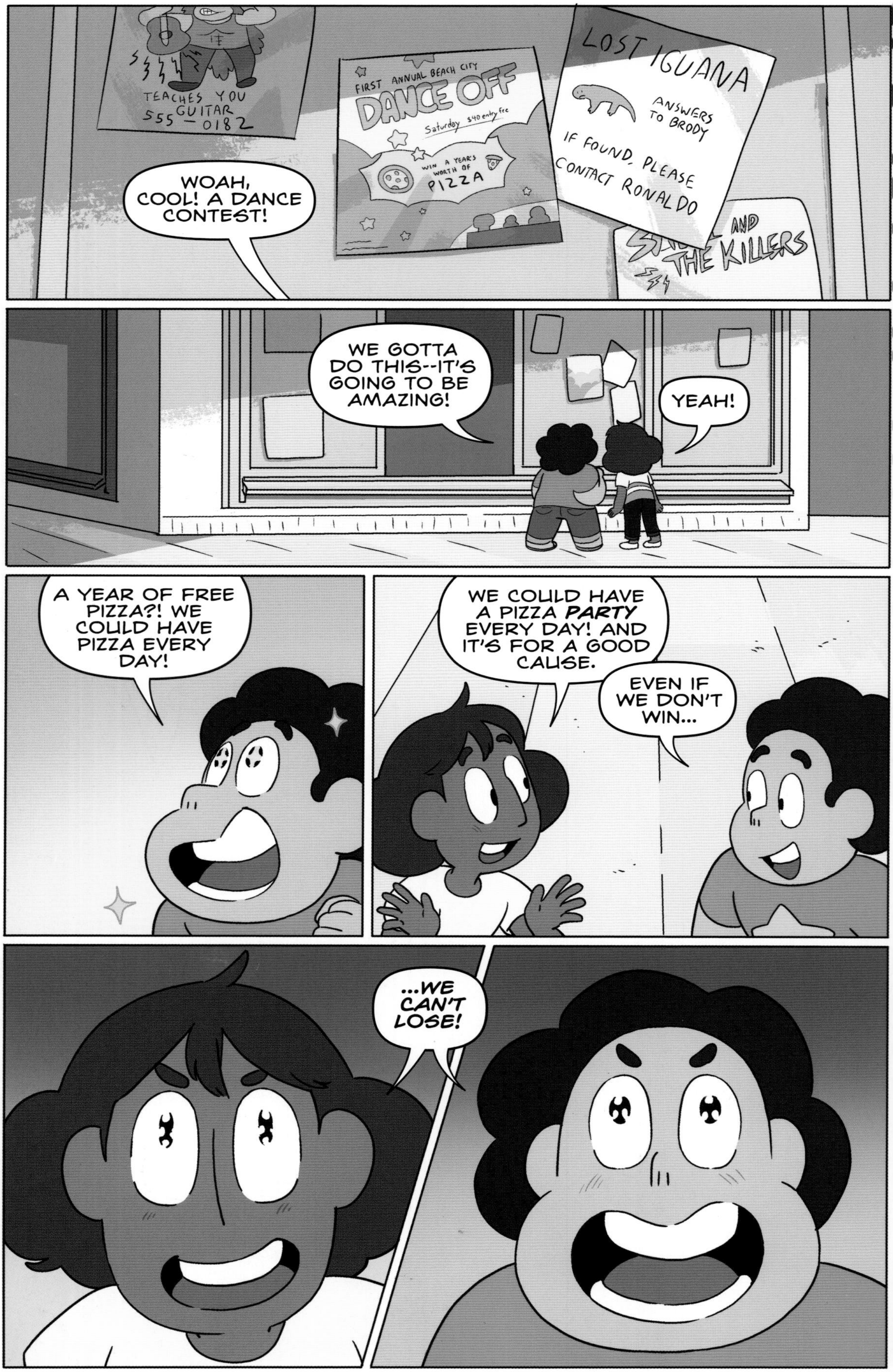
TEACHES YOU GUITAR 555-0182
FIRST ANNUAL BEACH CITY DANCE OFF
Saturday $40 entry fee
WIN A YEAR'S WORTH OF PIZZA
LOST IGUANA
ANSWERS TO BRODY
IF FOUND, PLEASE CONTACT RONALDO
AND THE KILLERS
WOAH, COOL! A DANCE CONTEST!
WE GOTTA DO THIS--IT'S GOING TO BE AMAZING!
YEAH!
A YEAR OF FREE PIZZA?! WE COULD HAVE PIZZA EVERY DAY!
WE COULD HAVE A PIZZA *PARTY* EVERY DAY! AND IT'S FOR A GOOD CAUSE.
EVEN IF WE DON'T WIN...
...WE CAN'T LOSE!

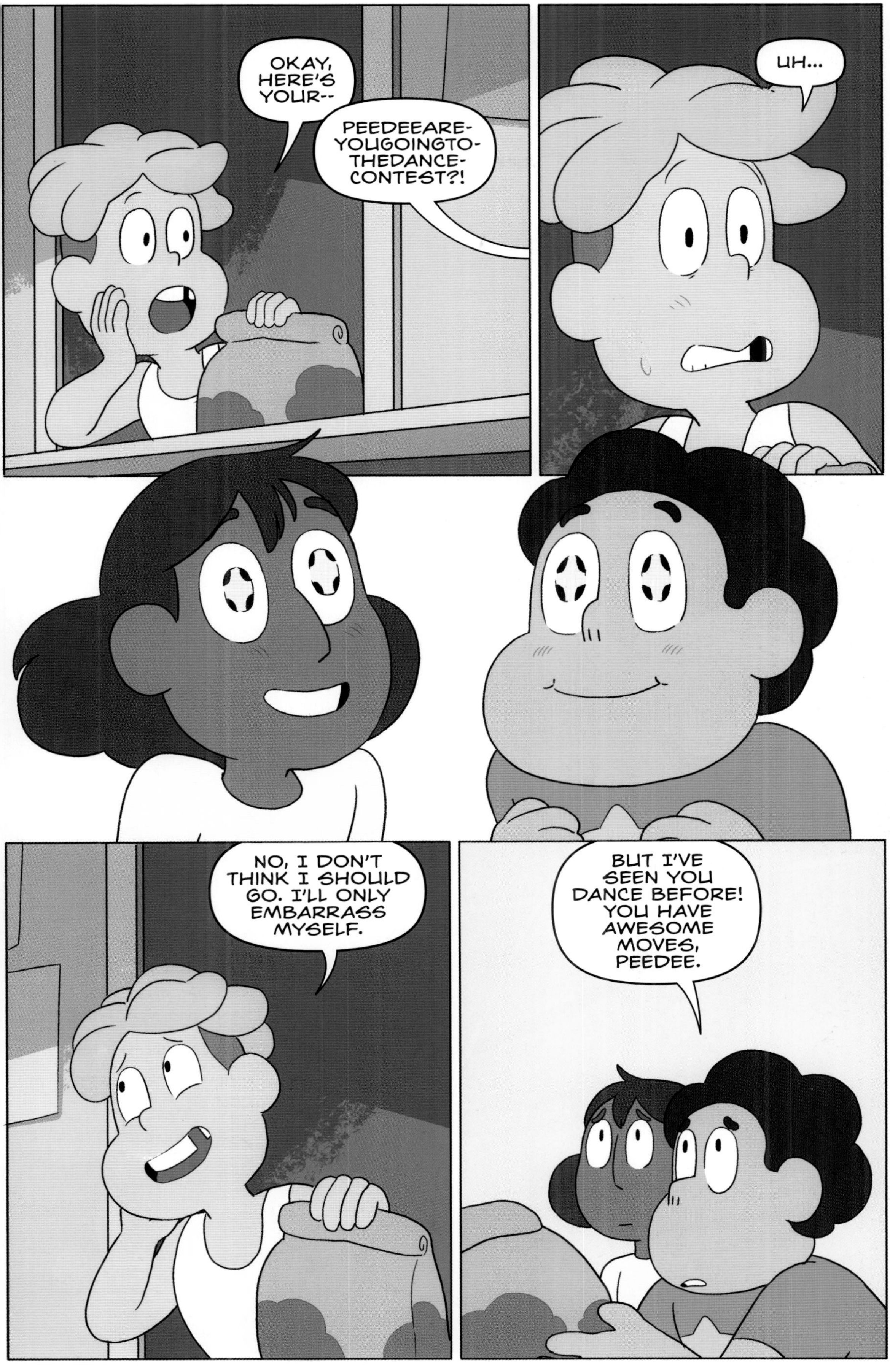
OKAY, HERE'S YOUR--
PEEDEEAREYOUGOINGTOTHEDANCECONTEST?!
UH...
NO, I DON'T THINK I SHOULD GO. I'LL ONLY EMBARRASS MYSELF.
BUT I'VE SEEN YOU DANCE BEFORE! YOU HAVE AWESOME MOVES, PEEDEE.

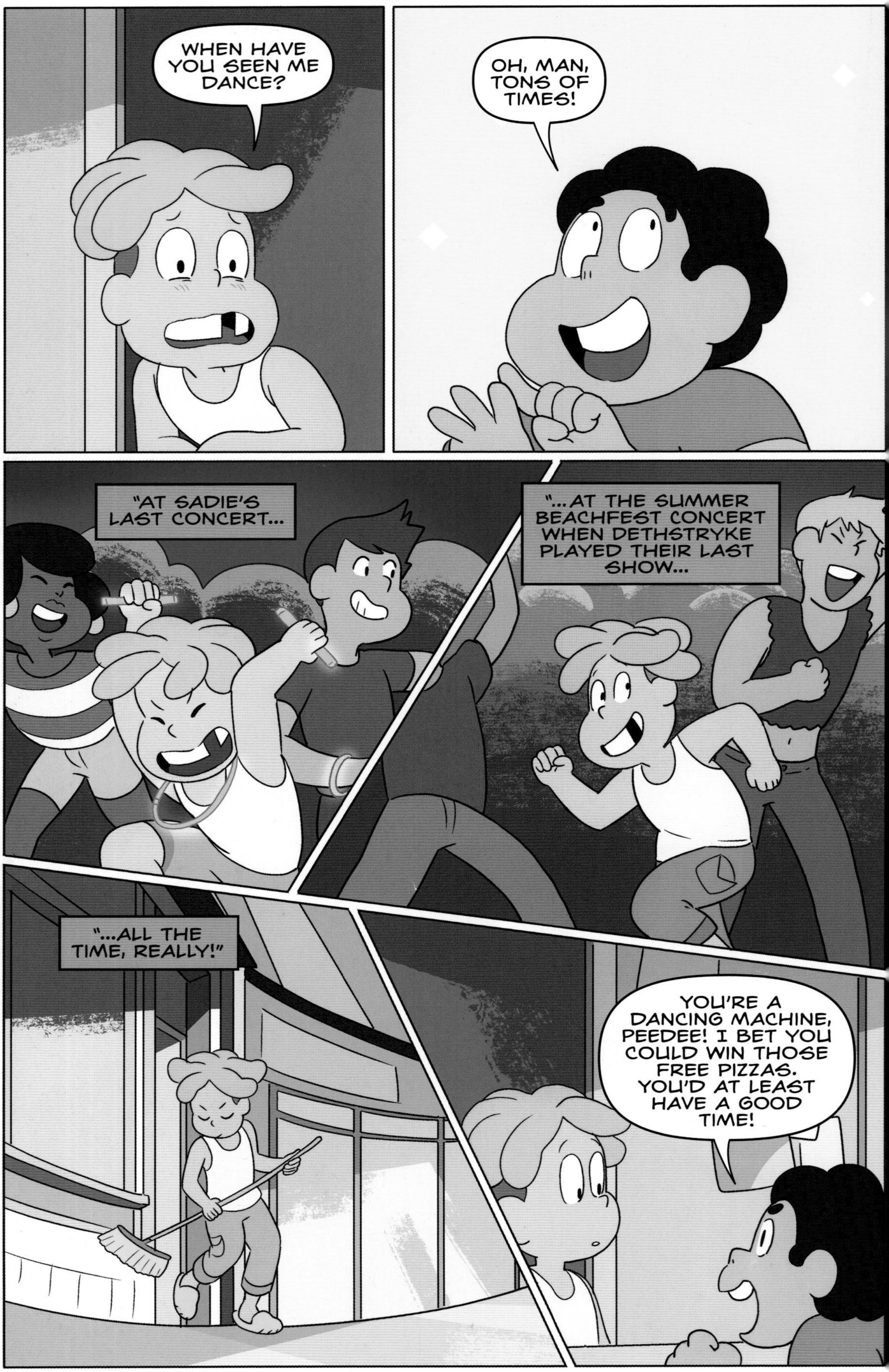
WHEN HAVE YOU SEEN ME DANCE?
OH, MAN, TONS OF TIMES!
"AT SADIE'S LAST CONCERT...
"...AT THE SUMMER BEACHFEST CONCERT WHEN DETHSTRYKE PLAYED THEIR LAST SHOW...
"...ALL THE TIME, REALLY!"
YOU'RE A DANCING MACHINE, PEEDEE! I BET YOU COULD WIN THOSE FREE PIZZAS. YOU'D AT LEAST HAVE A GOOD TIME!

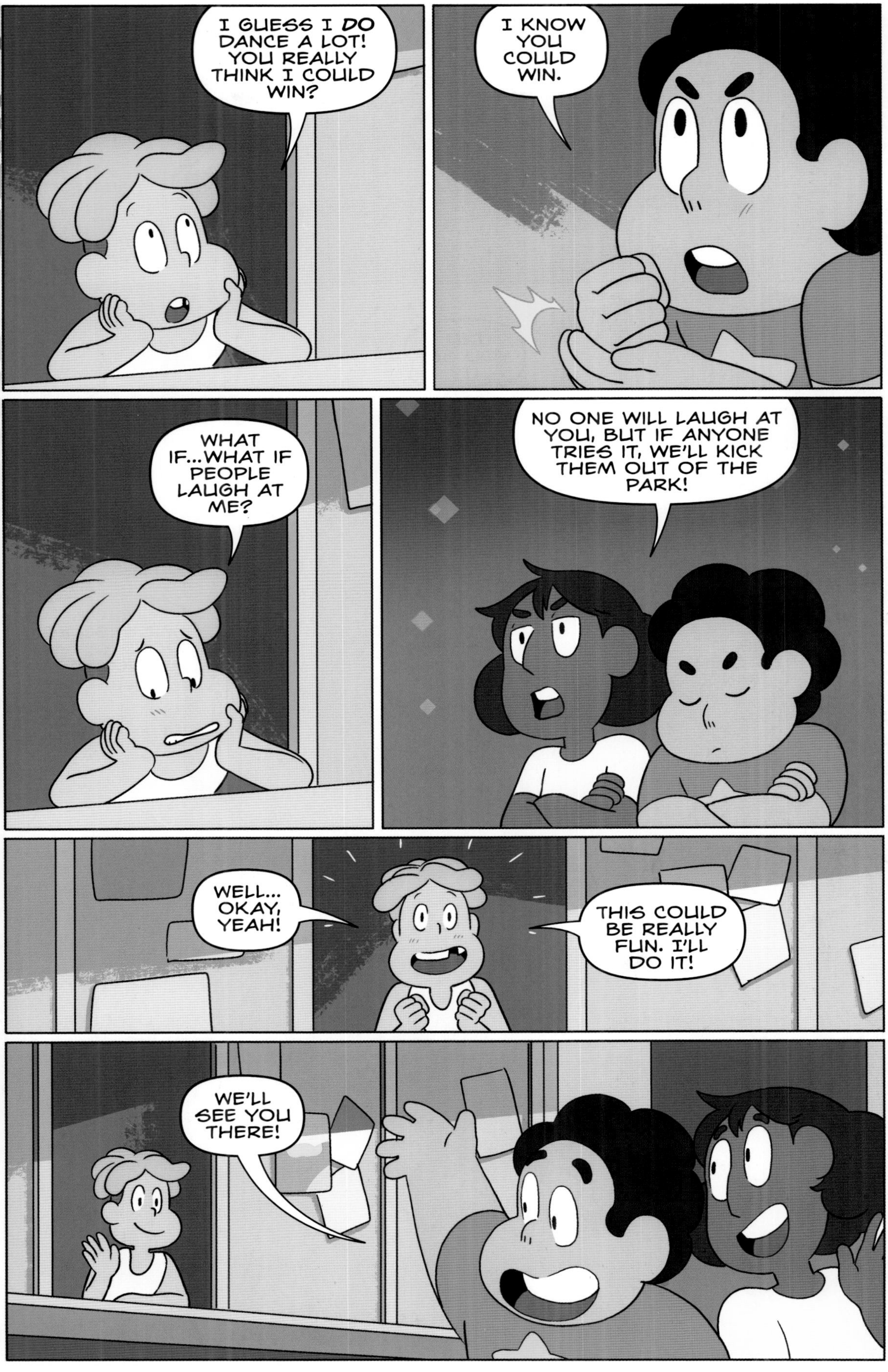
I GUESS I *DO* DANCE A LOT! YOU REALLY THINK I COULD WIN?
I KNOW YOU COULD WIN.
WHAT IF...WHAT IF PEOPLE LAUGH AT ME?
NO ONE WILL LAUGH AT YOU, BUT IF ANYONE TRIES IT, WE'LL KICK THEM OUT OF THE PARK!
WELL... OKAY, YEAH!
THIS COULD BE REALLY FUN. I'LL DO IT!
WE'LL SEE YOU THERE!

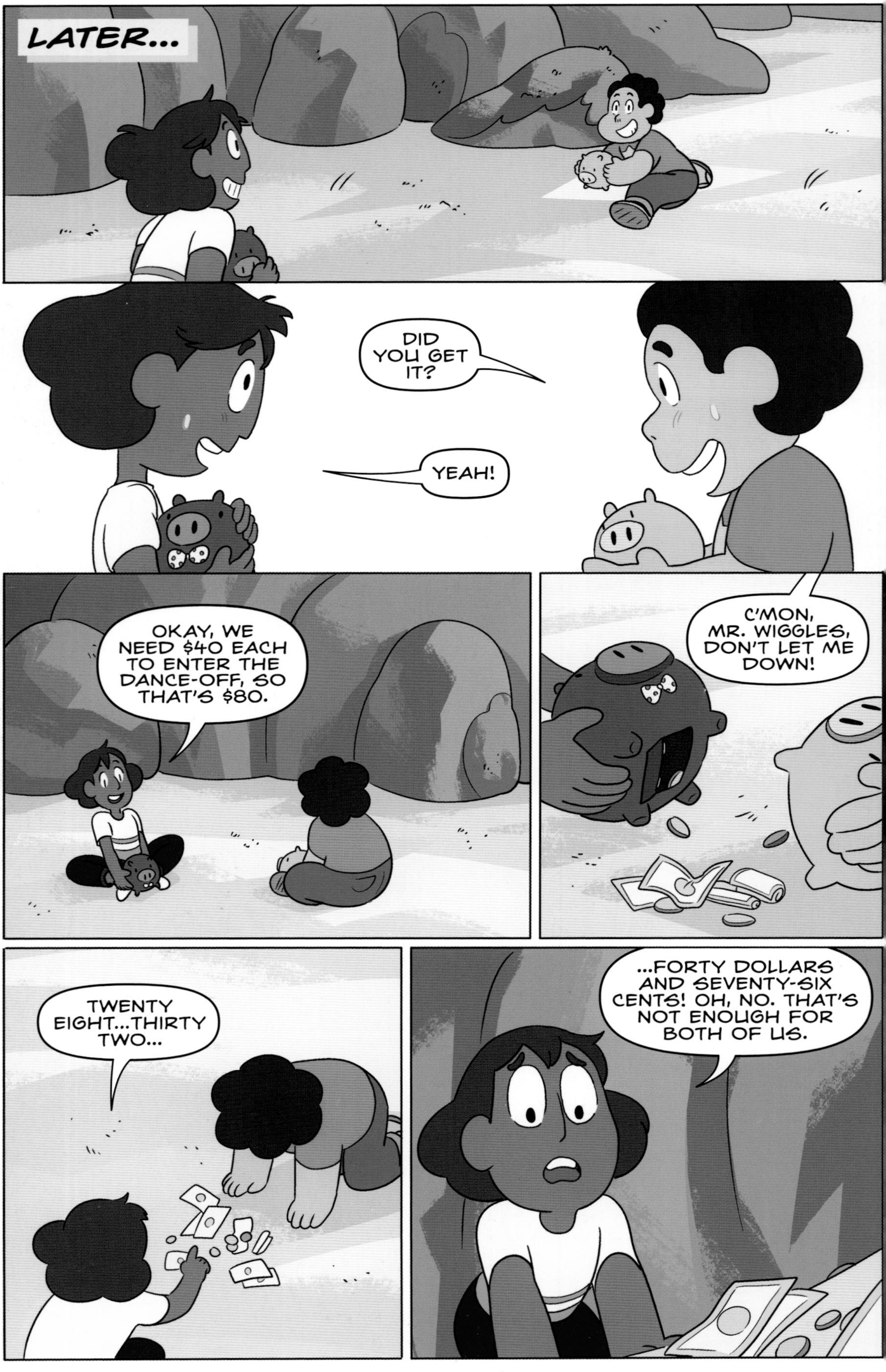
LATER...
DID YOU GET IT?
YEAH!
OKAY, WE NEED $40 EACH TO ENTER THE DANCE-OFF, SO THAT'S $80.
C'MON, MR. WIGGLES, DON'T LET ME DOWN!
TWENTY EIGHT...THIRTY TWO...
...FORTY DOLLARS AND SEVENTY-SIX CENTS! OH, NO. THAT'S NOT ENOUGH FOR BOTH OF US.

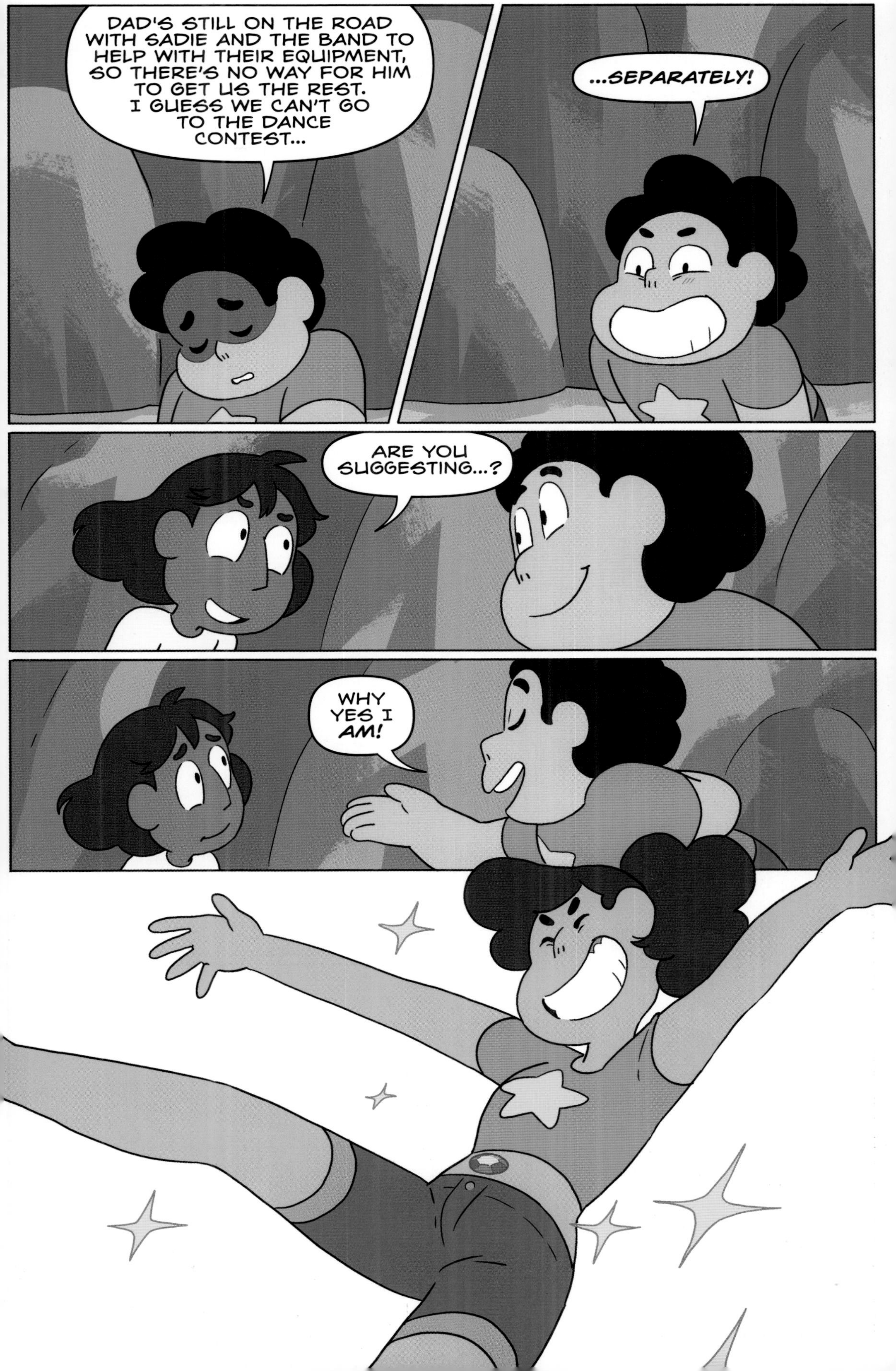
DAD'S STILL ON THE ROAD WITH SADIE AND THE BAND TO HELP WITH THEIR EQUIPMENT, SO THERE'S NO WAY FOR HIM TO GET US THE REST. I GUESS WE CAN'T GO TO THE DANCE CONTEST...
...SEPARATELY!
ARE YOU SUGGESTING...?
WHY YES I *AM!*

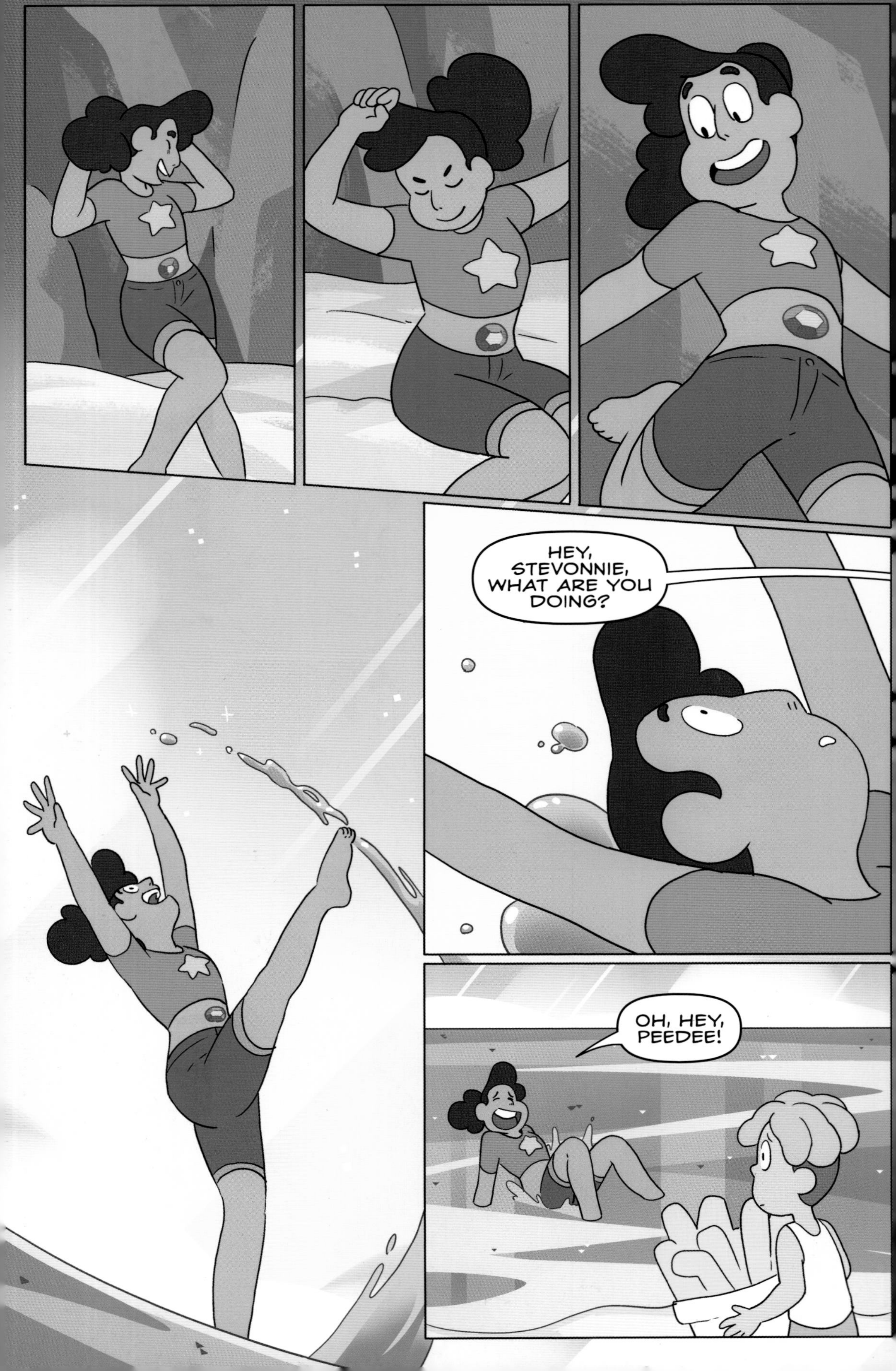
HEY, STEVONNIE, WHAT ARE YOU DOING?
OH, HEY, PEEDEE!

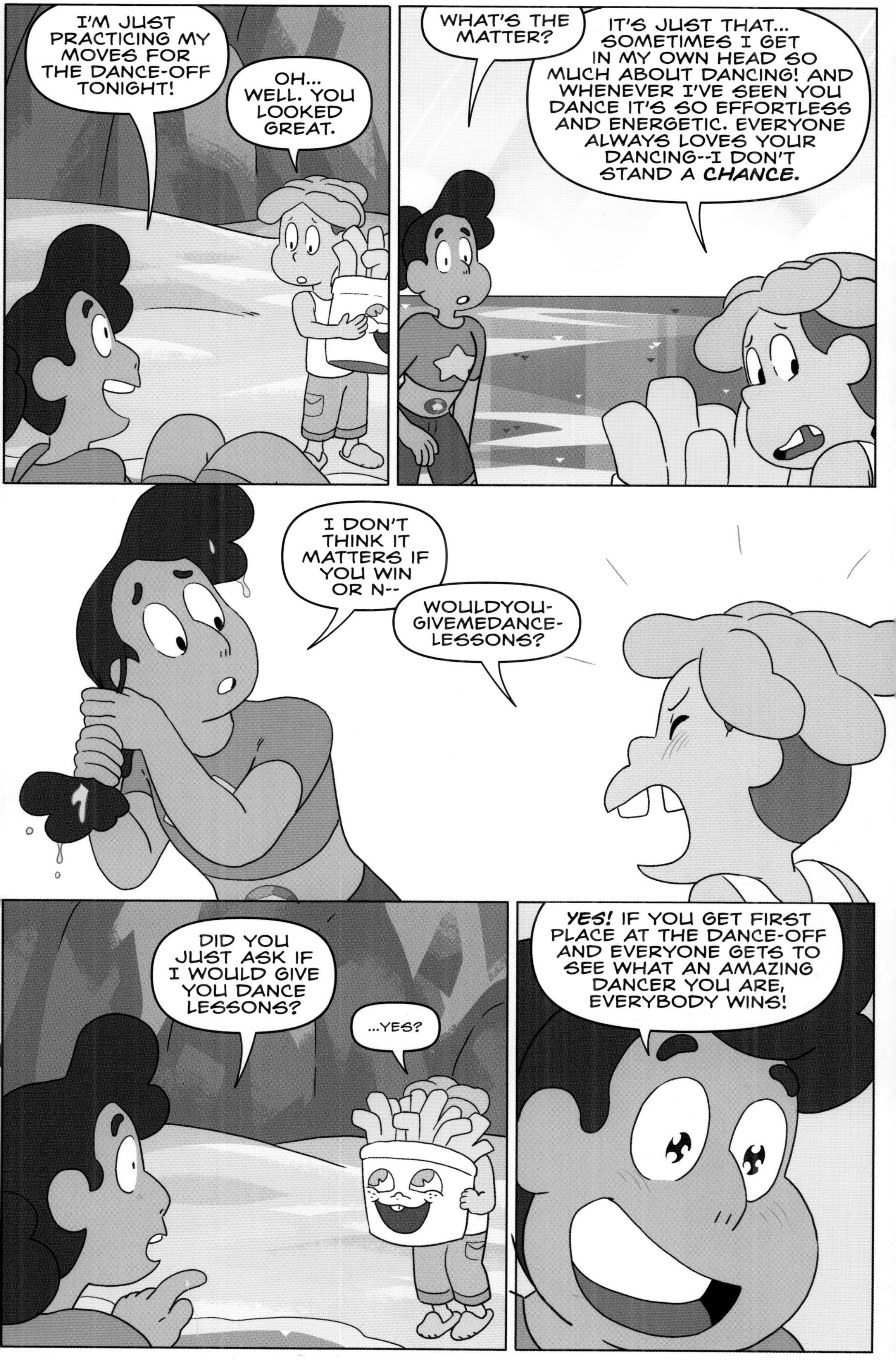
I'M JUST PRACTICING MY MOVES FOR THE DANCE-OFF TONIGHT!
OH... WELL. YOU LOOKED GREAT.
WHAT'S THE MATTER?
IT'S JUST THAT... SOMETIMES I GET IN MY OWN HEAD SO MUCH ABOUT DANCING! AND WHENEVER I'VE SEEN YOU DANCE IT'S SO EFFORTLESS AND ENERGETIC. EVERYONE ALWAYS LOVES YOUR DANCING--I DON'T STAND A *CHANCE.*
I DON'T THINK IT MATTERS IF YOU WIN OR N--
WOULDYOU-GIVEMEDANCE-LESSONS?
DID YOU JUST ASK IF I WOULD GIVE YOU DANCE LESSONS?
...YES?
YES! IF YOU GET FIRST PLACE AT THE DANCE-OFF AND EVERYONE GETS TO SEE WHAT AN AMAZING DANCER YOU ARE, EVERYBODY WINS!

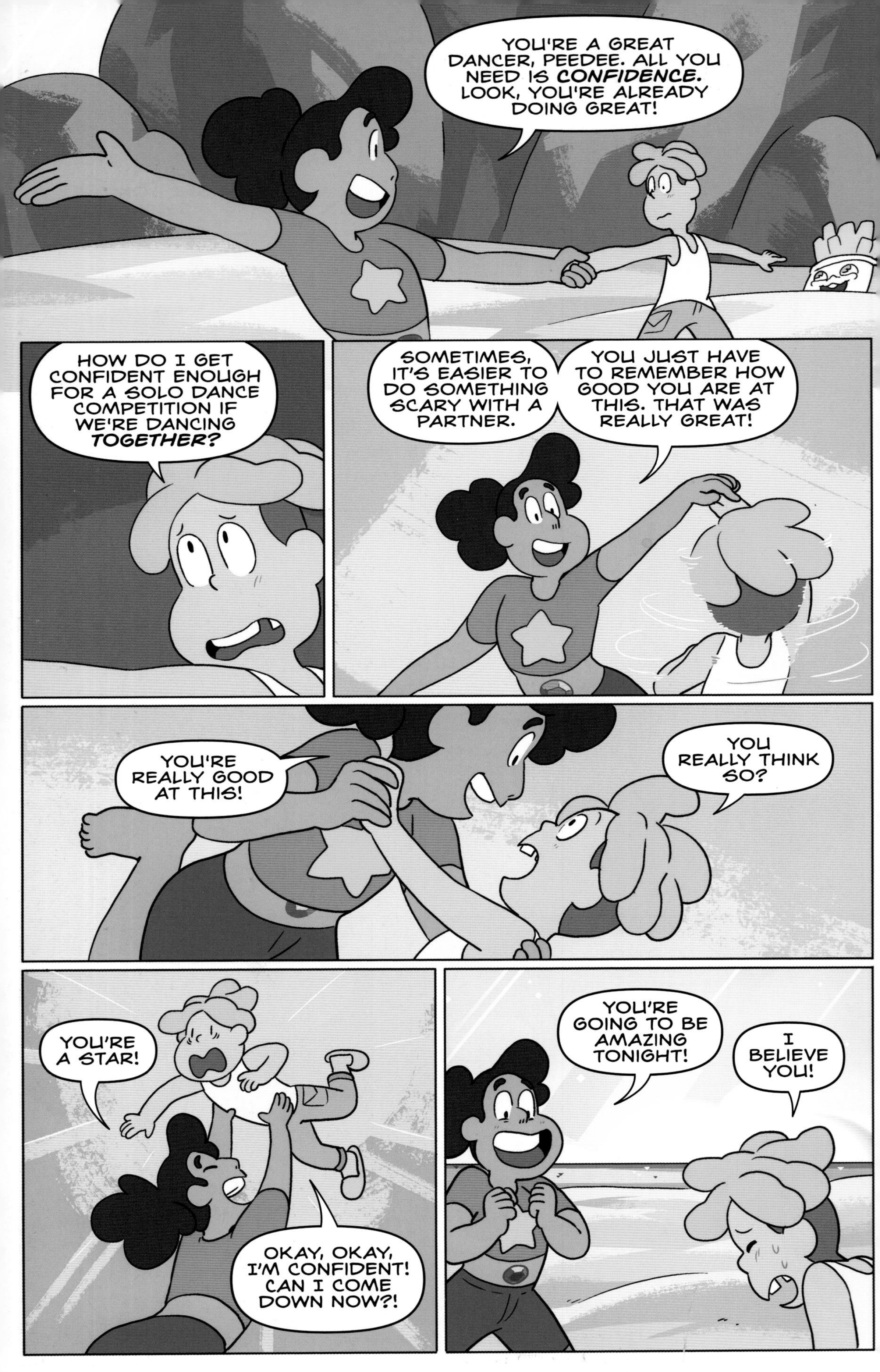
YOU'RE A GREAT DANCER, PEEDEE. ALL YOU NEED IS **CONFIDENCE.** LOOK, YOU'RE ALREADY DOING GREAT!
HOW DO I GET CONFIDENT ENOUGH FOR A SOLO DANCE COMPETITION IF WE'RE DANCING ***TOGETHER?***
SOMETIMES, IT'S EASIER TO DO SOMETHING SCARY WITH A PARTNER.
YOU JUST HAVE TO REMEMBER HOW GOOD YOU ARE AT THIS. THAT WAS REALLY GREAT!
YOU'RE REALLY GOOD AT THIS!
YOU REALLY THINK SO?
YOU'RE A STAR!
OKAY, OKAY, I'M CONFIDENT! CAN I COME DOWN NOW?!
YOU'RE GOING TO BE AMAZING TONIGHT!
I BELIEVE YOU!

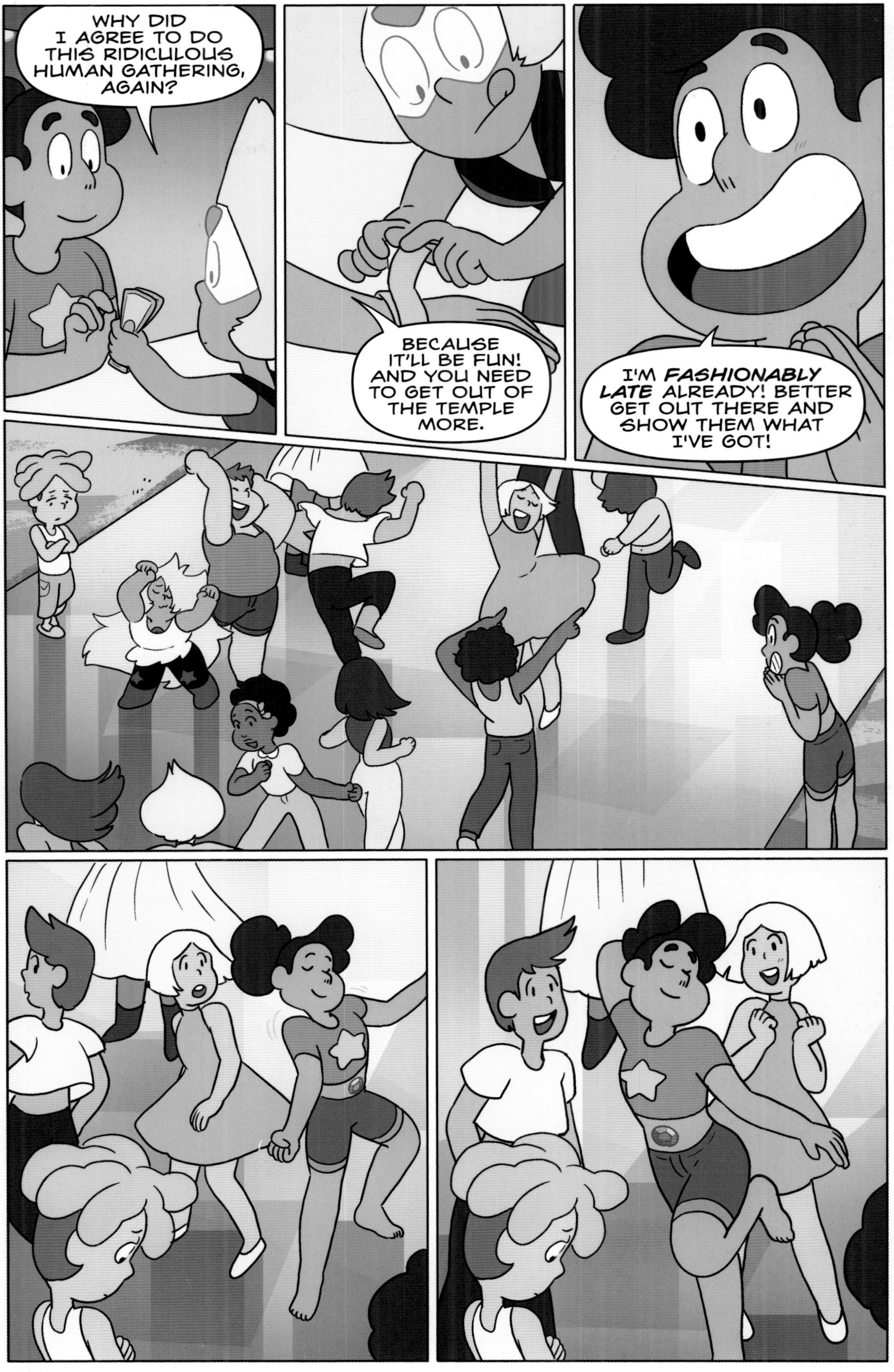
WHY DID I AGREE TO DO THIS RIDICULOUS HUMAN GATHERING, AGAIN?
BECAUSE IT'LL BE FUN! AND YOU NEED TO GET OUT OF THE TEMPLE MORE.
I'M *FASHIONABLY LATE* ALREADY! BETTER GET OUT THERE AND SHOW THEM WHAT I'VE GOT!

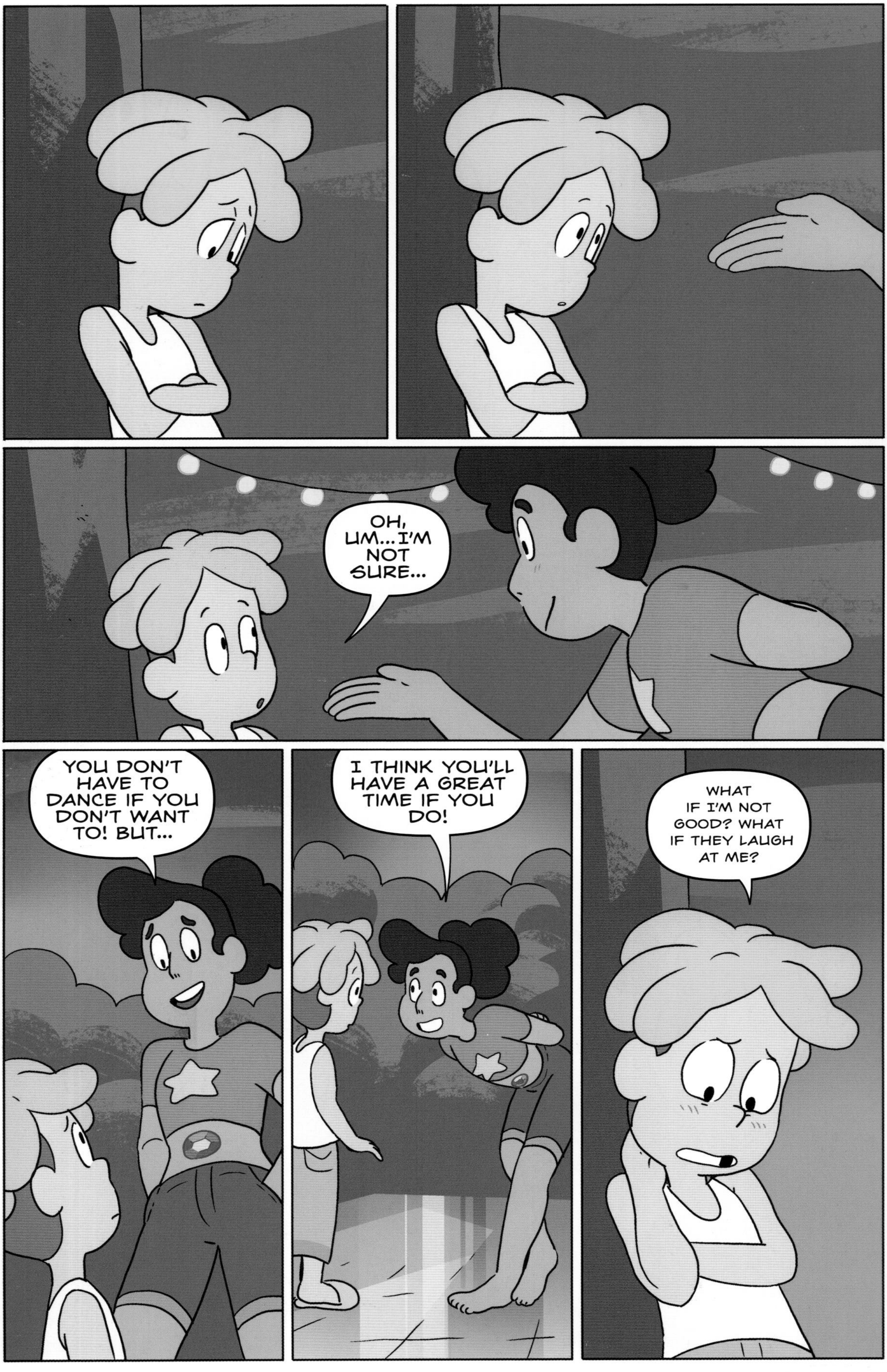
OH, UM...I'M NOT SURE...
YOU DON'T HAVE TO DANCE IF YOU DON'T WANT TO! BUT...
I THINK YOU'LL HAVE A GREAT TIME IF YOU DO!
WHAT IF I'M NOT GOOD? WHAT IF THEY LAUGH AT ME?

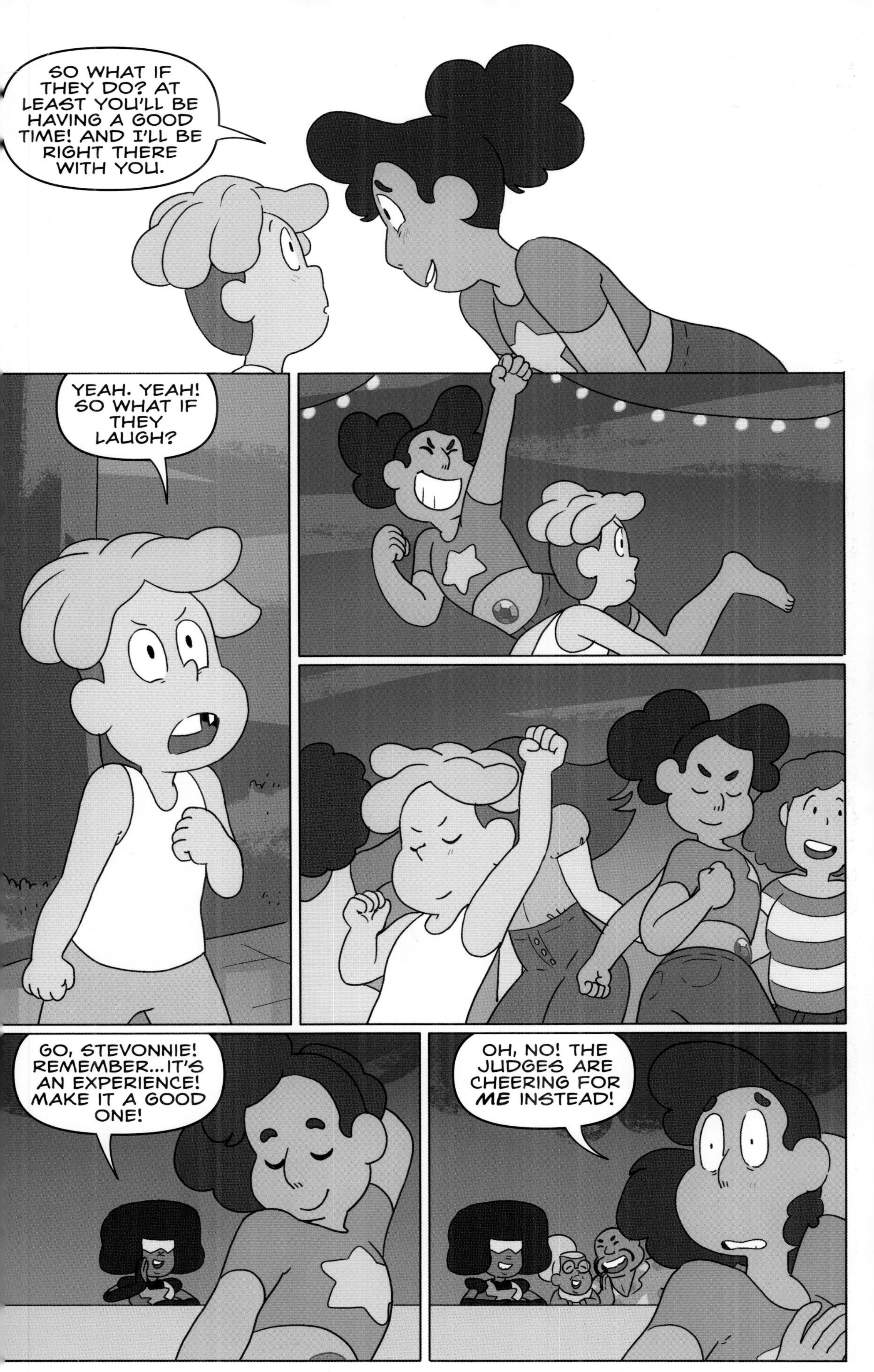
SO WHAT IF THEY DO? AT LEAST YOU'LL BE HAVING A GOOD TIME! AND I'LL BE RIGHT THERE WITH YOU.
YEAH. YEAH! SO WHAT IF THEY LAUGH?
GO, STEVONNIE! REMEMBER...IT'S AN EXPERIENCE! MAKE IT A GOOD ONE!
OH, NO! THE JUDGES ARE CHEERING FOR *ME* INSTEAD!

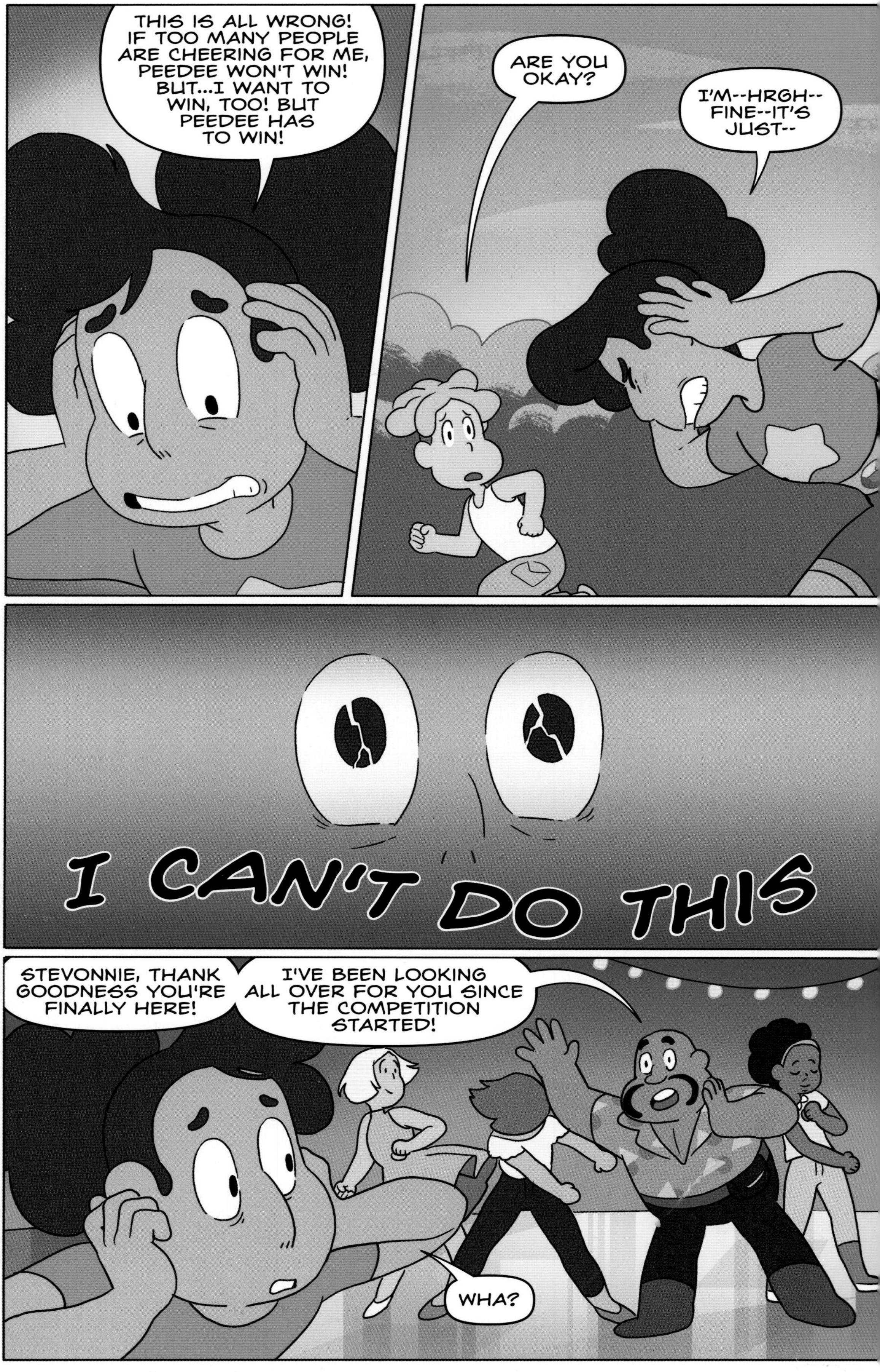
THIS IS ALL WRONG! IF TOO MANY PEOPLE ARE CHEERING FOR ME, PEEDEE WON'T WIN! BUT...I WANT TO WIN, TOO! BUT PEEDEE HAS TO WIN!
ARE YOU OKAY?
I'M--HRGH--FINE--IT'S JUST--
I CAN'T DO THIS
STEVONNIE, THANK GOODNESS YOU'RE FINALLY HERE!
I'VE BEEN LOOKING ALL OVER FOR YOU SINCE THE COMPETITION STARTED!
WHA?

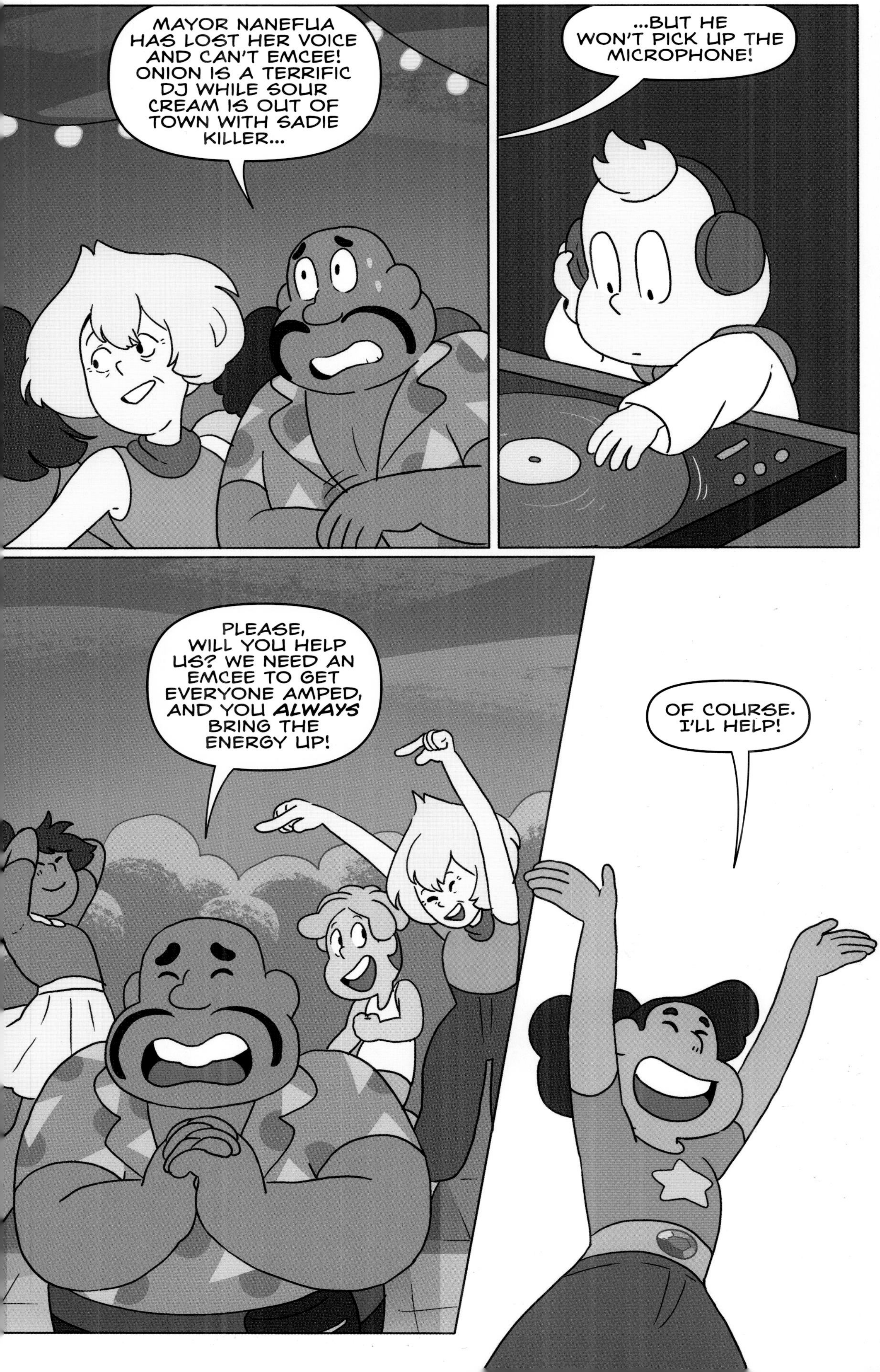
MAYOR NANEFUA HAS LOST HER VOICE AND CAN'T EMCEE! ONION IS A TERRIFIC DJ WHILE SOUR CREAM IS OUT OF TOWN WITH SADIE KILLER...
...BUT HE WON'T PICK UP THE MICROPHONE!
PLEASE, WILL YOU HELP US? WE NEED AN EMCEE TO GET EVERYONE AMPED, AND YOU *ALWAYS* BRING THE ENERGY UP!
OF COURSE. I'LL HELP!

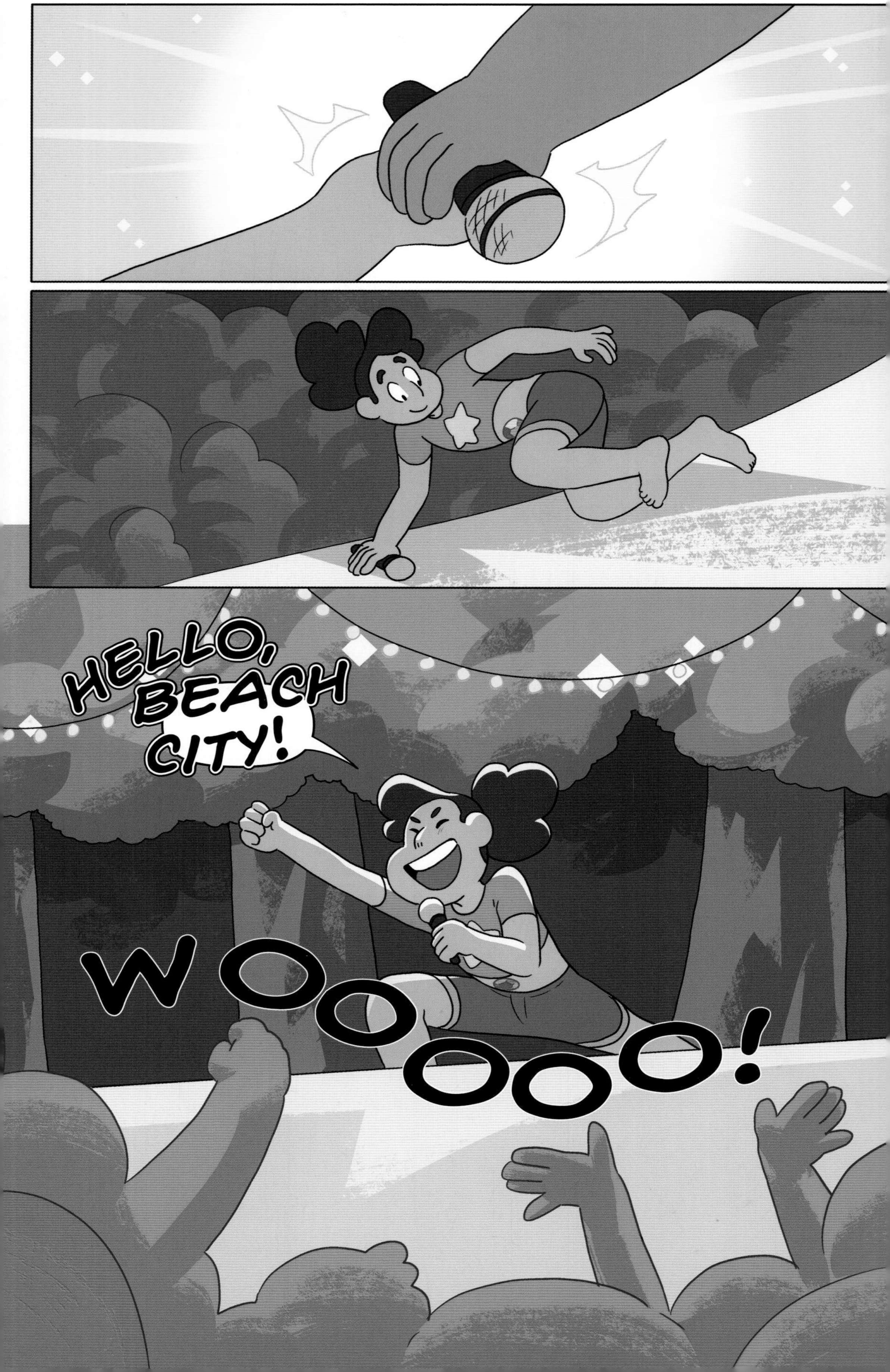
HELLO, BEACH CITY!
WOOOOOO!

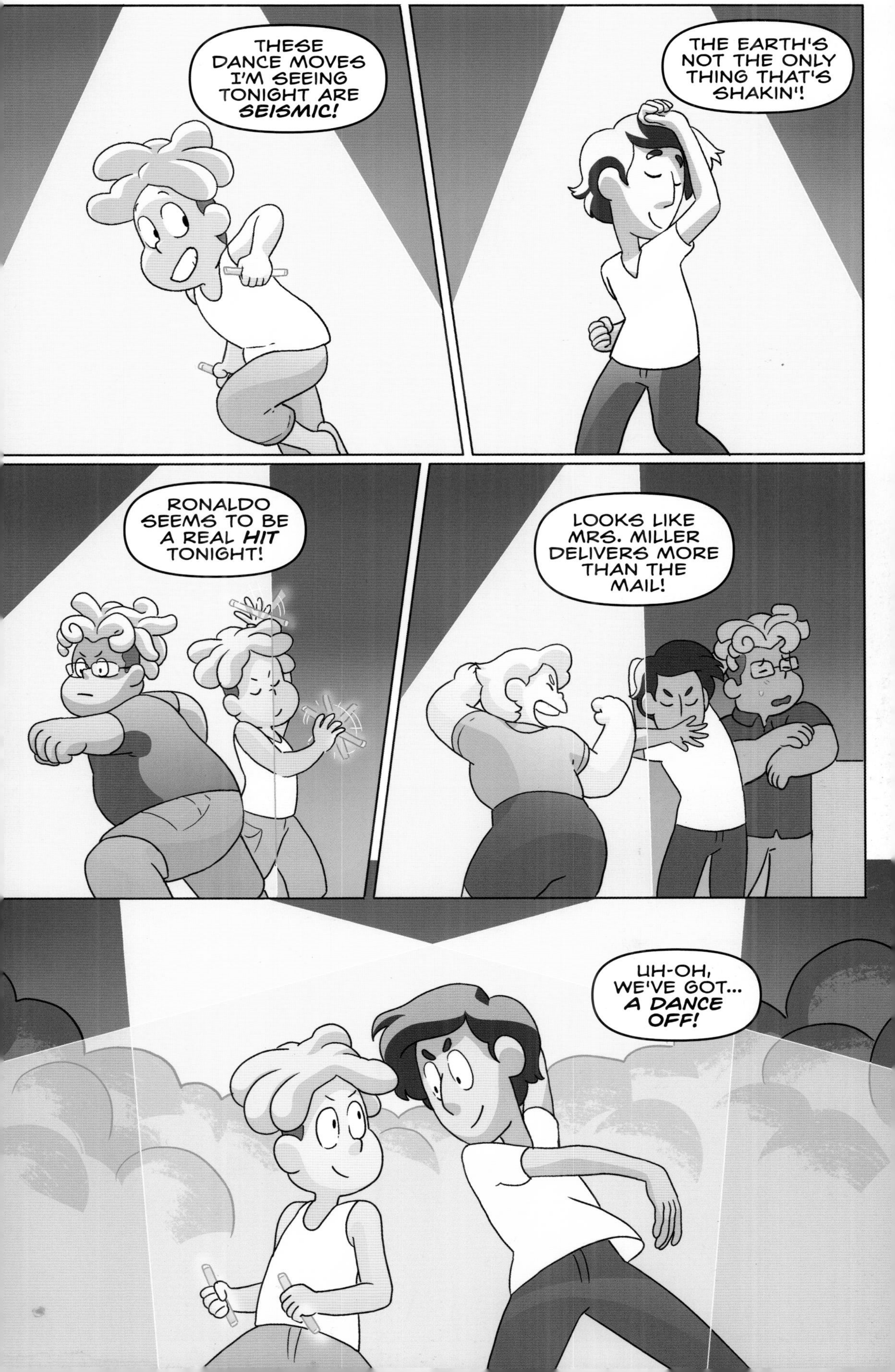
THESE DANCE MOVES I'M SEEING TONIGHT ARE SEISMIC!
THE EARTH'S NOT THE ONLY THING THAT'S SHAKIN'!
RONALDO SEEMS TO BE A REAL HIT TONIGHT!
LOOKS LIKE MRS. MILLER DELIVERS MORE THAN THE MAIL!
UH-OH, WE'VE GOT... A DANCE OFF!

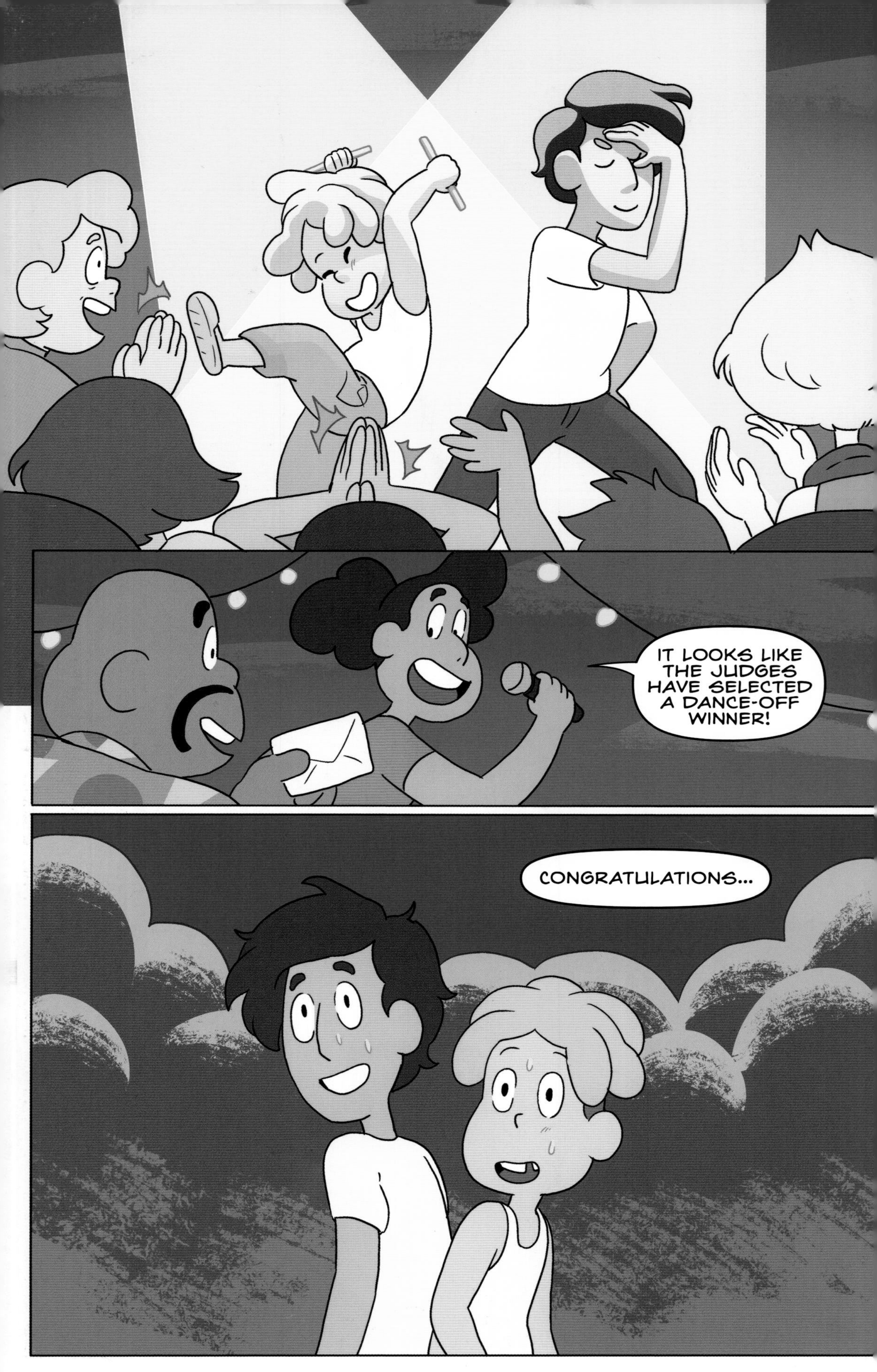
IT LOOKS LIKE THE JUDGES HAVE SELECTED A DANCE-OFF WINNER!
CONGRATULATIONS...

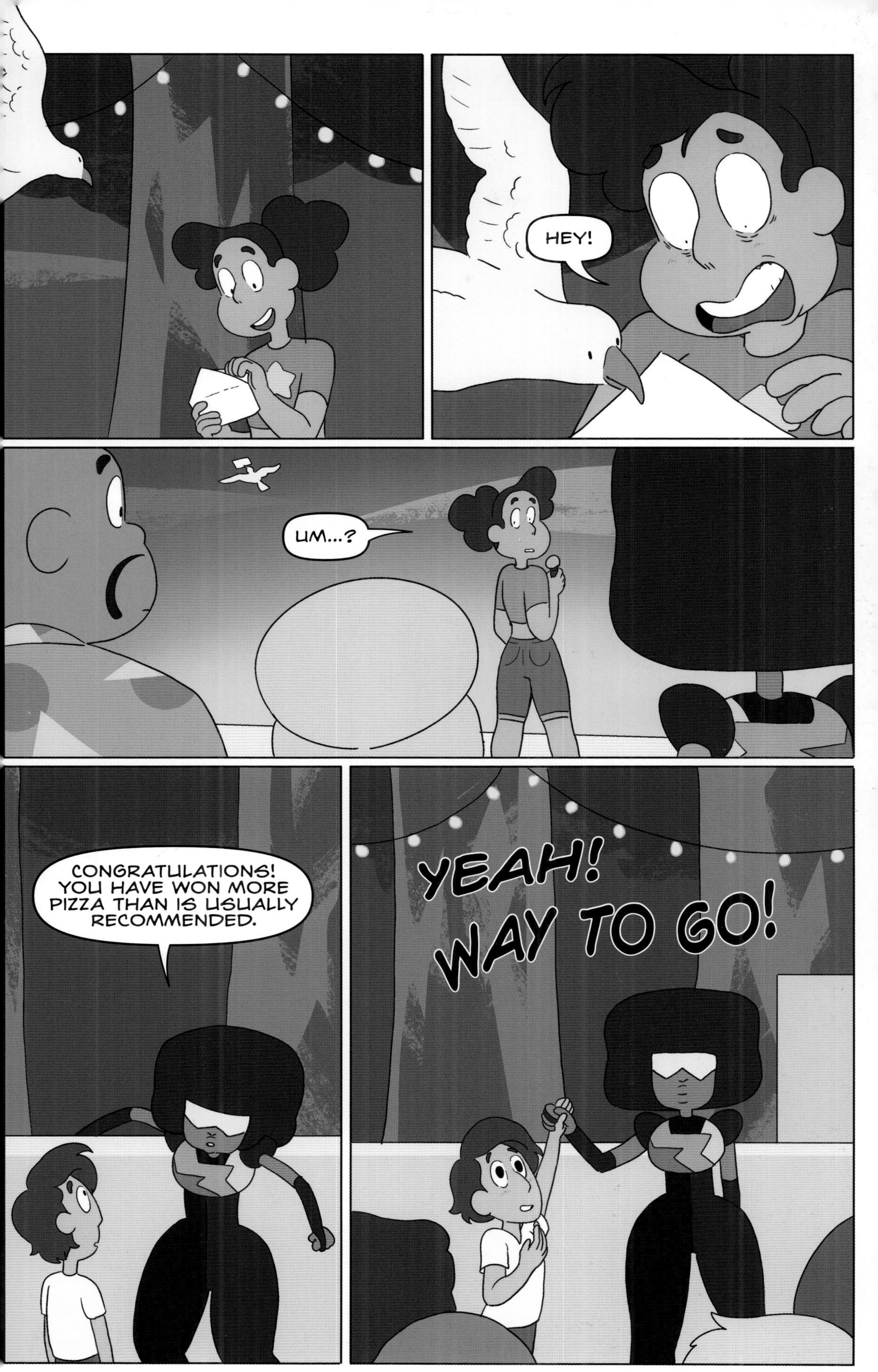
HEY!
UM...?
CONGRATULATIONS! YOU HAVE WON MORE PIZZA THAN IS USUALLY RECOMMENDED.
YEAH! WAY TO GO!

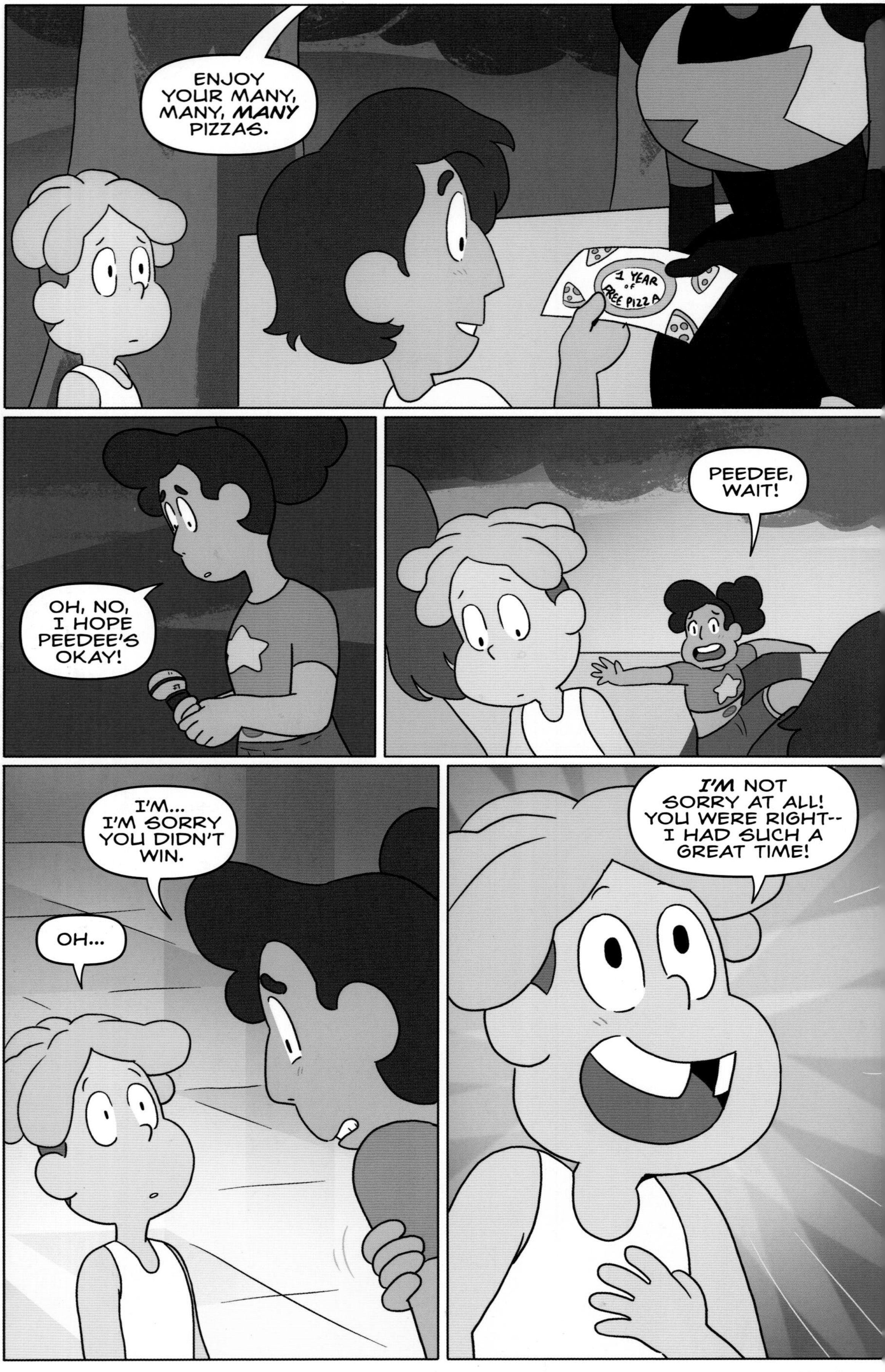
ENJOY YOUR MANY, MANY, *MANY* PIZZAS.
1 YEAR of FREE PIZZA
OH, NO, I HOPE PEEDEE'S OKAY!
PEEDEE, WAIT!
I'M... I'M SORRY YOU DIDN'T WIN.
OH...
I'M NOT SORRY AT ALL! YOU WERE RIGHT-- I HAD SUCH A GREAT TIME!

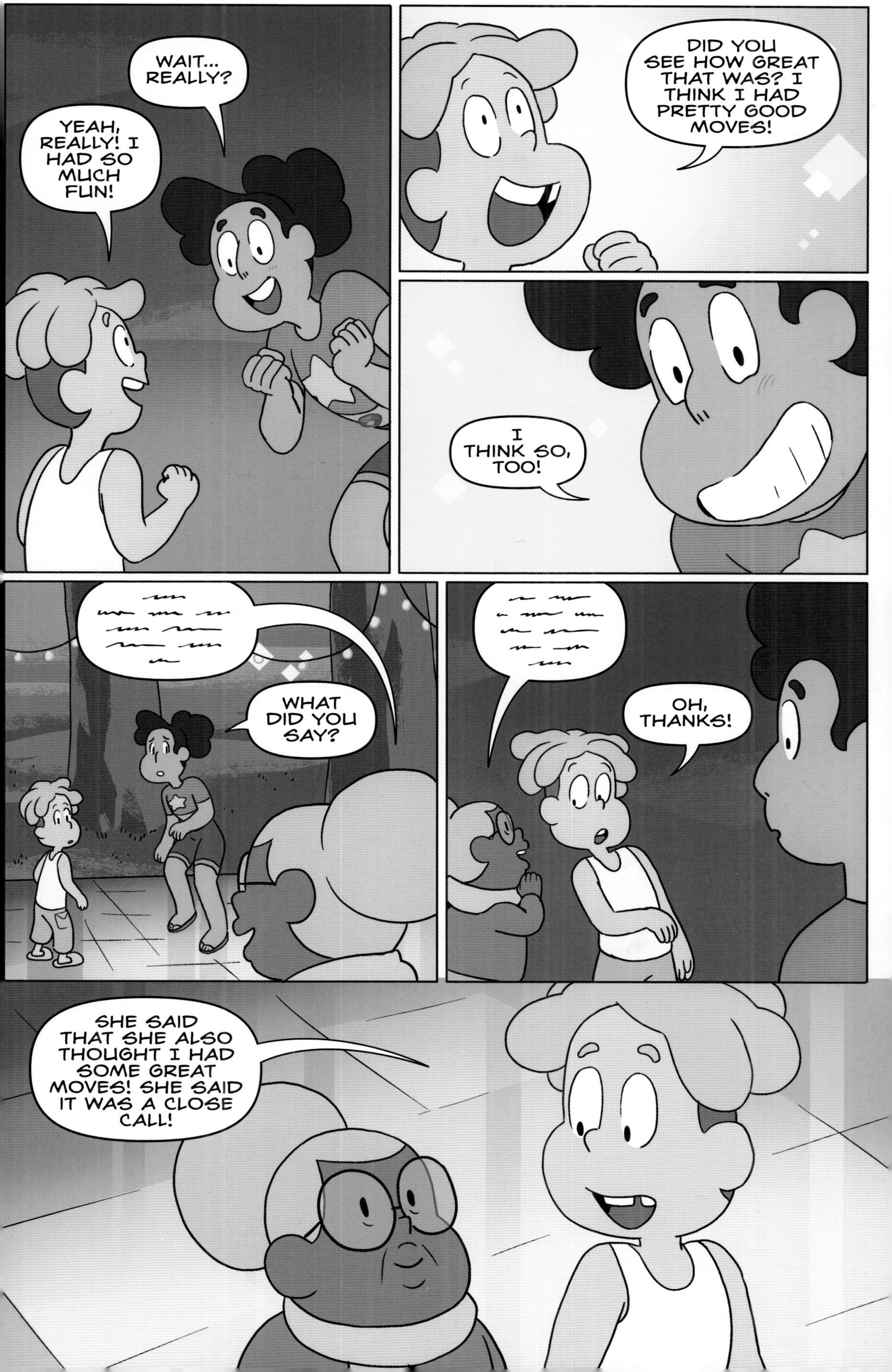
WAIT... REALLY?
YEAH, REALLY! I HAD SO MUCH FUN!
DID YOU SEE HOW GREAT THAT WAS? I THINK I HAD PRETTY GOOD MOVES!
I THINK SO, TOO!
WHAT DID YOU SAY?
OH, THANKS!
SHE SAID THAT SHE ALSO THOUGHT I HAD SOME GREAT MOVES! SHE SAID IT WAS A CLOSE CALL!

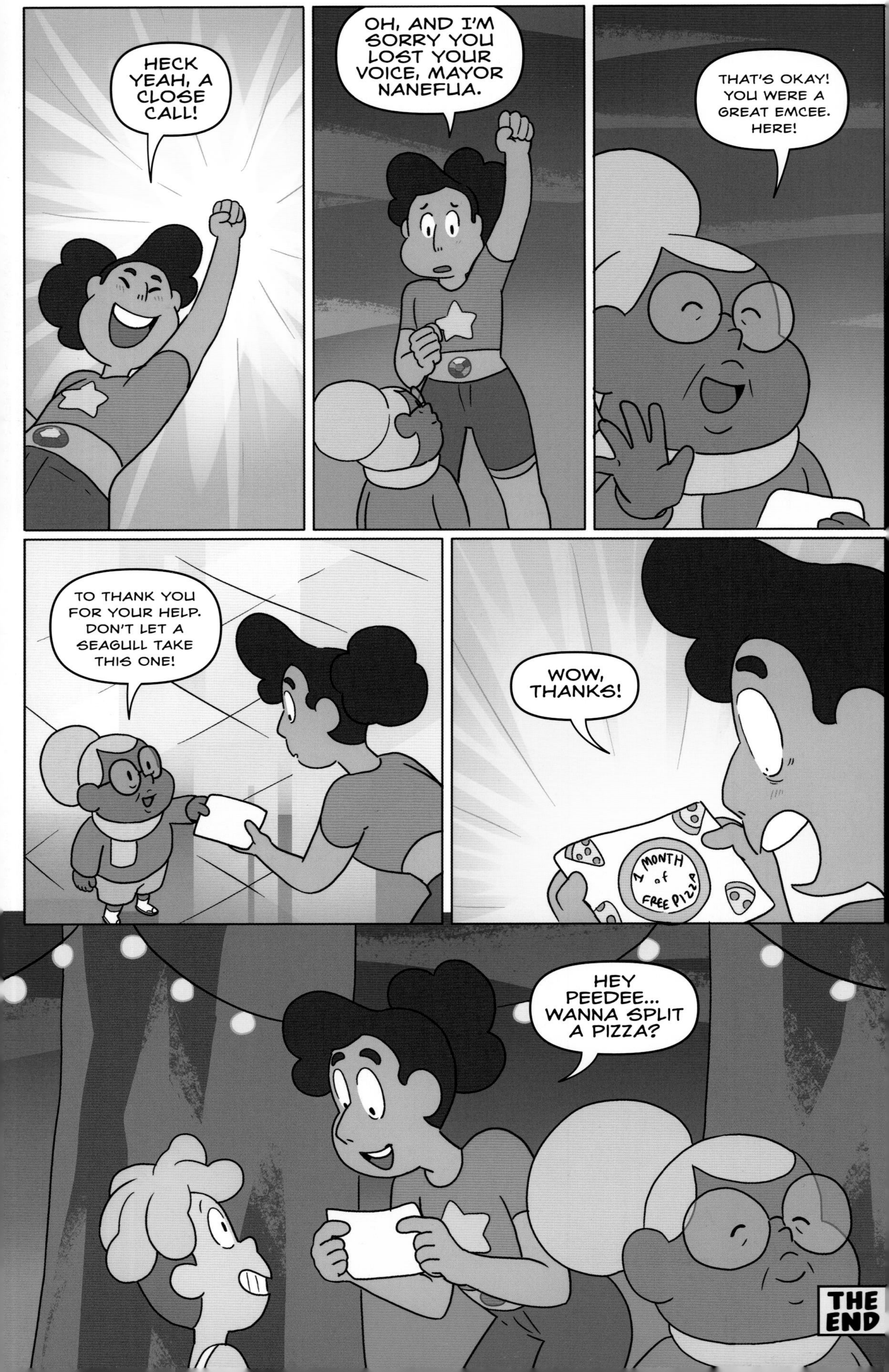
HECK YEAH, A CLOSE CALL!
OH, AND I'M SORRY YOU LOST YOUR VOICE, MAYOR NANEFUA.
THAT'S OKAY! YOU WERE A GREAT EMCEE. HERE!
TO THANK YOU FOR YOUR HELP. DON'T LET A SEAGULL TAKE THIS ONE!
WOW, THANKS!
1 MONTH of FREE PIZZA
HEY PEEDEE... WANNA SPLIT A PIZZA?
THE END

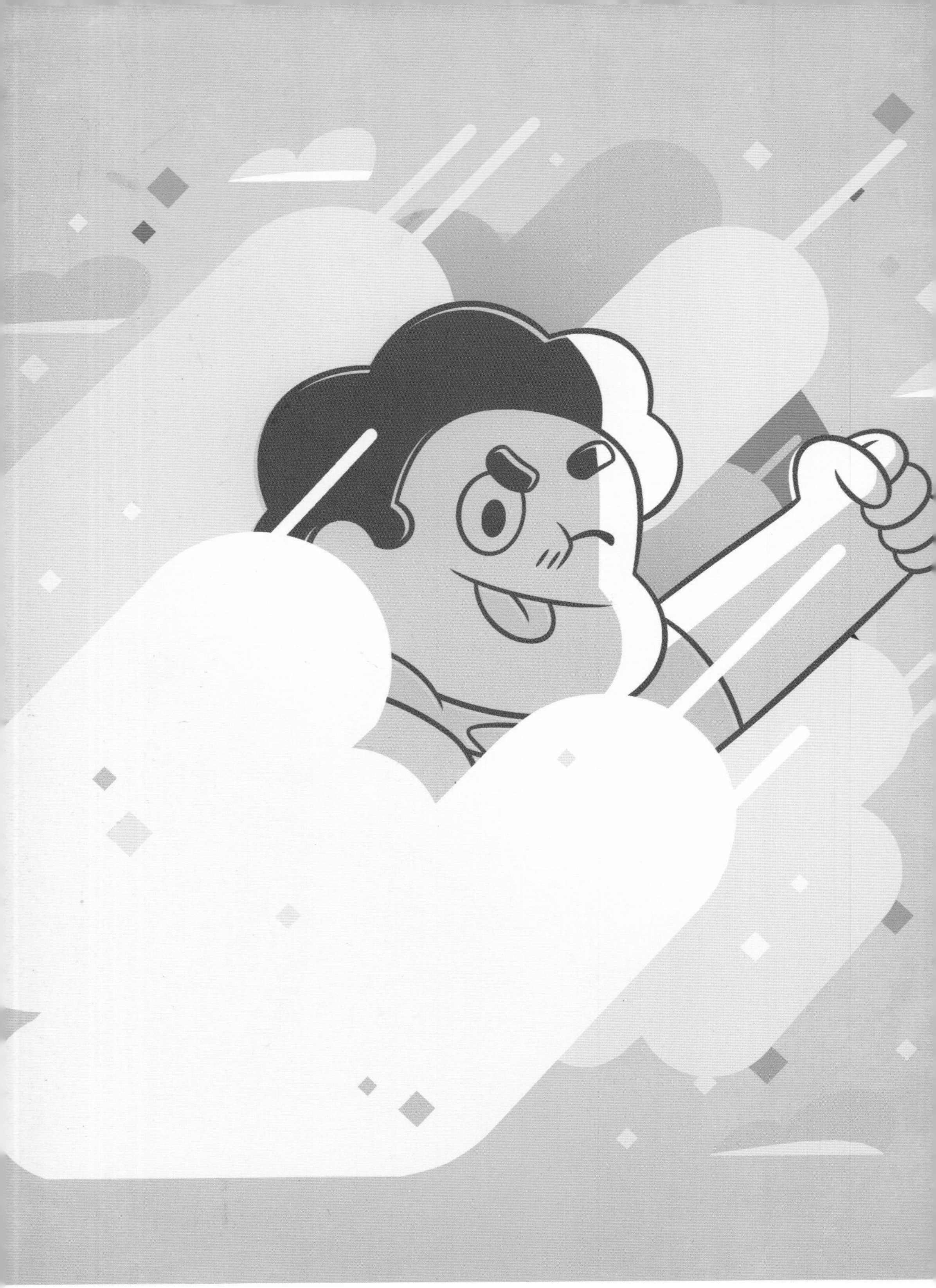

CHAPTER THIRTY-TWO

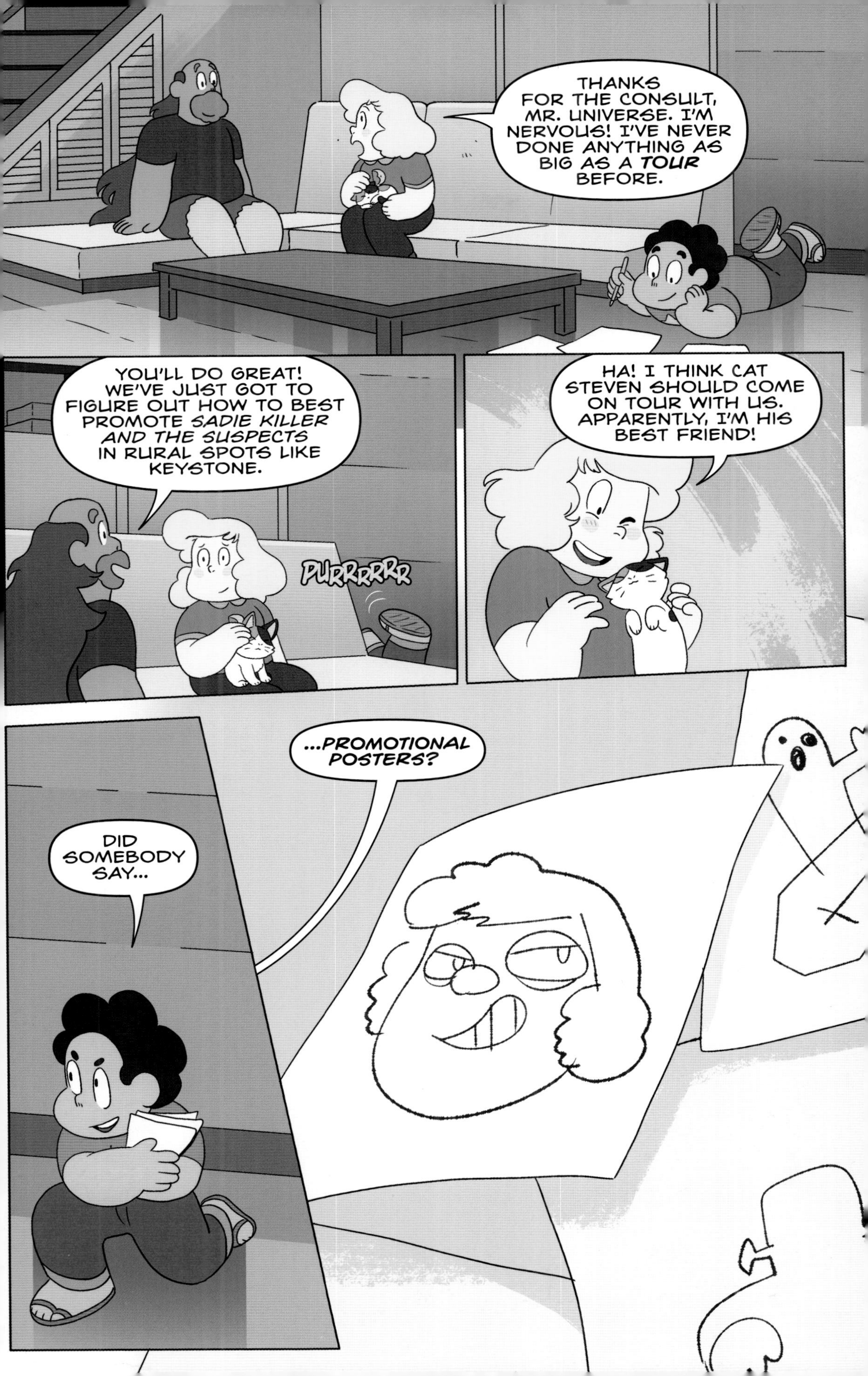
THANKS FOR THE CONSULT, MR. UNIVERSE. I'M NERVOUS! I'VE NEVER DONE ANYTHING AS BIG AS A *TOUR* BEFORE.
YOU'LL DO GREAT! WE'VE JUST GOT TO FIGURE OUT HOW TO BEST PROMOTE *SADIE KILLER AND THE SUSPECTS* IN RURAL SPOTS LIKE KEYSTONE.
PURRRRRR
HA! I THINK CAT STEVEN SHOULD COME ON TOUR WITH US. APPARENTLY, I'M HIS BEST FRIEND!
DID SOMEBODY SAY...
...PROMOTIONAL POSTERS?

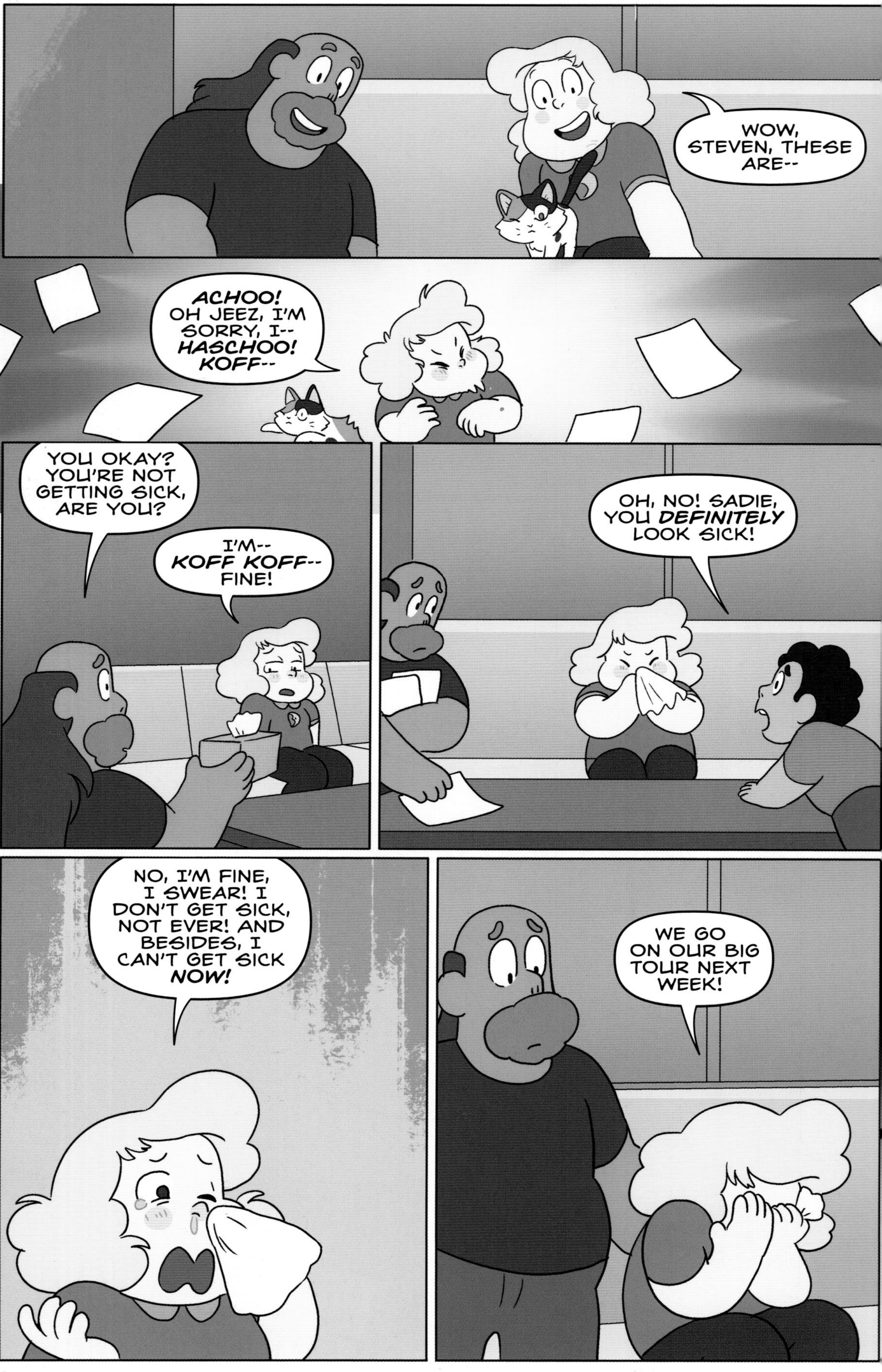
WOW, STEVEN, THESE ARE--
ACHOO! OH JEEZ, I'M SORRY, I-- HASCHOO! KOFF--
YOU OKAY? YOU'RE NOT GETTING SICK, ARE YOU?
I'M-- KOFF KOFF-- FINE!
OH, NO! SADIE, YOU DEFINITELY LOOK SICK!
NO, I'M FINE, I SWEAR! I DON'T GET SICK, NOT EVER! AND BESIDES, I CAN'T GET SICK NOW!
WE GO ON OUR BIG TOUR NEXT WEEK!

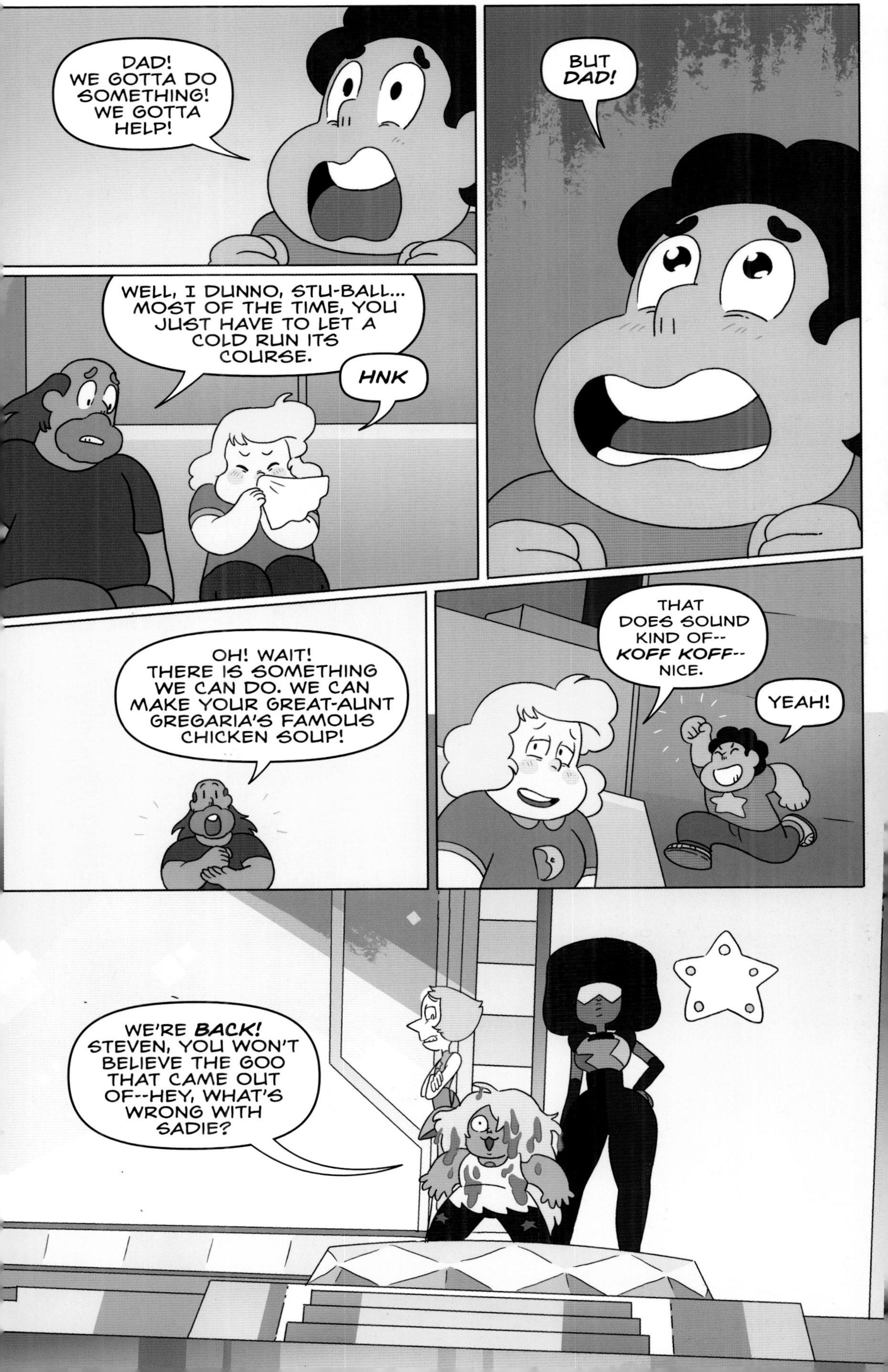
DAD! WE GOTTA DO SOMETHING! WE GOTTA HELP!
BUT DAD!
WELL, I DUNNO, STU-BALL... MOST OF THE TIME, YOU JUST HAVE TO LET A COLD RUN ITS COURSE.
HNK
OH! WAIT! THERE IS SOMETHING WE CAN DO. WE CAN MAKE YOUR GREAT-AUNT GREGARIA'S FAMOUS CHICKEN SOUP!
THAT DOES SOUND KIND OF-- KOFF KOFF-- NICE.
YEAH!
WE'RE BACK! STEVEN, YOU WON'T BELIEVE THE GOO THAT CAME OUT OF--HEY, WHAT'S WRONG WITH SADIE?

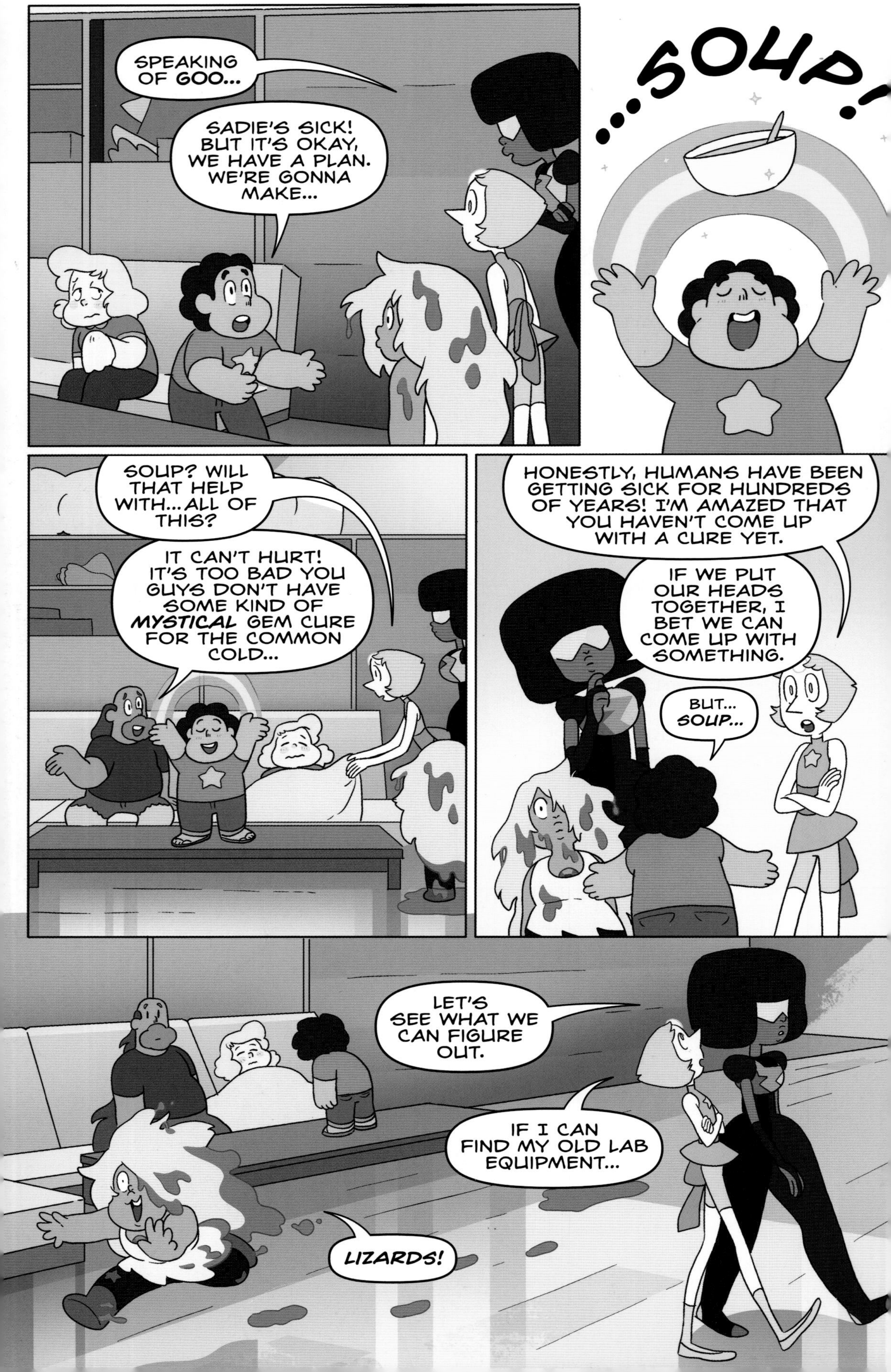
SPEAKING OF GOO...
SADIE'S SICK! BUT IT'S OKAY, WE HAVE A PLAN. WE'RE GONNA MAKE...
...SOUP!
SOUP? WILL THAT HELP WITH...ALL OF THIS?
IT CAN'T HURT! IT'S TOO BAD YOU GUYS DON'T HAVE SOME KIND OF MYSTICAL GEM CURE FOR THE COMMON COLD...
HONESTLY, HUMANS HAVE BEEN GETTING SICK FOR HUNDREDS OF YEARS! I'M AMAZED THAT YOU HAVEN'T COME UP WITH A CURE YET.
IF WE PUT OUR HEADS TOGETHER, I BET WE CAN COME UP WITH SOMETHING.
BUT... SOUP...
LET'S SEE WHAT WE CAN FIGURE OUT.
IF I CAN FIND MY OLD LAB EQUIPMENT...
LIZARDS!

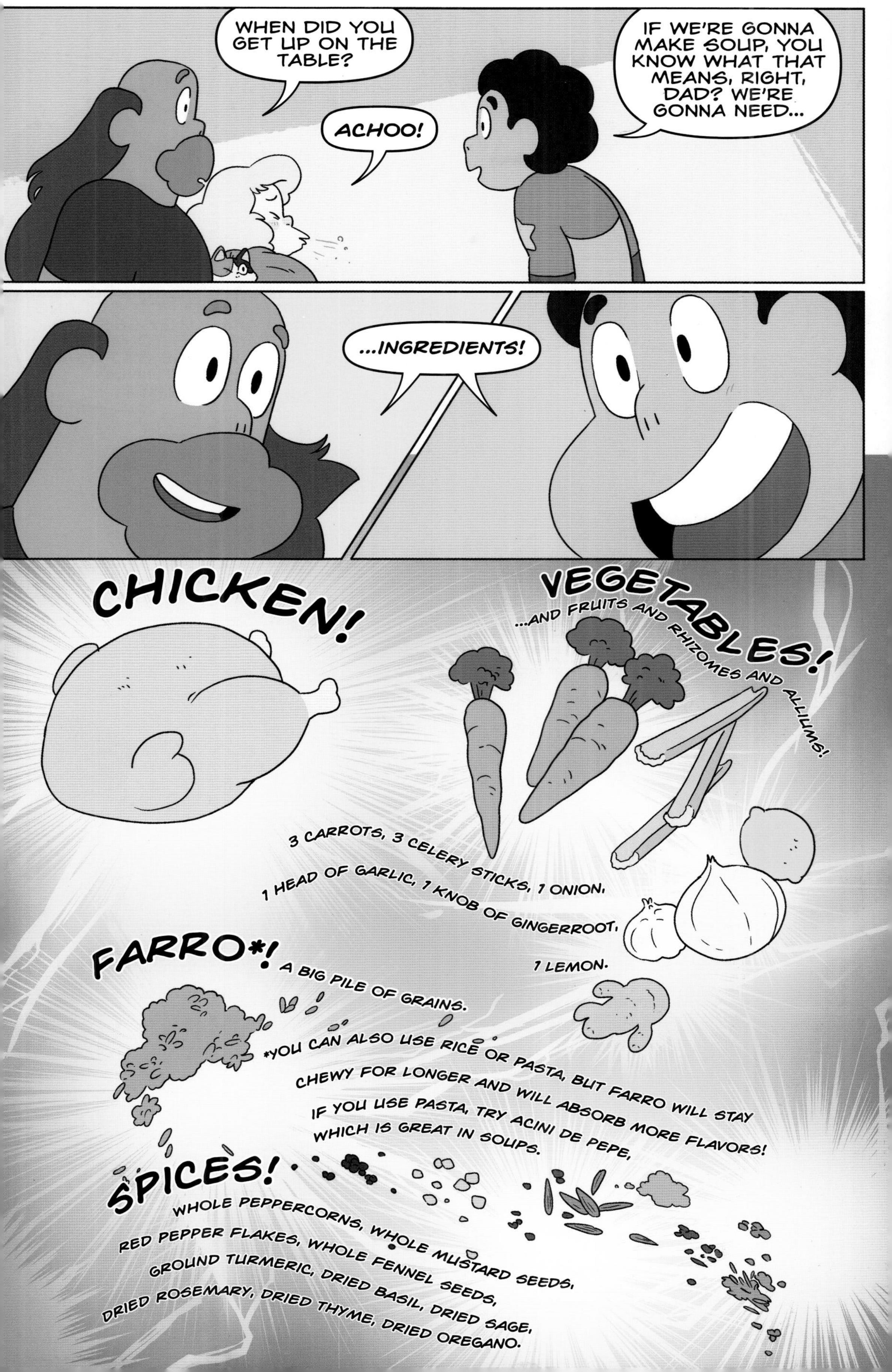
WHEN DID YOU GET UP ON THE TABLE?
ACHOO!
IF WE'RE GONNA MAKE SOUP, YOU KNOW WHAT THAT MEANS, RIGHT, DAD? WE'RE GONNA NEED...
...INGREDIENTS!
CHICKEN!
VEGETABLES!
...AND FRUITS AND RHIZOMES AND ALLIUMS!
3 CARROTS, 3 CELERY STICKS, 1 ONION,
1 HEAD OF GARLIC, 1 KNOB OF GINGERROOT,
1 LEMON.
FARRO*! A BIG PILE OF GRAINS.
*YOU CAN ALSO USE RICE OR PASTA, BUT FARRO WILL STAY CHEWY FOR LONGER AND WILL ABSORB MORE FLAVORS! IF YOU USE PASTA, TRY ACINI DE PEPE, WHICH IS GREAT IN SOUPS.
SPICES!
WHOLE PEPPERCORNS, WHOLE MUSTARD SEEDS,
RED PEPPER FLAKES, WHOLE FENNEL SEEDS,
GROUND TURMERIC, DRIED BASIL, DRIED SAGE,
DRIED ROSEMARY, DRIED THYME, DRIED OREGANO.

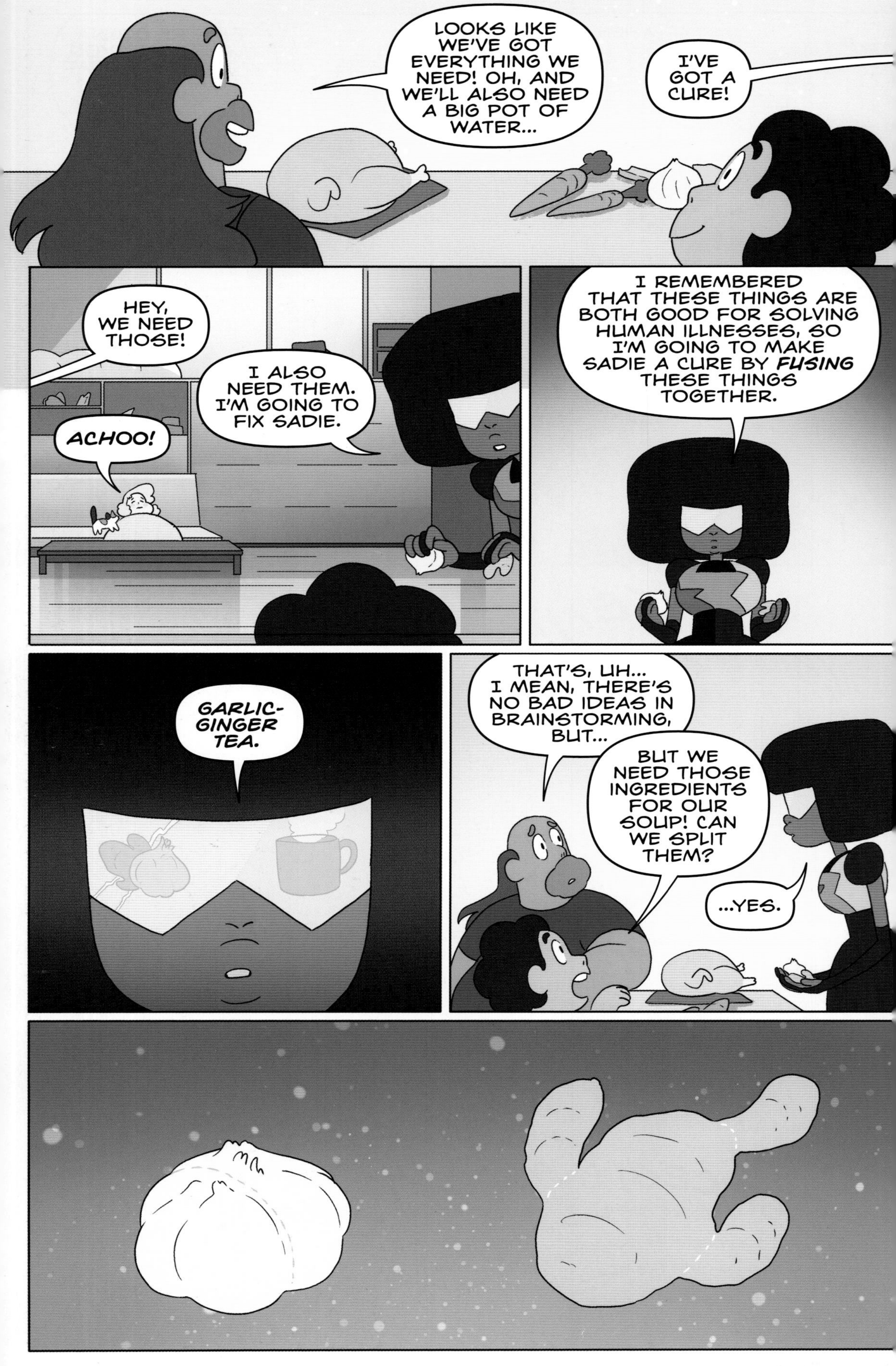
LOOKS LIKE WE'VE GOT EVERYTHING WE NEED! OH, AND WE'LL ALSO NEED A BIG POT OF WATER...
I'VE GOT A CURE!
HEY, WE NEED THOSE!
I ALSO NEED THEM. I'M GOING TO FIX SADIE.
ACHOO!
I REMEMBERED THAT THESE THINGS ARE BOTH GOOD FOR SOLVING HUMAN ILLNESSES, SO I'M GOING TO MAKE SADIE A CURE BY FUSING THESE THINGS TOGETHER.
GARLIC-GINGER TEA.
THAT'S, UH... I MEAN, THERE'S NO BAD IDEAS IN BRAINSTORMING, BUT...
BUT WE NEED THOSE INGREDIENTS FOR OUR SOUP! CAN WE SPLIT THEM?
...YES.

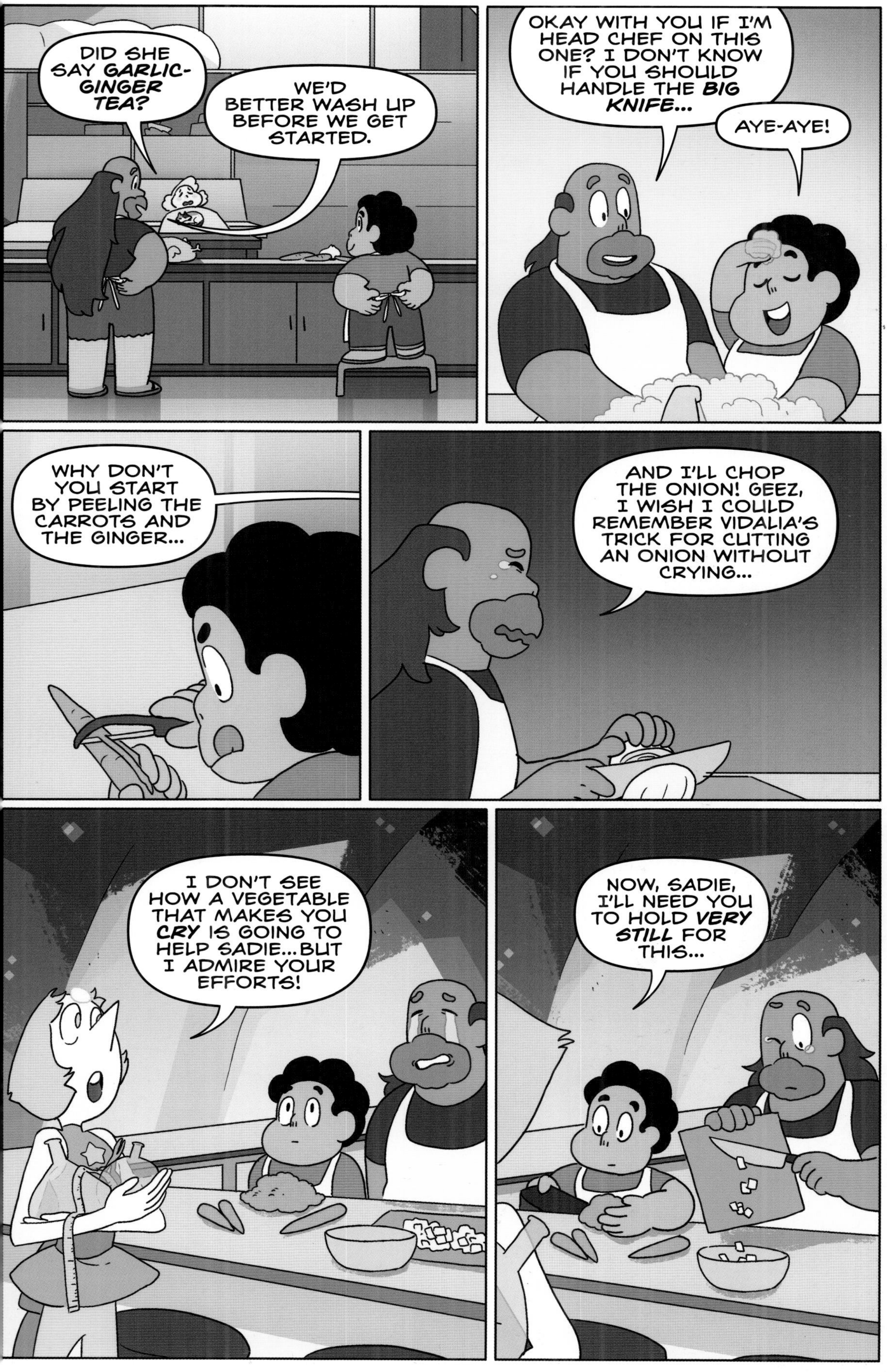
DID SHE SAY GARLIC-GINGER TEA?
WE'D BETTER WASH UP BEFORE WE GET STARTED.
OKAY WITH YOU IF I'M HEAD CHEF ON THIS ONE? I DON'T KNOW IF YOU SHOULD HANDLE THE BIG KNIFE...
AYE-AYE!
WHY DON'T YOU START BY PEELING THE CARROTS AND THE GINGER...
AND I'LL CHOP THE ONION! GEEZ, I WISH I COULD REMEMBER VIDALIA'S TRICK FOR CUTTING AN ONION WITHOUT CRYING...
I DON'T SEE HOW A VEGETABLE THAT MAKES YOU CRY IS GOING TO HELP SADIE...BUT I ADMIRE YOUR EFFORTS!
NOW, SADIE, I'LL NEED YOU TO HOLD VERY STILL FOR THIS...

STEVEN, CAN YOU PEEL ALL THAT GARLIC WHILE I CHOP UP THESE VEGGIES?

OH YEAH?

OH, I LEARNED A TRICK FOR THIS FROM MR. MAHESWARAN!

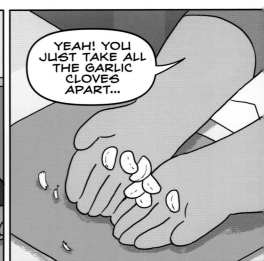
YEAH! YOU JUST TAKE ALL THE GARLIC CLOVES APART...

AND THEN YOU PUT THEM IN A JAR...

AND THEN YOU *SHAKE THEM UP A LOT!*

...AND THEN THEY PEEL THEMSELVES!

WOAH! COOL!

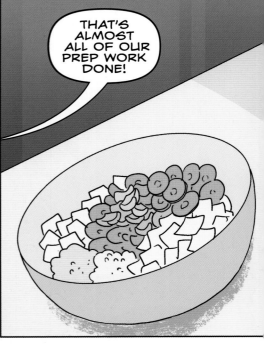
THAT'S ALMOST ALL OF OUR PREP WORK DONE!

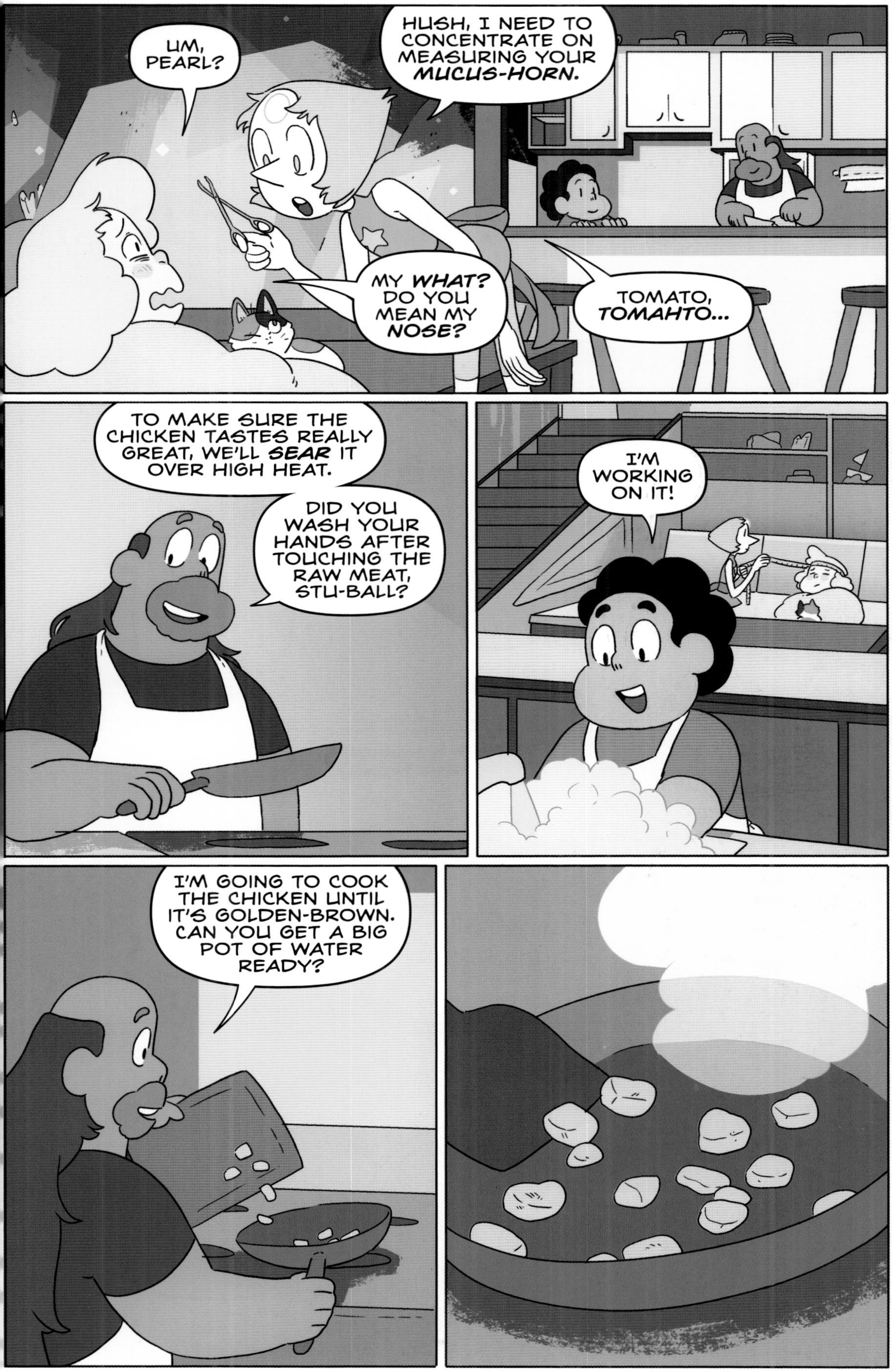
UM, PEARL?
HUSH, I NEED TO CONCENTRATE ON MEASURING YOUR MUCUS-HORN.
MY WHAT? DO YOU MEAN MY NOSE?
TOMATO, TOMAHTO...
TO MAKE SURE THE CHICKEN TASTES REALLY GREAT, WE'LL SEAR IT OVER HIGH HEAT.
DID YOU WASH YOUR HANDS AFTER TOUCHING THE RAW MEAT, STU-BALL?
I'M WORKING ON IT!
I'M GOING TO COOK THE CHICKEN UNTIL IT'S GOLDEN-BROWN. CAN YOU GET A BIG POT OF WATER READY?

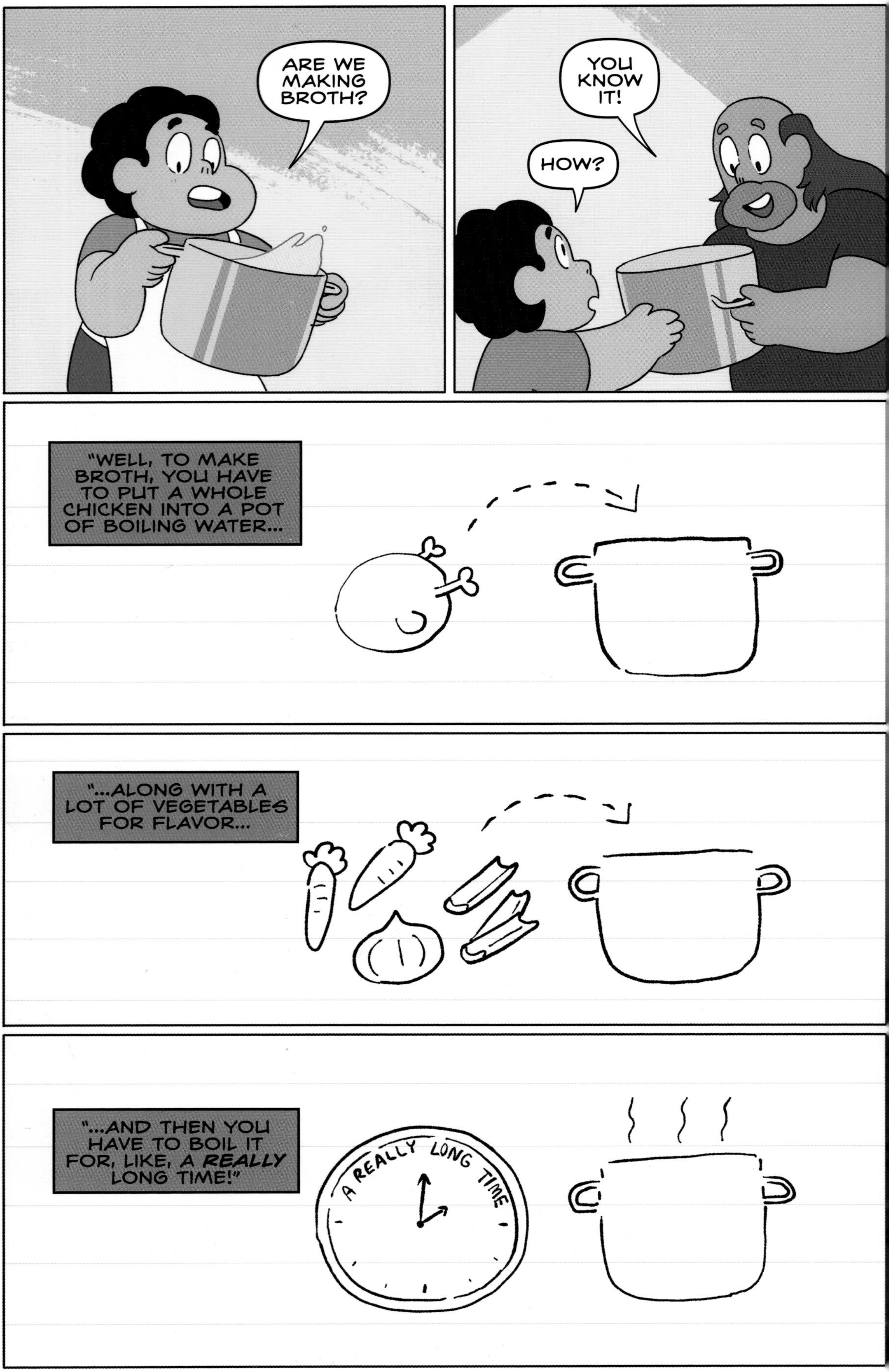
ARE WE MAKING BROTH?
YOU KNOW IT!
HOW?
"WELL, TO MAKE BROTH, YOU HAVE TO PUT A WHOLE CHICKEN INTO A POT OF BOILING WATER...
"...ALONG WITH A LOT OF VEGETABLES FOR FLAVOR...
"...AND THEN YOU HAVE TO BOIL IT FOR, LIKE, A *REALLY* LONG TIME!"
A REALLY LONG TIME

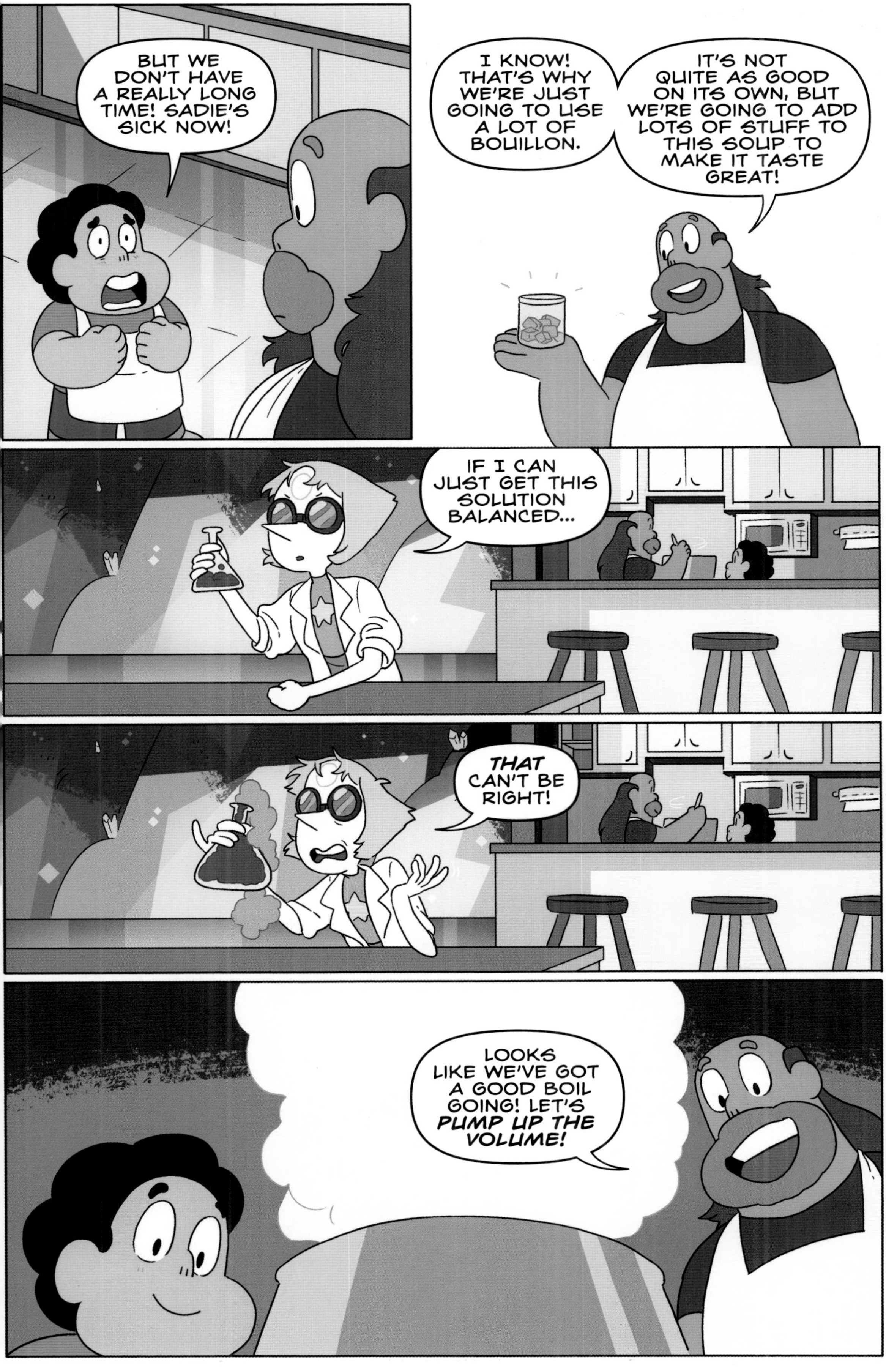
BUT WE DON'T HAVE A REALLY LONG TIME! SADIE'S SICK NOW!
I KNOW! THAT'S WHY WE'RE JUST GOING TO USE A LOT OF BOUILLON.
IT'S NOT QUITE AS GOOD ON ITS OWN, BUT WE'RE GOING TO ADD LOTS OF STUFF TO THIS SOUP TO MAKE IT TASTE GREAT!
IF I CAN JUST GET THIS SOLUTION BALANCED...
THAT CAN'T BE RIGHT!
LOOKS LIKE WE'VE GOT A GOOD BOIL GOING! LET'S *PUMP UP THE VOLUME!*

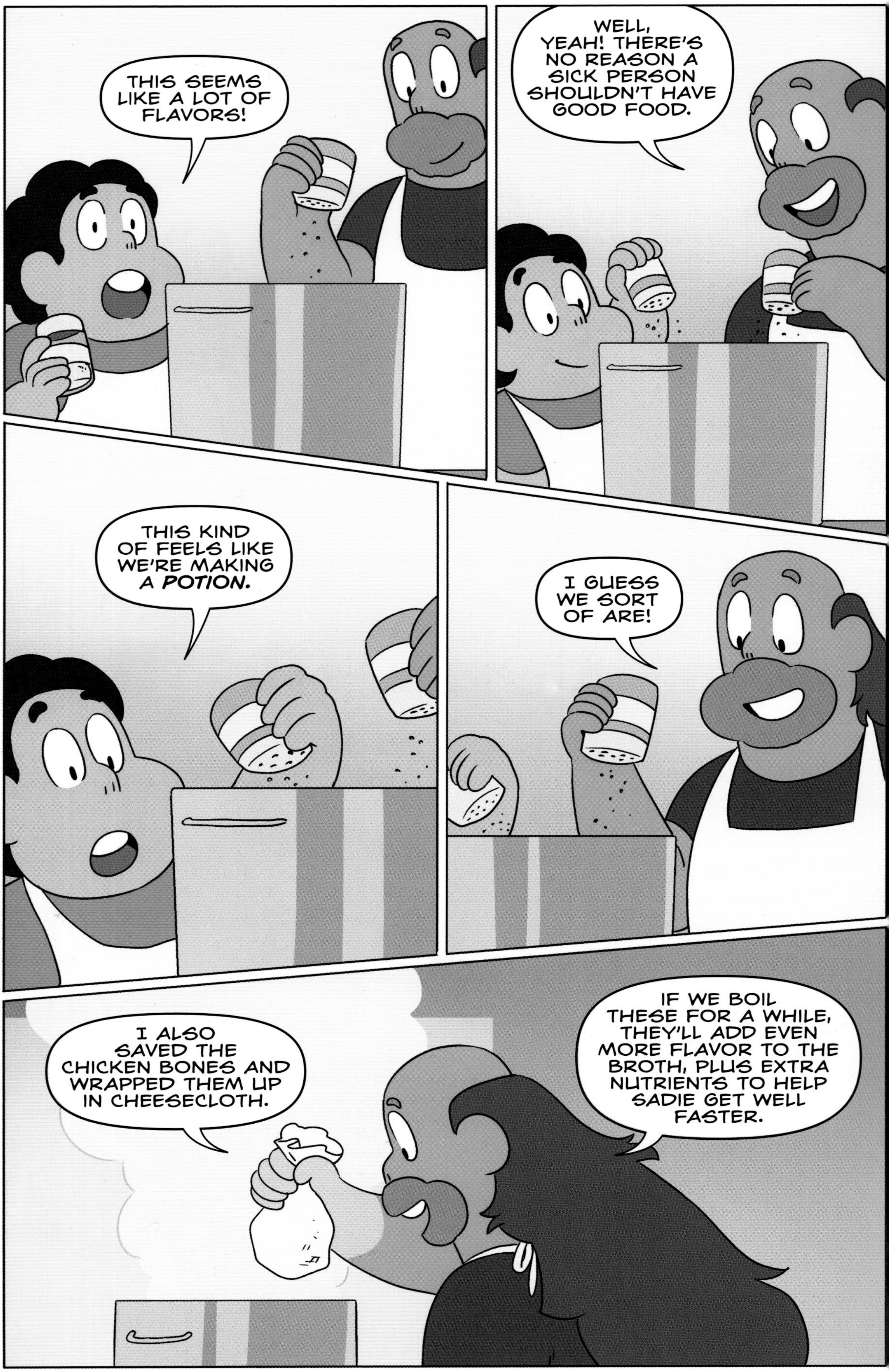
THIS SEEMS LIKE A LOT OF FLAVORS!
WELL, YEAH! THERE'S NO REASON A SICK PERSON SHOULDN'T HAVE GOOD FOOD.
THIS KIND OF FEELS LIKE WE'RE MAKING A *POTION.*
I GUESS WE SORT OF ARE!
I ALSO SAVED THE CHICKEN BONES AND WRAPPED THEM UP IN CHEESECLOTH.
IF WE BOIL THESE FOR A WHILE, THEY'LL ADD EVEN MORE FLAVOR TO THE BROTH, PLUS EXTRA NUTRIENTS TO HELP SADIE GET WELL FASTER.

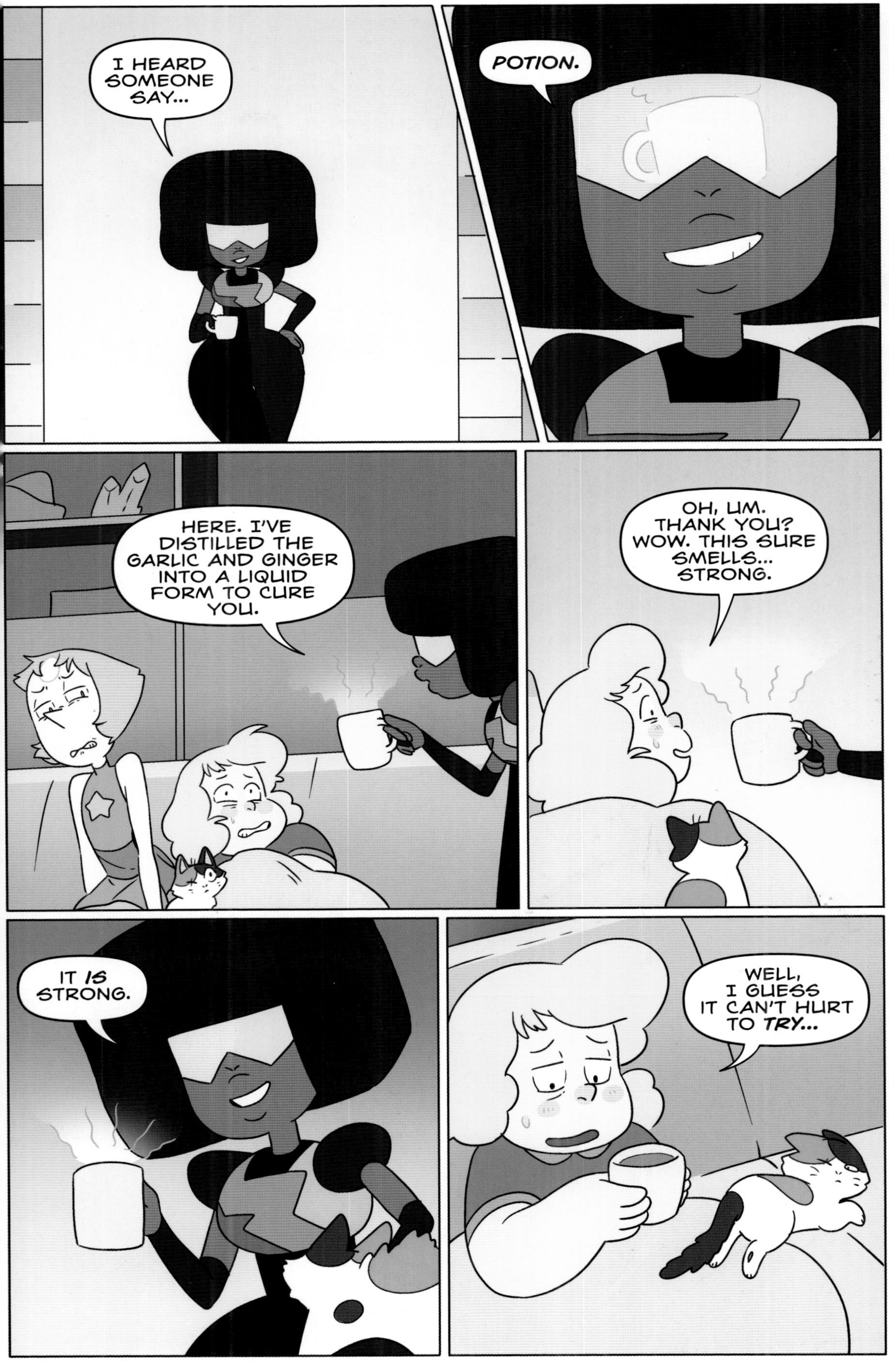
I HEARD SOMEONE SAY...
POTION.
HERE. I'VE DISTILLED THE GARLIC AND GINGER INTO A LIQUID FORM TO CURE YOU.
OH, UM. THANK YOU? WOW. THIS SURE SMELLS... STRONG.
IT IS STRONG.
WELL, I GUESS IT CAN'T HURT TO TRY...

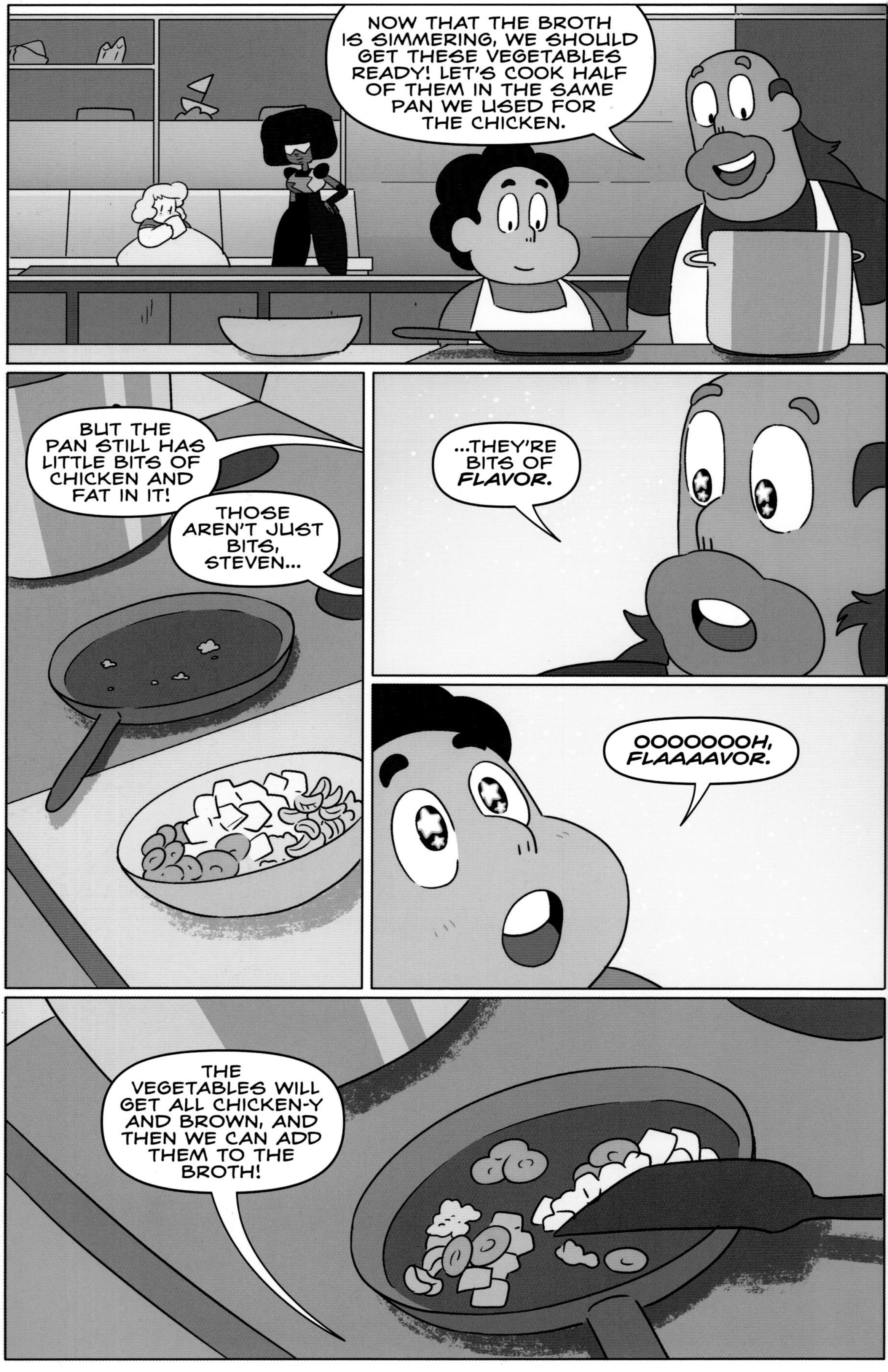
NOW THAT THE BROTH IS SIMMERING, WE SHOULD GET THESE VEGETABLES READY! LET'S COOK HALF OF THEM IN THE SAME PAN WE USED FOR THE CHICKEN.
BUT THE PAN STILL HAS LITTLE BITS OF CHICKEN AND FAT IN IT!
THOSE AREN'T JUST BITS, STEVEN...
...THEY'RE BITS OF *FLAVOR.*
OOOOOOOH, FLAAAAVOR.
THE VEGETABLES WILL GET ALL CHICKEN-Y AND BROWN, AND THEN WE CAN ADD THEM TO THE BROTH!

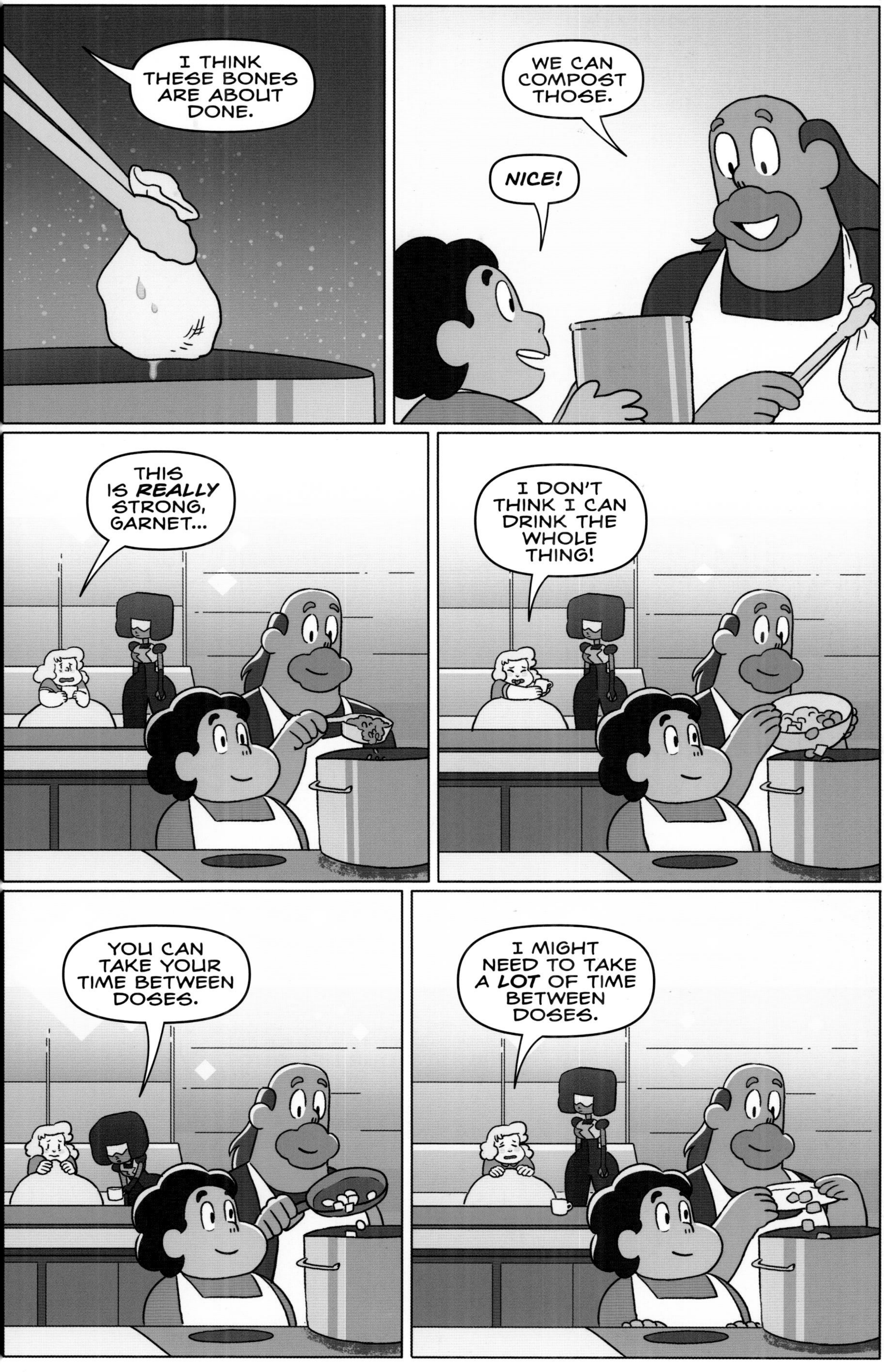
I THINK THESE BONES ARE ABOUT DONE.
WE CAN COMPOST THOSE.
NICE!
THIS IS REALLY STRONG, GARNET...
I DON'T THINK I CAN DRINK THE WHOLE THING!
YOU CAN TAKE YOUR TIME BETWEEN DOSES.
I MIGHT NEED TO TAKE A LOT OF TIME BETWEEN DOSES.

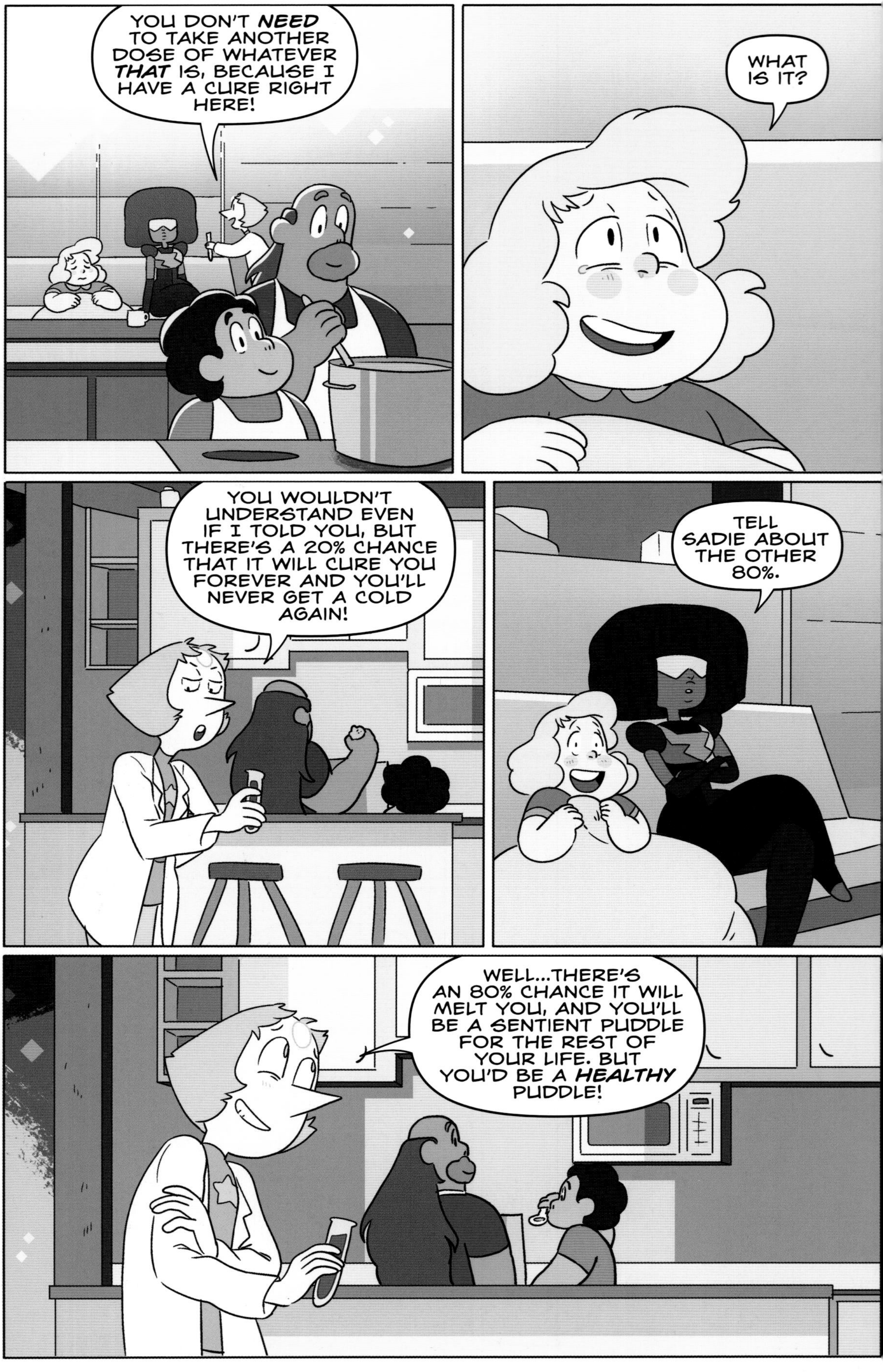
YOU DON'T NEED TO TAKE ANOTHER DOSE OF WHATEVER THAT IS, BECAUSE I HAVE A CURE RIGHT HERE!
WHAT IS IT?
YOU WOULDN'T UNDERSTAND EVEN IF I TOLD YOU, BUT THERE'S A 20% CHANCE THAT IT WILL CURE YOU FOREVER AND YOU'LL NEVER GET A COLD AGAIN!
TELL SADIE ABOUT THE OTHER 80%.
WELL...THERE'S AN 80% CHANCE IT WILL MELT YOU, AND YOU'LL BE A SENTIENT PUDDLE FOR THE REST OF YOUR LIFE. BUT YOU'D BE A HEALTHY PUDDLE!

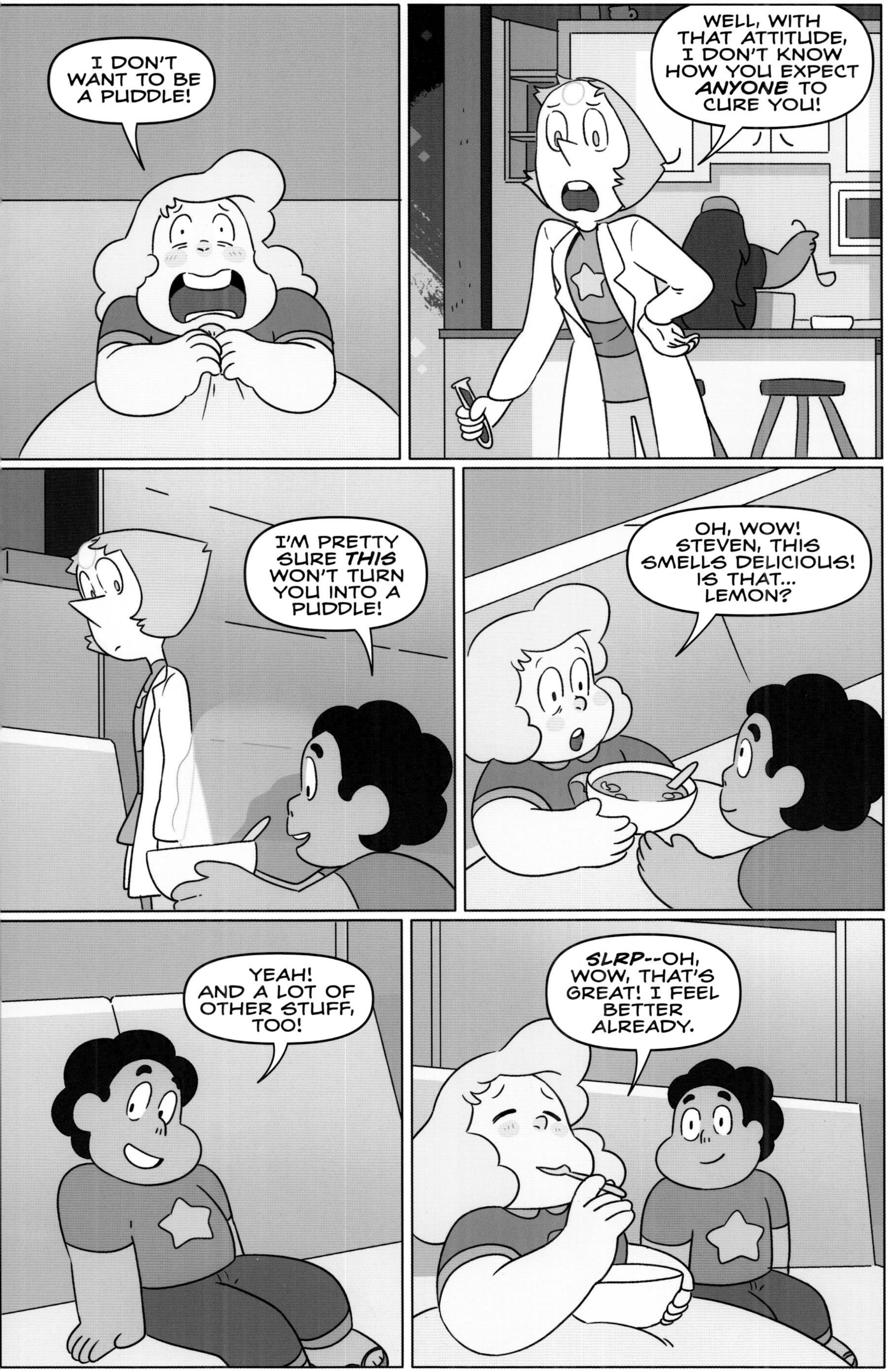
I DON'T WANT TO BE A PUDDLE!
WELL, WITH THAT ATTITUDE, I DON'T KNOW HOW YOU EXPECT ANYONE TO CURE YOU!
I'M PRETTY SURE THIS WON'T TURN YOU INTO A PUDDLE!
OH, WOW! STEVEN, THIS SMELLS DELICIOUS! IS THAT... LEMON?
YEAH! AND A LOT OF OTHER STUFF, TOO!
SLRP--OH, WOW, THAT'S GREAT! I FEEL BETTER ALREADY.

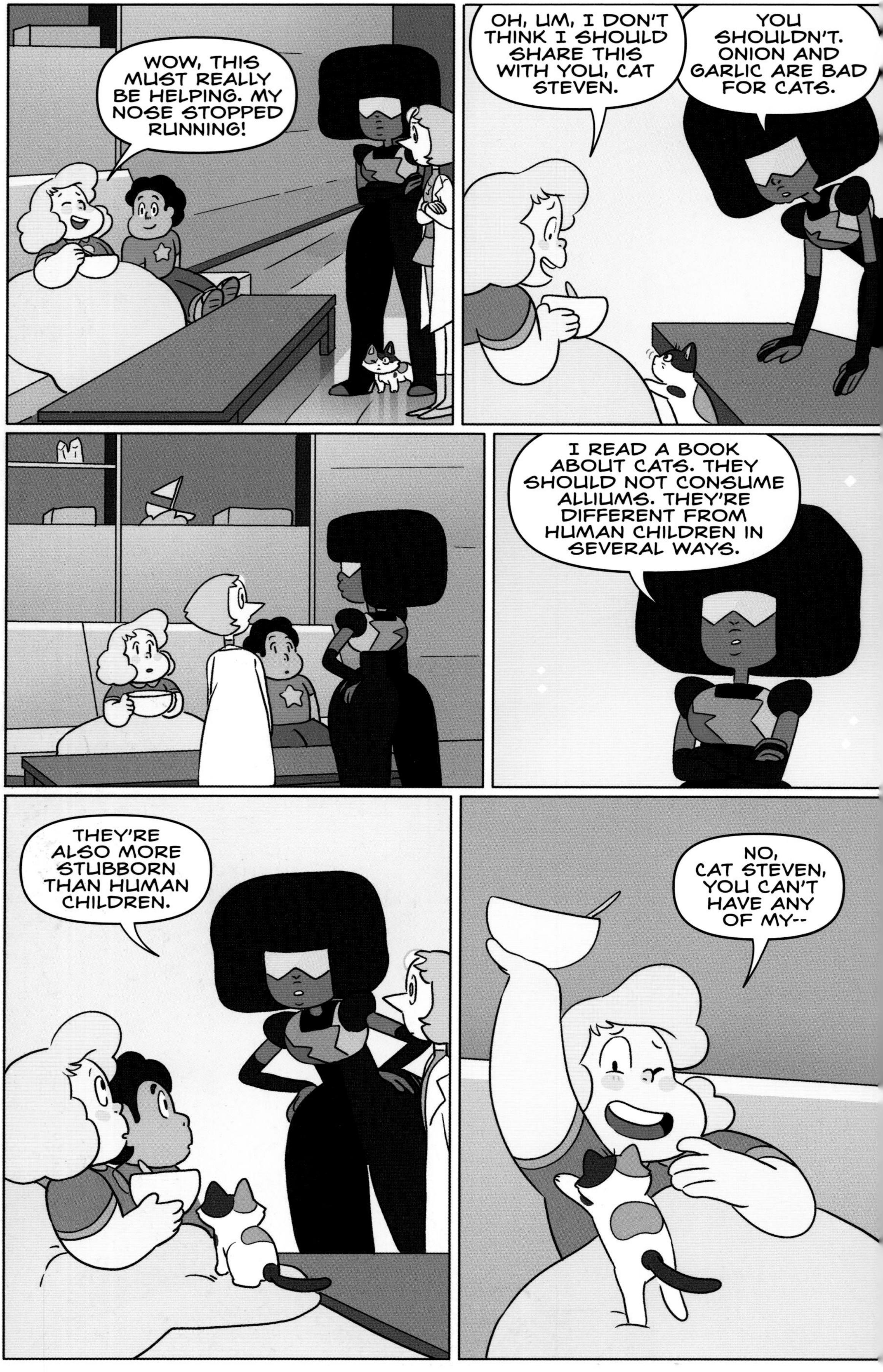
WOW, THIS MUST REALLY BE HELPING. MY NOSE STOPPED RUNNING!
OH, UM, I DON'T THINK I SHOULD SHARE THIS WITH YOU, CAT STEVEN.
YOU SHOULDN'T. ONION AND GARLIC ARE BAD FOR CATS.
I READ A BOOK ABOUT CATS. THEY SHOULD NOT CONSUME ALLIUMS. THEY'RE DIFFERENT FROM HUMAN CHILDREN IN SEVERAL WAYS.
THEY'RE ALSO MORE STUBBORN THAN HUMAN CHILDREN.
NO, CAT STEVEN, YOU CAN'T HAVE ANY OF MY--

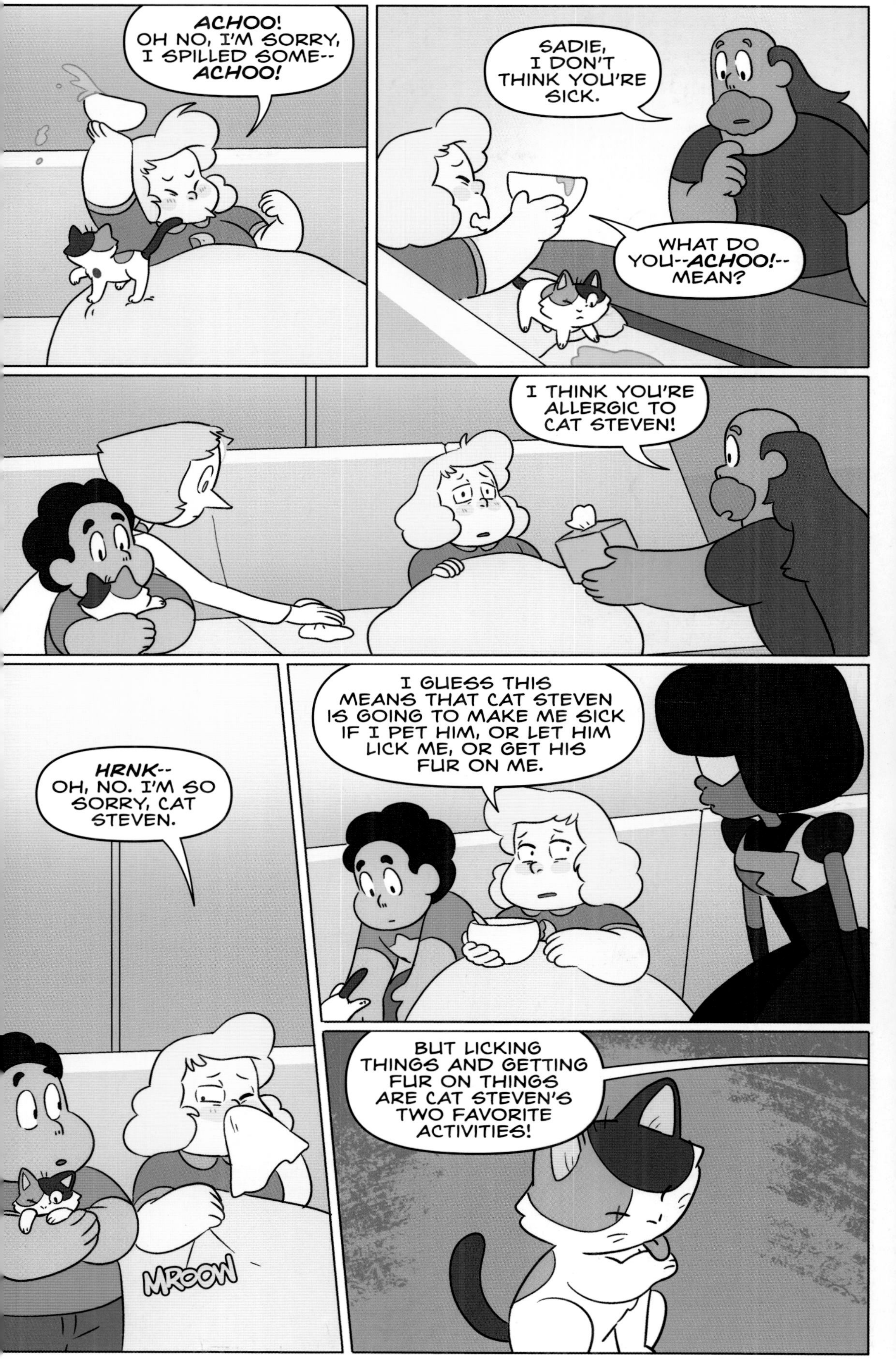
ACHOO! OH NO, I'M SORRY, I SPILLED SOME-- ACHOO!
SADIE, I DON'T THINK YOU'RE SICK.
WHAT DO YOU--ACHOO!-- MEAN?
I THINK YOU'RE ALLERGIC TO CAT STEVEN!
I GUESS THIS MEANS THAT CAT STEVEN IS GOING TO MAKE ME SICK IF I PET HIM, OR LET HIM LICK ME, OR GET HIS FUR ON ME.
HRNK-- OH, NO. I'M SO SORRY, CAT STEVEN.
MROOW
BUT LICKING THINGS AND GETTING FUR ON THINGS ARE CAT STEVEN'S TWO FAVORITE ACTIVITIES!

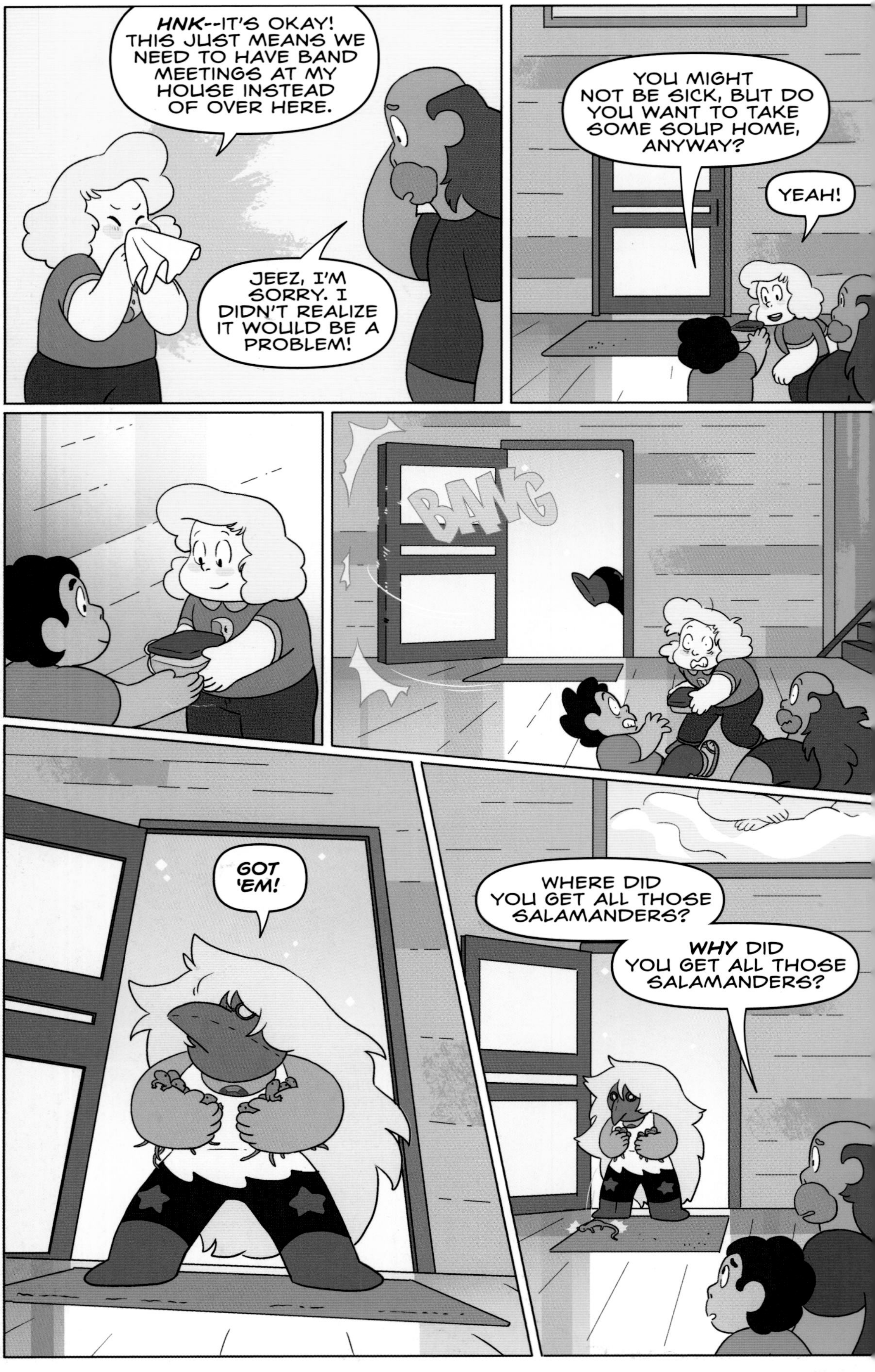

HNK--IT'S OKAY! THIS JUST MEANS WE NEED TO HAVE BAND MEETINGS AT MY HOUSE INSTEAD OF OVER HERE.
JEEZ, I'M SORRY. I DIDN'T REALIZE IT WOULD BE A PROBLEM!
YOU MIGHT NOT BE SICK, BUT DO YOU WANT TO TAKE SOME SOUP HOME, ANYWAY?
YEAH!
BANG
GOT 'EM!
WHERE DID YOU GET ALL THOSE SALAMANDERS?
WHY DID YOU GET ALL THOSE SALAMANDERS?

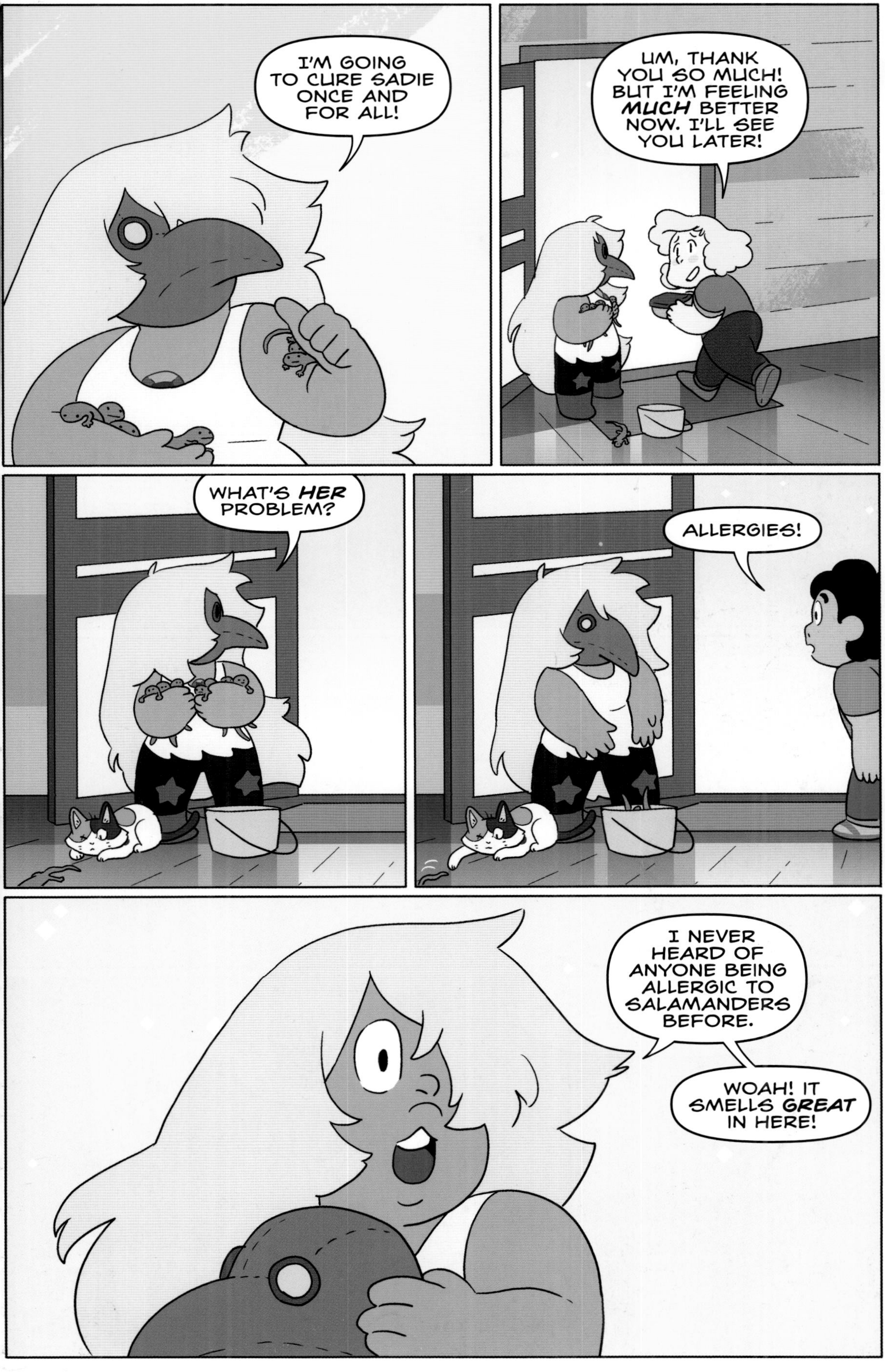
I'M GOING TO CURE SADIE ONCE AND FOR ALL!
UM, THANK YOU SO MUCH! BUT I'M FEELING MUCH BETTER NOW. I'LL SEE YOU LATER!
WHAT'S HER PROBLEM?
ALLERGIES!
I NEVER HEARD OF ANYONE BEING ALLERGIC TO SALAMANDERS BEFORE.
WOAH! IT SMELLS GREAT IN HERE!

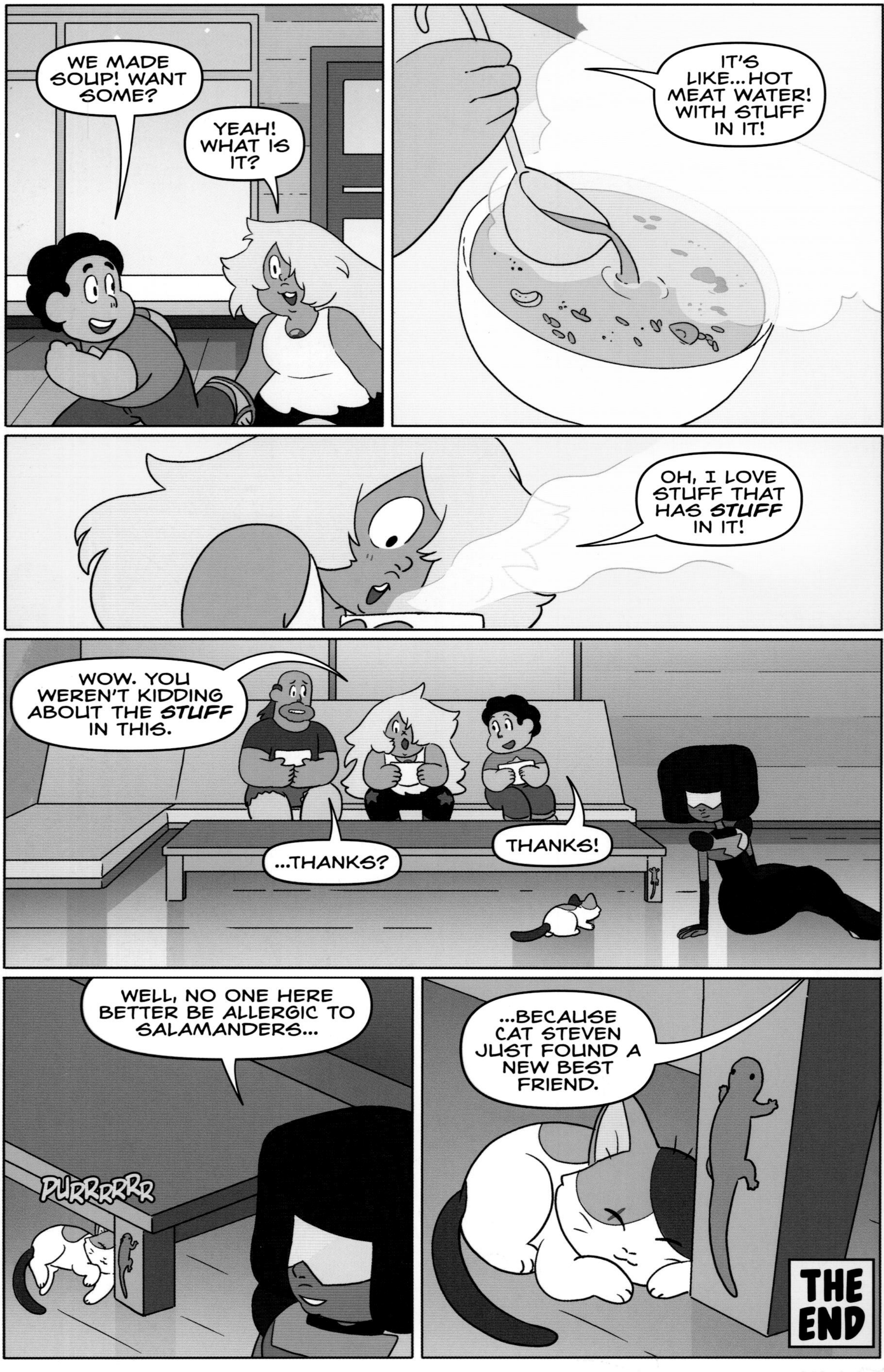
WE MADE SOUP! WANT SOME?
YEAH! WHAT IS IT?
IT'S LIKE...HOT MEAT WATER! WITH STUFF IN IT!
OH, I LOVE STUFF THAT HAS *STUFF* IN IT!
WOW. YOU WEREN'T KIDDING ABOUT THE *STUFF* IN THIS.
...THANKS?
THANKS!
WELL, NO ONE HERE BETTER BE ALLERGIC TO SALAMANDERS...
PURRRRRR
...BECAUSE CAT STEVEN JUST FOUND A NEW BEST FRIEND.
THE END

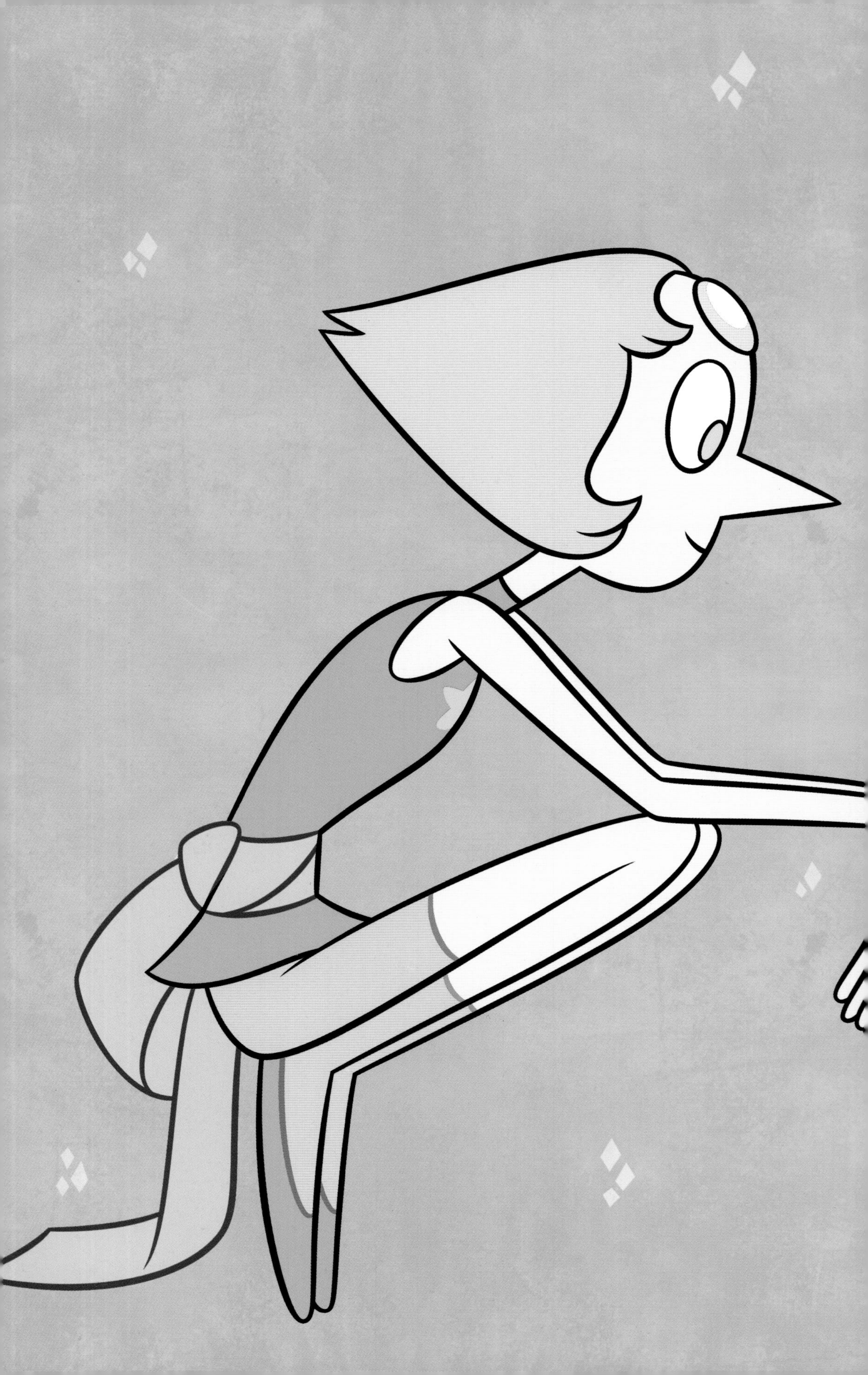

COVER GALLERY

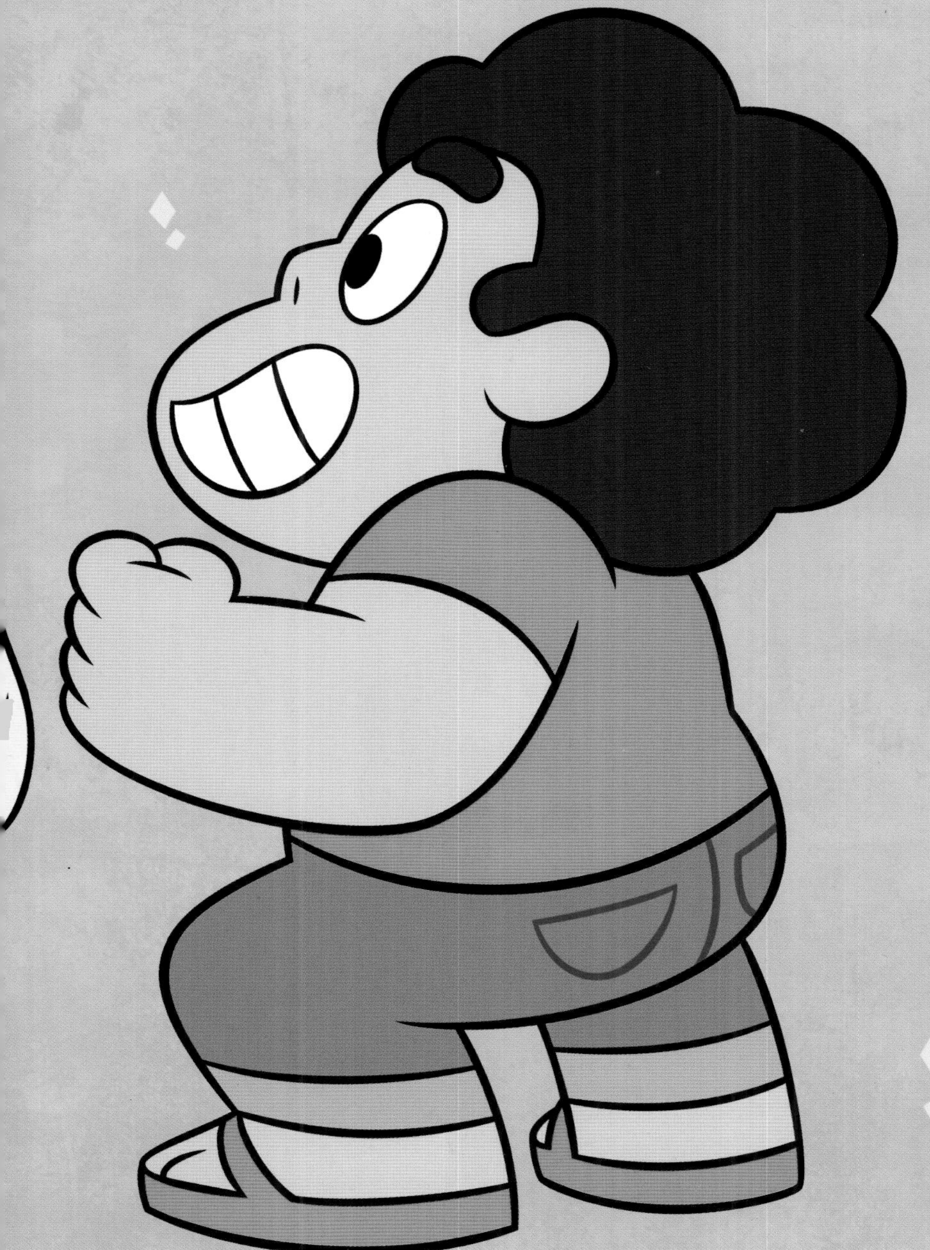

Issue Twenty-Nine Main Cover
MISSY PEÑA

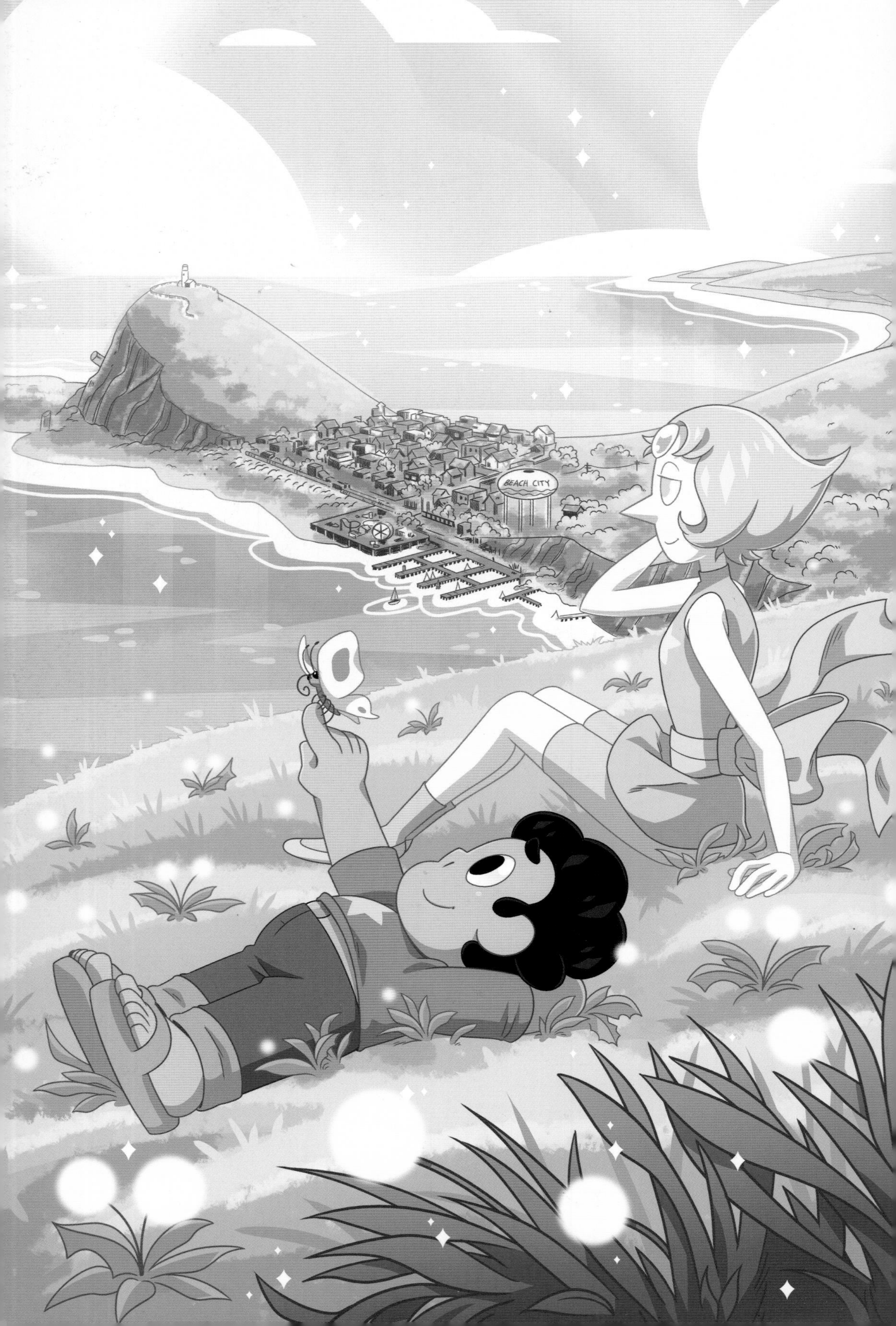
BEACH CITY

Issue Twenty-Nine Preorder Cover
JAMIE LOUGHRAN

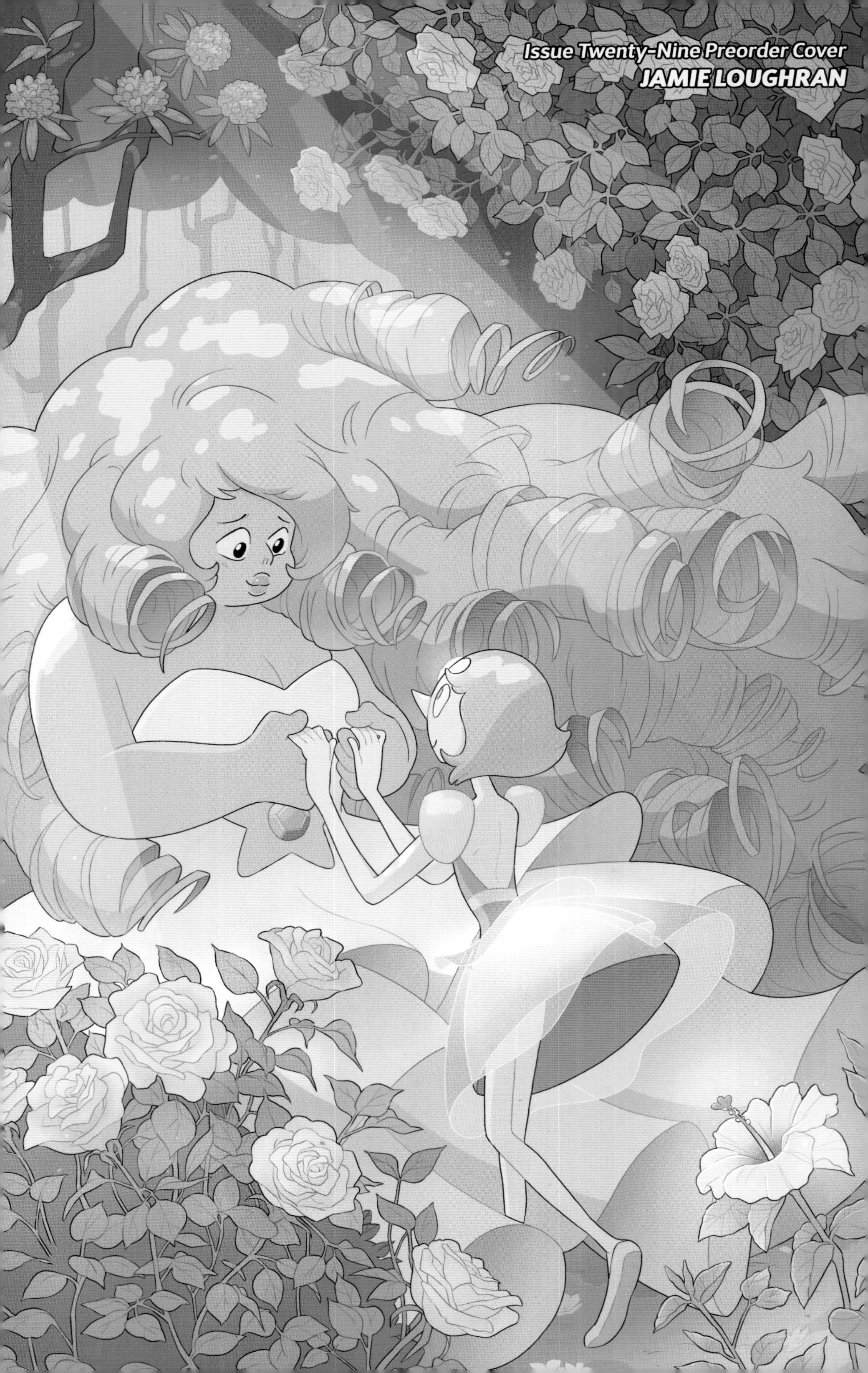

Issue Thirty Main Cover

MISSY PEÑA

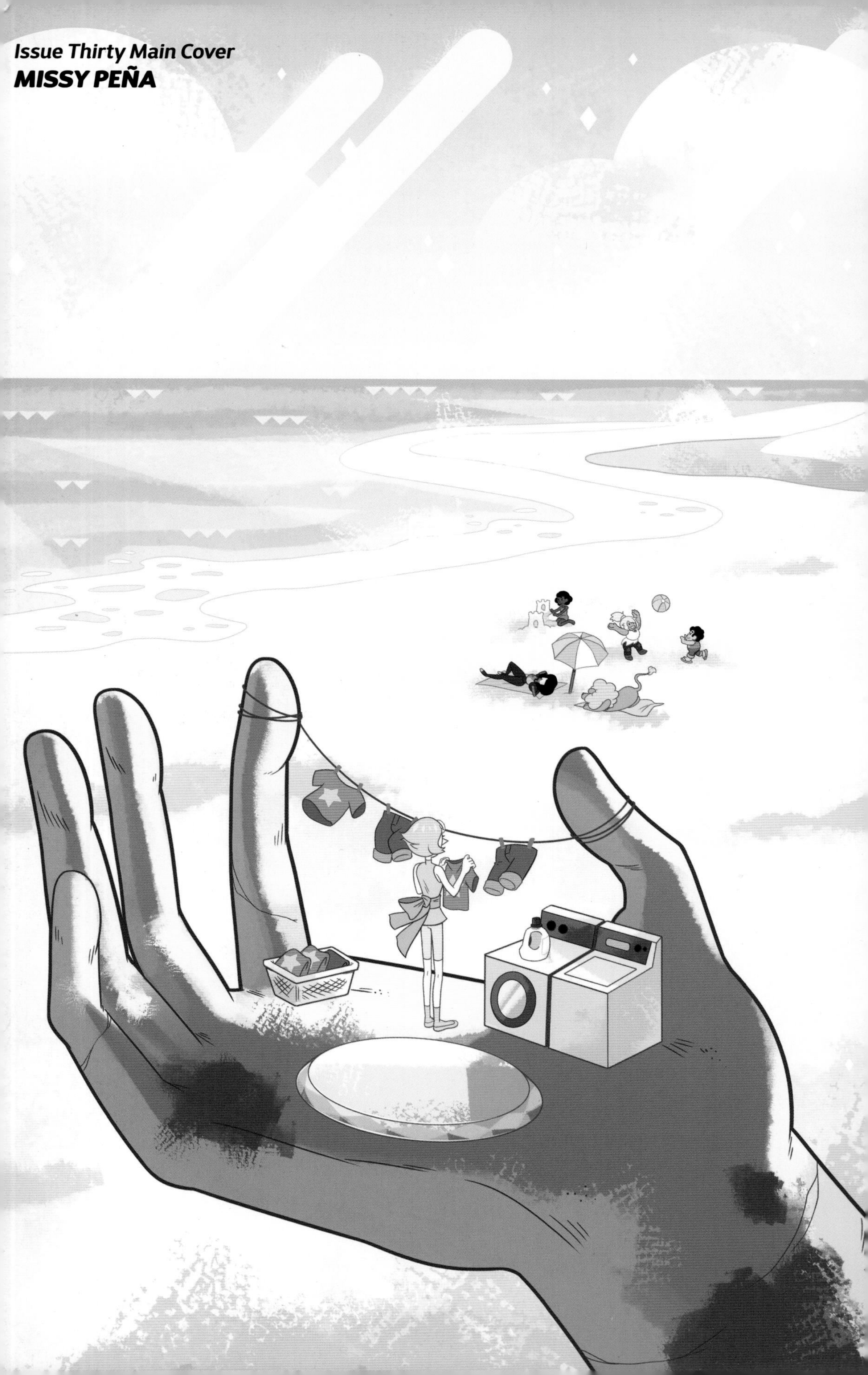

Issue Thirty Preorder Cover
ARI W. NORTH

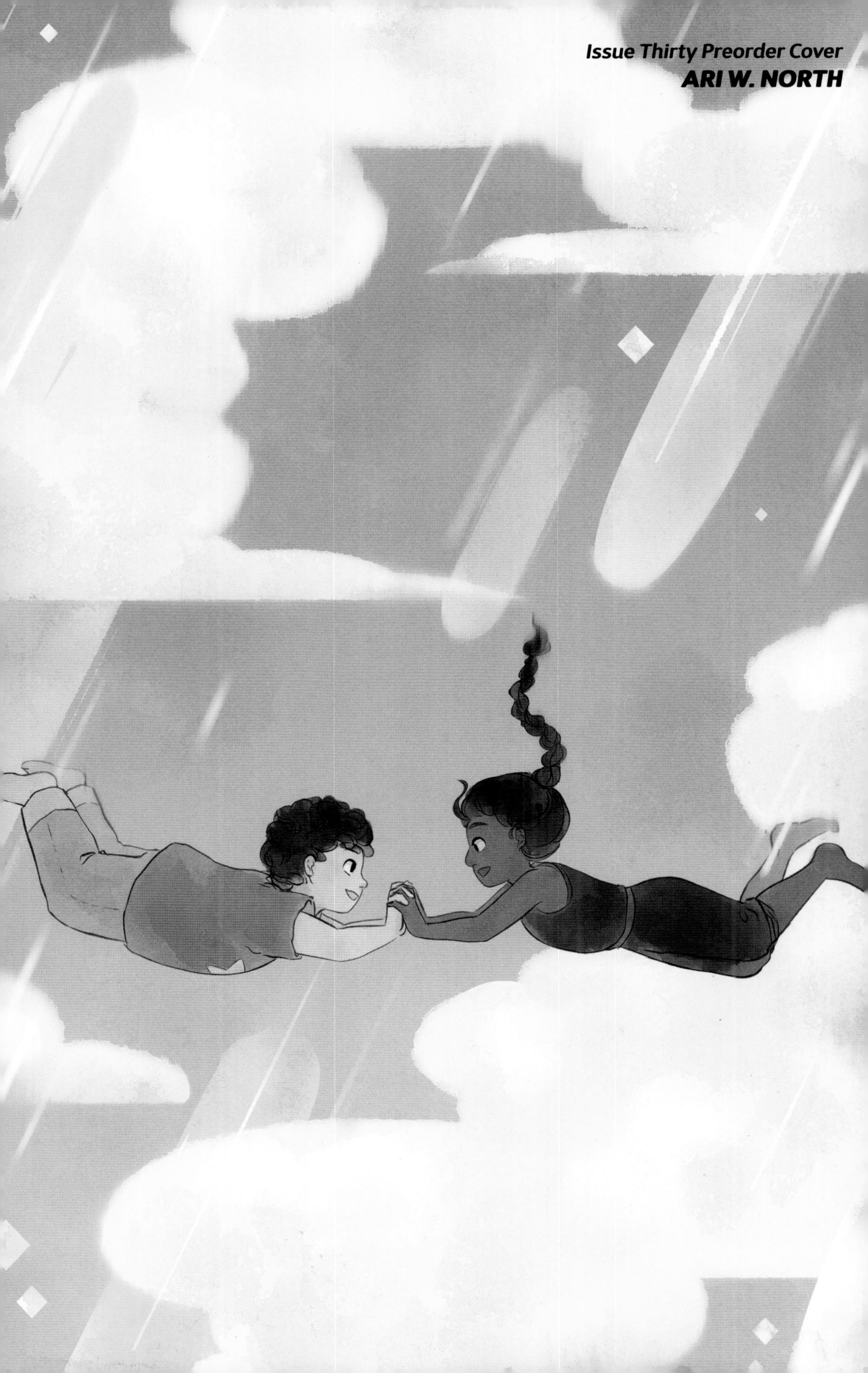

Issue Thirty-One Main Cover
MISSY PEÑA

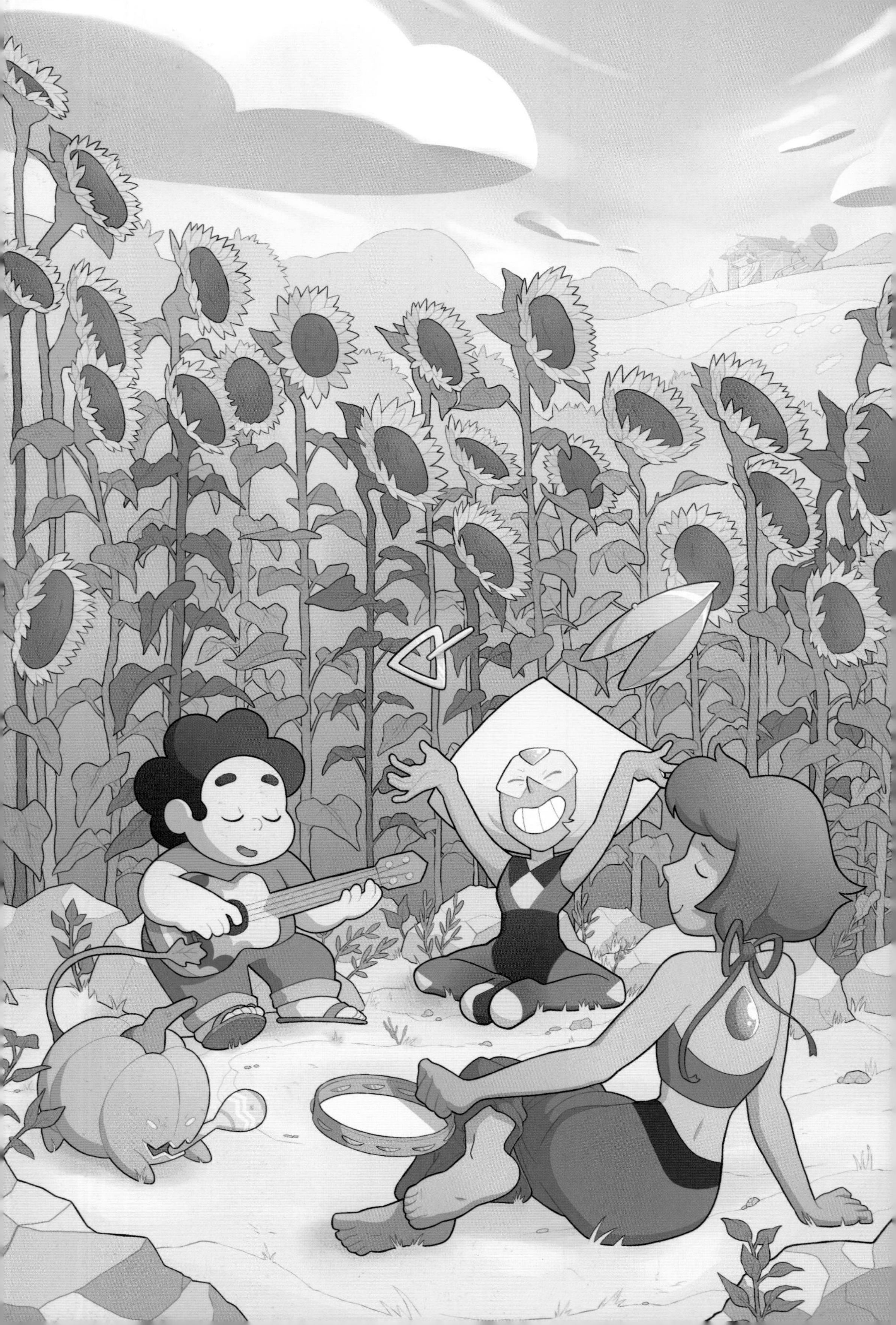

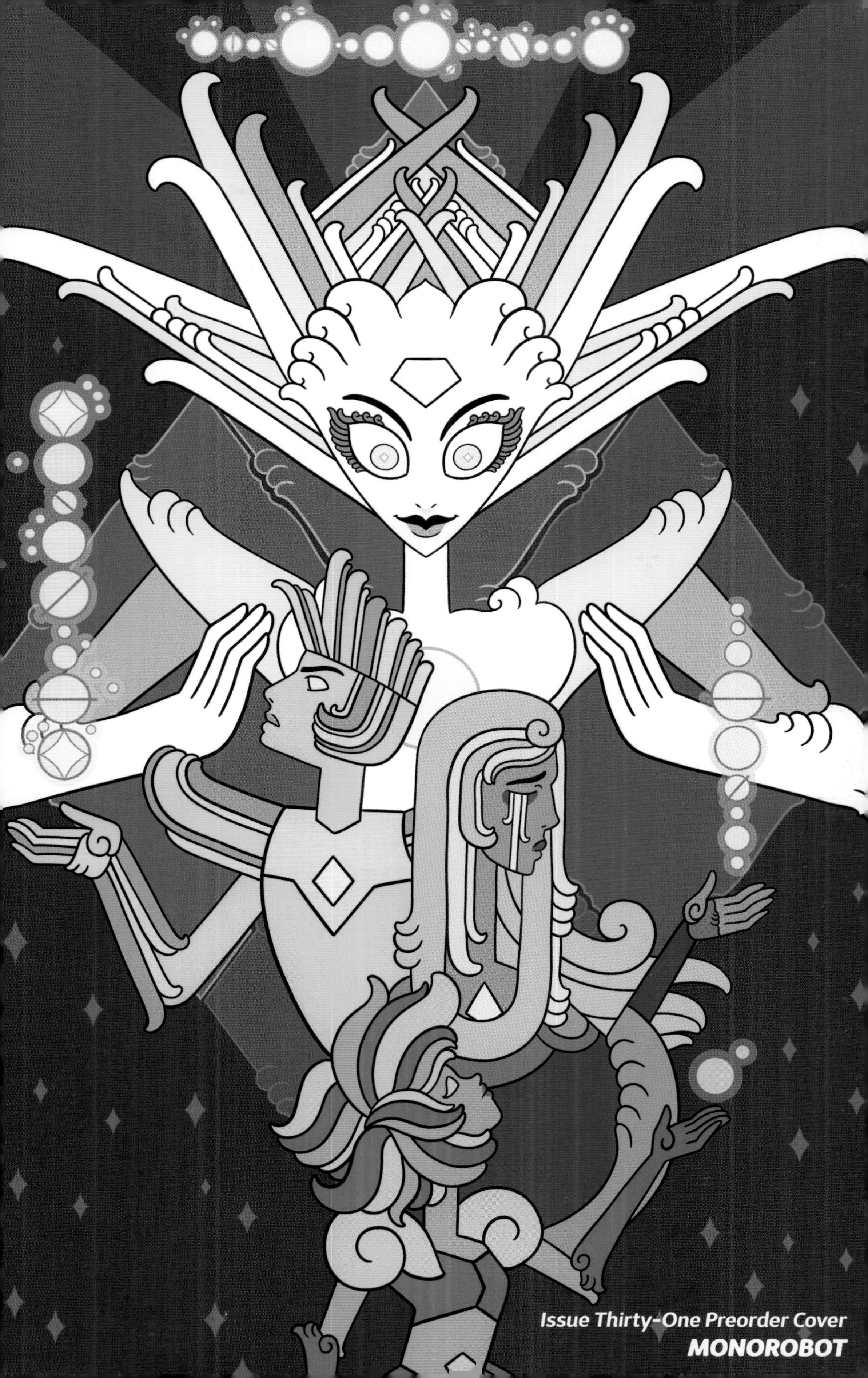

Issue Thirty-One Preorder Cover
MONOROBOT

Issue Thirty-Two Main Cover
MISSY PEÑA

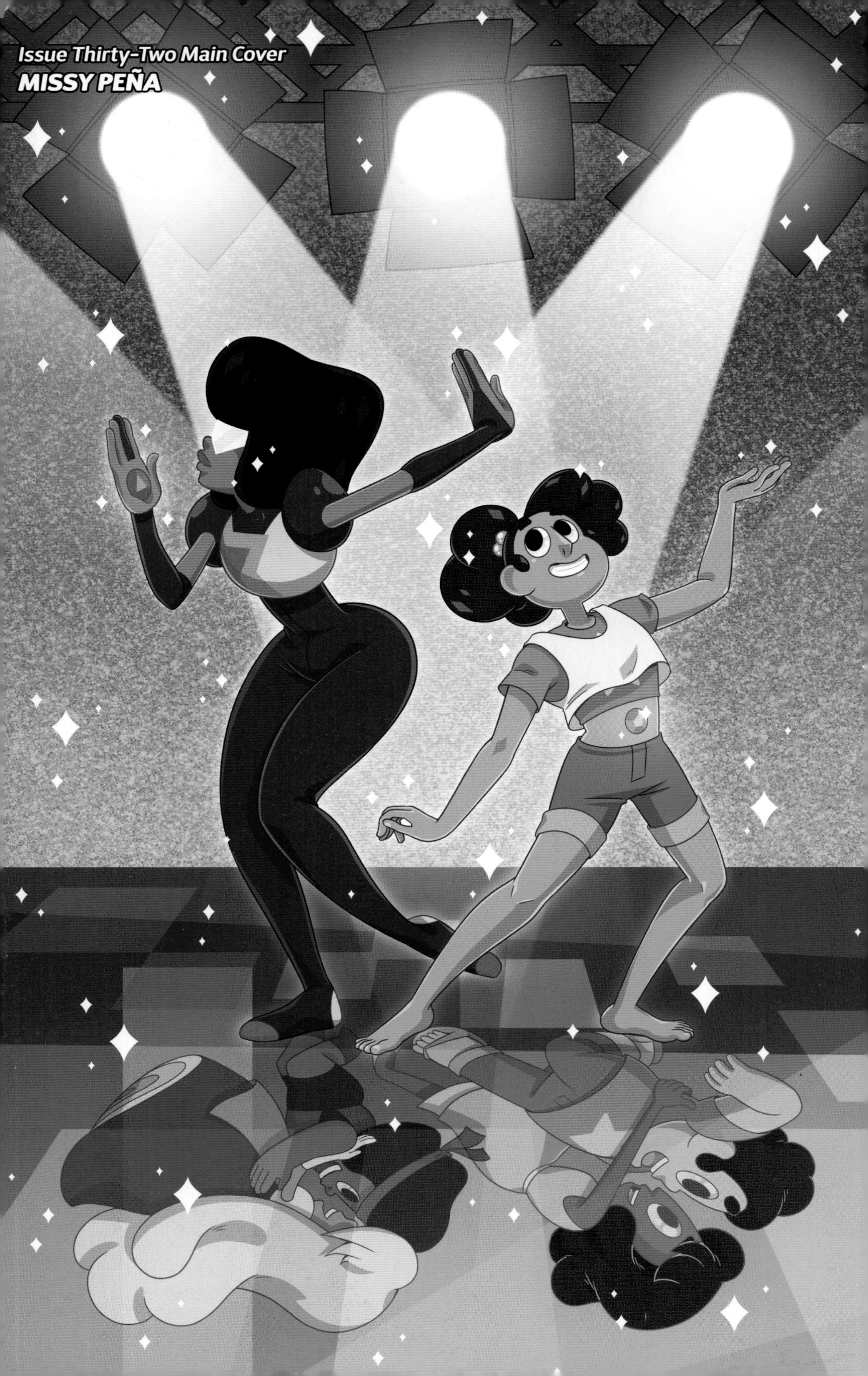

Issue Thirty-Two Preorder Cover
SLOANE LEONG

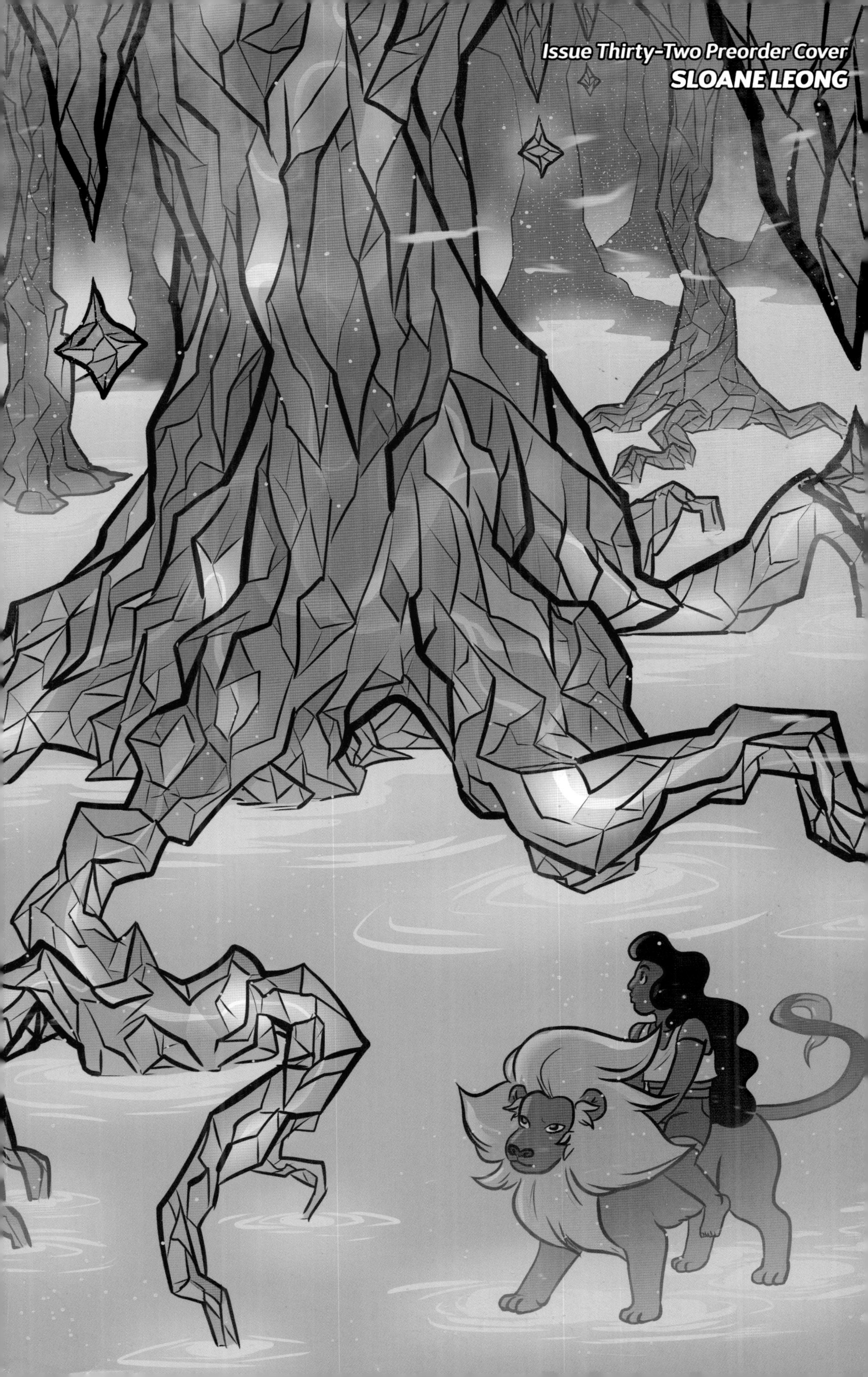

DISCOVER EXPLOSIVE NEW WORLDS

Adventure Time
Pendleton Ward and Others
Volume 1
ISBN: 978-1-60886-280-1 | $14.99 US
Volume 2
ISBN: 978-1-60886-323-5 | $14.99 US
Adventure Time: Islands
ISBN: 978-1-60886-972-5 | $9.99 US

The Amazing World of Gumball
Ben Bocquelet and Others
Volume 1
ISBN: 978-J-60886-488-1 | $14.99 US
Volume 2
ISBN: 978-1-60886-793-6 | $14.99 US

Brave Chef Brianna
Sam Sykes, Selina Espiritu
ISBN: 978-1-68415-050-2 | $14.99 US

Mega Princess
Kelly Thompson, Brianne Drouhard
ISBN: 978-1-68415-007-6 | $14.99 US

The Not-So Secret Society
Matthew Daley, Arlene Daley,
Wook Jin Clark
ISBN: 978-1-60886-997-8 | $9.99 US

Over the Garden Wall
Patrick McHale, Jim Campbell
and Others
Volume 1
ISBN: 978-1-60886-940-4 | $14.99 US
Volume 2
ISBN: 978-1-68415-006-9 | $14.99 US

Steven Universe
Rebecca Sugar and Others
Volume 1
ISBN: 978-1-60886-706-6 | $14.99 US
Volume 2
ISBN: 978-1-60886-796-7 | $14.99 US

Steven Universe & The Crystal Gems
ISBN: 978-1-60886-921-3 | $14.99 US

Steven Universe: Too Cool for School
ISBN: 978-1-60886-771-4 | $14.99 US

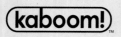

AVAILABLE AT YOUR LOCAL COMICS SHOP AND BOOKSTORE
To find a comics shop in your area, visit www.comicshoplocator.com
WWW.BOOM-STUDIOS.COM